AMERICAN SYCAMORE

AMERICAN SYCAMORE

A NOVEL

CHARLES KENNEY

Arcade Publishing • New York

First Edition

This is a work of fiction. Names, places, characters, and incidents are either the products of the author's imagination or are used fictitiously.

Arcade Publishing books may be purchased in bulk at special discounts for sales promotion, corporate gifts, fund-raising, or educational purposes. Special editions can also be created to specifications. For details, contact the Special Sales Department, Arcade Publishing, 307 West 36th Street, 11th Floor, New York, NY 10018 or arcade@skyhorsepublishing.com.

Arcade Publishing® is a registered trademark of Skyhorse Publishing, Inc.®, a Delaware corporation.

Visit our website at www.arcadepub.com.

10 9 8 7 6 5 4 3 2 1

Library of Congress Cataloging-in-Publication Data is available on file.
Library of Congress Control Number: 2023946953

Cover design by Elizabeth S. Kenney
Front cover and title page photo Cavan Images/Getty

ISBN: 978-1-956763-98-0
Ebook ISBN: 978-1-64821-008-2

Printed in the United States of America

To my daughter, Elizabeth

My wife, Anne

And in memory of my son,
1st Lt. Charles F. Kenney (1987–2012)
United States Marine Corps
7th Marine Regiment Headquarters Company
Regimental Combat Team 7
29 Palms California

Contents

PART TWO

PART
ONE

1

The White Light

Rob Barrow believed in America. He believed in her mission, vision, and aspirational nature. And in her resilience. Hadn't this nation, inspired by the Enlightenment, descended from Locke and Voltaire, overcome existential threats, foreign and domestic, for two and a half centuries? Rob had devoted his professional life to constitutional scholarship—research, writing, teaching, and arguing fundamental constitutional questions before the highest court in the land. Never in his nearly fifty years of studying this historic document, with its visionary aspirations, had it failed to thrill him.

Now, in the fraught year of 2021, Rob needed the reassurance of America's foundational strength more than ever. Some days it was harder to summon than others. As he reclined in the surgical prep area on September 16, 2021, his seventieth birthday, Harvard professor Robert Barrow sought comfort in the nation's historical resilience. He had to get his mind off what was about to happen: a scalpel through his abdomen to remove his cancerous prostate gland in the hope of finding, *please, God*, that the malevolent rogue cells had not escaped the prostate capsule.

"It is going to be fine, it's going to work out well," Julia Barrow had assured her husband early that morning as she drove him into the medical center. While waiting in the pre-op area, Rob had been scrolling through a newsfeed on his iPad when he stumbled upon an article likening America's twenty-first-century tumult to the period of unrest in 1970 when he had been a law student. It had followed the assassinations of the Kennedys and Martin Luther King Jr., protests and riots, Molotov cocktails, bombings of university buildings, the Tet offensive, My Lai. Now, too, the forces of illiberalism seemed about to bust open the American experiment and expose it for the sham that the doubters always said it was.

"We will survive," Rob muttered to himself. "We will survive."

A nurse at his bedside looked at him quizzically.

"Almost everyone survives this procedure," she said.

"No I meant . . ." said Rob. "What do you mean *'almost'*?"

But she didn't answer. Instead, she said, "In just a minute I'm going to give you a little medicine to relax."

"Propofol?" he asked.

"Express to *lala* land!" she said.

Rob had been briefed by his friend and next-door neighbor, Dr. Raymond Witter, dean of the medical school. Ray had told Rob that before surgery he would be given propofol, which worked by sedating the neurotransmitter system that regulated the brain.

"Nerve cells talk to one another through a particular protein," Ray explained. "It's not clear that propofol is all that healthy for the protein."

"So what kind of risks am I taking?" Rob asked.

"Depends on a lot of things. You'll be okay," said Ray.

"But the brain's communication system . . . ?"

"You worry too much," said Ray.

Propofol slowed the ability of cells to communicate by somehow disrupting the protein. What if it was permanent? Rob wondered. Were there cases of that?

"A little pinch," said the nurse, inserting the IV. A propofol drip, to be exact, kicking in within a minute and he felt himself rising, slowly,

comfortably floating above the bed, through the ceiling, above the buildings, on his way to the sky to heaven and he wondered whether he was
free now, released from it all, free of the earthly suffering, freed from
any physical sensation other than the ecstasy of lightness, of lifting, rising via some unseen power with no exertion on his part, no energy or
thrust, but rising nonetheless, looking around and seeing the clouds and
feeling protected from reality and certain that he never wanted this to
end. He had been in the pre-op area with the nurse who inserted his IV,
but now she was with him, rising next to him trying to get his attention.
Nurse Sheila, dark-haired, freckled, a big girl.

"Robert, tell me again please what is your date of birth?" Heavy
Boston accent—Ro*bit* rather than Ro*bert*.

He felt her touch his hand and wondered why she was rising with
him, alongside him, up and up.

"Robit? Mr. Barrow?"

He felt that she loved him very much and he wondered whether he
was supposed to love her as well.

"Robit?"

"June 18," he said. "Paul McCartney."

She looked puzzled.

"McCartney's birthday," he said.

She seemed amused by this and he thought he heard her say something to another nurse and he heard them both laugh and he kept rising, warm air lifting him, no sound, vivid colors everywhere, the ribbon
of greenery that was Olmsted's Emerald Necklace parkland weaving its
way through Boston, and he was high enough now to see the sun glint
off the waters of the Charles River to the west and he felt himself floating over Fenway Park and the lovingly tended expanse of outfield and
he realized Updike was right that it really did seem like "a lyric little
band box of a ballpark" and he felt a jab of sadness that Updike was
gone, had been gone now for a number of years, and he recalled the
time he had met the great man in Concord, New Hampshire. During

dinner with a friend all those years ago, Rob and his pal argued about the relative merits of the *Rabbit* series. Rob ardently defended the brilliance of the portrait and recalled the lancing moment on the outdoor basketball court when Harry Angstrom, shooting hoops alone, felt the hammering in his chest, occluded blood flow, clamping heart muscle, sending him to the grave at fifty-five.

"No, *your* date of birth, *Robit*," Sheila insisted.

He had not attended Woodstock—couldn't afford it. He was trying to tell her about McCartney and the Beatles not having been there and neither had the Stones and he wanted to explain why both bands had skipped it but he couldn't quite recall why and he made a mental note to ask Julia because it was exactly the sort of thing she would know. It was the strangest sensation, for Rob now realized that he was in a bed, reclining in pre-op at the hospital, yet he felt that at the same time he was not there, but outside, quite a warm September day.

Dr. Steve Chen, the surgeon, a young, hefty fellow, had been introduced to Rob by his friend Ray. Supposed to be the best, but all these people Ray recommended were supposed to be the best. How was Rob to know? What if Chen's worst day ever in an OR was destined to be today? What if Chen was hung over? Had a fight with his wife that morning? Was getting divorced, had become addicted to some opiate? How often did these surgeons make mistakes that got covered up as "complications"? Ray had talked about that through the years, had harped on it actually, how mistakes were made and papered over with money and nondisclosure agreements—*sorry we cut off the wrong leg here's a bucket of money instead.*

But with propofol coursing through the system, why worry? Rob had been on edge about all this but now embraced it because he had never been lifted, carried so gently ever in his life. Maybe the nuns were right that he had a guardian angel. Everyone was supposed to have one, but he had never before been aware of one, not in any tangible way, but maybe this was the force he felt. He was floating over the Charles gazing down upon a lone sculler in steady rhythm. And then suddenly, there was Julia, Rob's beloved wife, Julia, who had driven him to the hospital that morning, now floating by him within a pinkish cloud! She was rising, smiling at him! Then, *oh blessed Lord*, there was his son, Thomas! *Oh my God it was Thomas*, here, in the midst of a soft, silvery cloud and Rob reached out but Thomas was floating just beyond his grasp, smiling at him looking for all the world like his mother. Rob had never been into drugs, not even weed, but he thought maybe this feeling was why people got addicted. Everything now made perfect sense to him.

He noticed that Dr. Chen was at the foot of the bed saying some things and Rob responded rationally and he realized he had bifurcated somehow, that his rational self was in the bed conversing with Chen while the other part of him—*it must be my soul*, he thought—was rising still, moving in defiance of the laws of physics. There was no energy source that he could see so really he should not be moving, but he *was*, rising still, without propulsion, gliding past other pre-op beds, through swinging doors, along a hallway past men and women in scrubs and colorful surgical caps. It was hushed and it felt busy and everyone was smiling except the people who were deadly serious, but most of the people he could see were having fun and he was having fun too, and in fact he thought he wanted this feeling to go on forever no matter what even if it meant that he was passing through a new realm into wherever it was that he and his soul were destined to go.

And he recalled that night in Concord, New Hampshire, when he was expressing his appreciation for the *Rabbit* series, a midwinter blizzard raging outside, when his friend looked toward the restaurant entrance and said, "Here's your man now." And in walked Updike along with another man and a woman and the three sat at a table eight feet away and it so happened that Updike's new novel, *The Coup*, was in Rob's car outside and he got up without a word, retrieved the bright green–jacketed novel, approached the author, and asked for an autograph. His nose, Updike's, was as prominent in person as it was in the dust jacket photos, but Rob did not expect the crooked-tooth smile, so warm, appreciative that someone here in this random place admired his work. *To Robert Barrow, here in Concord. John Updike.* He still had the book.

Into the OR, the massive overhead lights—*the white light! Oh, My God*, Rob thought, *this is it! Portal to the other side! The final destination!* The light luring him onward, seducing him. Though he had always tended toward stoicism, he now felt a surge of emotion as he headed straight for the light where he would at long last escape the earthly pull and the cruelty of human memory. He was flying now, weightless, above everything, looking down on the roofs of the buildings and Fenway Park empty this day and he wanted only for this feeling to continue. And then a young woman by his side, very young, he thought, too young to be in the OR. Was it bring your child to work day? he wondered. But no, it was just that some of these physicians seemed so youthful to Rob's aging eyes. She was saying something to him about the anesthesia and the operation, asking him to count backward from one hundred and he tried, but the mask was over his nose and mouth and everything went dark.

2

Rita B

It had started back in early August as a routine part of his annual physical, with a standard blood test measuring whether a statin had succeeded in lowering his LDL cholesterol. The number came up on his computer screen and he was pleased with the progress, but when he scanned the other numbers he noticed that his PSA had climbed to a value of 5.6. Like many other seventy-year-old men in America in the third decade of the twenty-first century, Rob knew about prostate-specific antigen, more commonly known as the PSA value. PSA is a protein that, when spiked, can indicate the presence of cancer of the prostate. Rob was a cerebral being. He possessed the lanky frame and easy manner of an athlete, but he preferred living in the world of the mind. He was blessed with a quick, inquisitive intellect combined with a steady reliability, but this number on his cell phone screen had unnerved him. He had never been sick with anything more than a cold, had never spent a night in a hospital, had never even seen a specialist. But now he was driving to the hospital for a follow-up blood test to determine whether the spiked PSA might have been an outlier. It was three days after the first elevated PSA, and already, Rob felt as though something had changed in his life. He was one of those steady-as-she-goes people who could handle anything, had handled anything

and everything. But now he was rattled. The hospital was twenty minutes from his home, and he knew the area well, but he got confused on
the way and then got lost inside the hospital. It was nerves; he wasn't
paying attention. He rode up to the fourth floor, realized his mistake,
and took the stairs back down to two. A masked receptionist—everyone
was masked—greeted him cheerfully, asking for his name and date of
birth. She consulted her computer screen and nodded.

"Do you have a port, sir?" she asked.

"A port?"

"For infusions, sir."

"Not that I know of," Rob said.

The receptionist smiled. "You'd probably know if you had one, sir!"

"Right, now, of course, I, ah, no, I do not have a port, I—" Nerves.

"Are you suffering from any cold or flu symptoms today?"

"I don't think so."

She wrapped a band with his name and date of birth around his
wrist and directed him to a waiting area, and that was when he saw
her. She was one of maybe fifty people stretched down a wide hallway
that led to a spacious waiting area. Chairs and sofas lined the walls dis-
playing framed works of commercial art. The lighting was soft, not too
harsh as was frequently the case in hospitals. The place felt like a mid-
range hotel—a sense of faux elegance, cherry-accented wood, lamps
with cream-colored shades, multicolored carpeting.

The woman in a wheelchair was listing to one side, seemingly
unable to hold herself up. She wore a kerchief, red and blue squares,
wrapped in back and tied in front the way they wore them on *I Love
Lucy*. She was swathed in a blanket and wheeled to her place in the
waiting area by a middle-aged woman, a daughter, he thought. The
woman in the chair sipped water from a plastic bottle and seemed to
get some caught in her throat. A coughing fit ensued, during which she
held her hand to her chest as she leaned forward and coughed, bits of
moisture spraying with each desperate bark. The daughter handed her

tissues, which the older woman used to wipe her mouth. Rob noticed that others watched her as he did, and he knew they were thinking what came into his mind—that she was very far down the road. When she dropped the tissue box, it tumbled down her legs and ricocheted onto the carpeted aisle in front of Rob. Instinctively, he scooped it up and went over and handed it to her. A weary half smile, a nod. *She's at a point where speaking is a chore*, he thought. He stood looking down at her, uncertain what to do. He wanted to say something, but nothing came to mind. He was, for the moment, transfixed. Her face was gaunt, shiny, the skin papery in spots, tugging at the eyes and jaw. She was so emaciated that her skin struggled to cover her bone structure. Strands of her hair, white and wispy, stuck out from the kerchief. The daughter looked up at him and offered a curt *Thank you*, although the tone conveyed the message that maybe he should stop staring at her as though she was on exhibit.

"Good luck," he said in a soft voice. It was involuntary, the words out before he knew what they were.

The gaunt woman—Rob guessed she was just about his age— regarded him with a quizzical look, and then, a bony shoulder escaping as the blanket slipped to one side, she shrugged. And he knew she was telling him that, *yes, this is what it looks like; this is what it comes to.*

"Rita B! Rita B!" one of the technicians called out. Every minute or so a technician would summon a patient for the blood draw by calling out a first name and last initial. Rita B, in her wheelchair, turned away from Rob without another look and was wheeled by her daughter into the clinical area to measure whatever it was in her bloodstream that was killing her.

He was supposed to call the doctor's office to find out what the next steps might be, but he knew that if the PSA was elevated a biopsy would be scheduled. He hoped this could be avoided, of course, but less than an hour after his blood was drawn, as he sat nervously sipping coffee at a Starbucks near the hospital, he received an email alert. He logged into his MyHealth account containing his medical records and clicked on TEST RESULTS. He paused. This seemed kind of amazing. He was about to look at a number that would tell him how likely it was that he had cancer. This was the modern world. In the old days, you would receive such news in person from your doctor in the comfort and privacy of his office. The troubling news would be accompanied by words of reassurance, whether sincere or not. But in the new world it had to be digital. If it wasn't digital, it wasn't real. Rob was not surprised when he clicked and saw that the number was even a bit worse than five days earlier. He had not finished his coffee before he received a call from the urologist's office scheduling the biopsy for the following week.

"Better to do it sooner rather than later," the secretary said.

"Oh, it's that bad?" he asked her.

"Well . . . I mean, it gets busy, and the doctor has openings, so better to get you in when we can. Could you do the twenty-first?"

"Of?" Rob asked.

"August," she said.

"The twenty-first," he said. "I think so." It seemed so soon. Did she know something she wasn't supposed to reveal? Had the doctor said something to her, some indication of a problem? The prospect of a biopsy did not excite him. The prostate, he had learned, was positioned alongside the bladder, rectum, and urethra. He phoned Ray and asked whether the procedure was painful.

"Well, they are poking needles up your ass, Rob, so I doubt it feels great!" Ray said with a laugh. "Stop worrying. You'll be okay."

Rob was guided to a changing room, where he hung up his pants and put on a hospital gown, open at the back, the cotton ties impossible to reach and secure. He was unable to see his bony ass, but he knew it was half hanging out the back, and what difference did it make because it would all be exposed during the biopsy anyway? It was over in fifteen minutes. The sheet he was given as he was leaving instructed: "Drink plenty of fluids to prevent blood clots and infection in the bladder. Avoid strenuous exercise such as jogging, heavy lifting"—as though he did any heavy lifting anyway—"golfing, and bike riding for at least seven days. Take your antibiotics as directed and complete the full dose given. Do not drink alcoholic beverages until after completing your antibiotics." Since when was golf a strenuous activity? he wondered. He would take the antibiotics, but the idea that he would wait until the full course before consuming alcohol—that was funny. Certainly, Ray would over-rule that on his behalf.

Rob realized he was experiencing the essential reality of aging, the body gradually yielding to the wear and tear of life. Rob Barrow was a fastidious man, an inveterate note-taker, a chronicler of events that mattered in his life:

August 12, 2021, PSA spike
August 15, spike confirmed
August 21, biopsy

At home with Julia, he tried to present a cheerful front, but he was distracted. He had never been a morbid man, but now, the thought of leaving her in the world without his love and support frightened him. What about his work? Who would teach his courses on Constitutional Law? Who would complete the journal articles? Who would argue the case scheduled before the First Circuit Court of Appeals in Washington in October? He was an accomplished man, a respected Harvard Law School professor known for expertise in constitutional law, valued in certain legal circles for his scholarship, and here he was haunted by irrational fears. Or maybe they weren't so irrational. He could not get the vision of Rita B out of his mind—her mournful look of defeat. Her shrug had been a signal, a warning that this woeful state, this degrada-tion—*this is the road ahead.*

It was happening so fast. Six days after the biopsy Rob was back in the hospital to learn the results. He got lost in the building again, finally making his way to the second floor, where he encountered a mass of people, wheelchairs, bald heads, surgical masks, oxygen tanks—baby boomers sick with cancer. Rob focused on the faces of all those boomers crowding the Cancer Center, awaiting a blood draw to be studied, analyzed, submitted to the medical jury, which would render a verdict on their fate. This was what it had come to—this was where the generation gathered now. No longer in parks for free concerts, love-ins, demonstrations for civil rights, for peace. No. Now the assemblies happened in hospitals and physician offices throughout the land; in rehabilitation facilities where patients were taught to walk after insertion of a new knee or hip; in rehab beds where others engaged in the arduous process of recovering from a stroke, learning for the second time in their lives how to speak or form a coherent thought.

He had intended to go to the eleventh floor for his appointment with a medical oncologist, but he was lost in thought as the elevator moved down to the subbasement, and he got off thinking it was the lobby where he could find some coffee. The hallways in this subterranean world extended in several directions, with men and women in surgical clothing moving quickly this way and that, all business, in the moment, an atmosphere infused with palpable intensity; an aura of tension underneath the world, everyone down here in ciel blue scrubs. Was it a sign that he had managed, in his confusion, to wind up in this place where complex surgical procedures were performed? Was this to be his fate? This was where patients were saved and where people who were brought to be saved sometimes died. Why do they wear ciel blue? He knew *ciel* meant "sky" or "heaven," which was where souls were destined to go in the afterlife.

He was twenty-five minutes early for the appointment and found his way to the lobby, where he bought a small cup of black coffee. The bustle through the main hospital entrance was nonstop. Couples, families in groups queuing up to ask for directions, the receptionists patiently answering questions for the thousandth time. As he watched people coming into the hospital, he tried to figure out which ones were the patients, the lead actors in this day's drama that was a visit to the hospital, the central character to whom others deferred. Sometimes it was obvious. Beacon Hospital and the Cancer Center were across the street from one another and collaborated on treatment of cancer patients. Also within Beacon was an active maternity practice and some of the visitors came through the lobby with balloons, smiles, a giddy sense of possibility. Most of the rest of the patients, though, tended toward grayscale, their expressions ranging from serious to determined, apprehensive to ashen. He kept his eye out for Rita B, hoping to catch a glimpse of her, but he worried that her deterioration had continued to the point where she was unable to leave home to make it to the hospital, or worse. He was disappointed in himself. The anxiety he felt worked as a kind of jamming device, disrupting his mind, fueling apprehension. He did not hunt or fish or play sports anymore. Other than an easy jog in the morning, he focused on ideas. He was about comprehension and analysis, and throughout his adult life he had mastered the ability to think through even the most complex legal questions. He could feel a bit of damp sweat on his forehead and wondered about the interaction of brain cells signaling the central nervous system to produce beads of moisture due to emotional stress rather than physical exertion.

He focused on the task at hand and rode an elevator to the eleventh floor and checked in. The receptionist went through the list—*name, date of birth, did he have a port, was he feeling as though he had a cold or flu?* She wrapped the ID bracelet around his wrist, and he found a seat in a waiting alcove with a view out over the Longwood medical area. He could see the Charles River and the merge of Brookline Avenue and the Riverway. He noticed the old Sears building where he had worked in college loading trucks, the building long since converted to other uses—movie theater, retail stores, offices, a restaurant. It was a massive structure, a city block long and nine stories high. He recalled some of the men with whom he had worked on the overnight crew. There were a few younger lads making some money while they searched for something better, but most of the crew was composed of men in their forties and fifties for whom the job was a career. This was the human landscape at its most uneven, the massive variation throughout the land in the power of each individual human brain, limited by circumstance or nature, the yawning variation in intelligence and opportunity—there was something particularly cruel in that, Rob thought. He tried to focus. There was a chance he could walk out of the hospital with a clean bill of health—negative biopsy result—and return to normal life. A positive result, however, would mean something else entirely: confirmation that cancer cells were active within his body. This would start him down a pathway of tests, procedures, physicians with various specialties, appointment after appointment with an oncologist, maybe a surgeon, maybe a radiation oncologist. Who knew where this would lead? The coffee cup sat untouched at his elbow.

It was forty minutes past the scheduled time for his appointment. What doctors did not understand was that patients awaiting results of a frightening test arrived at the hospital with near maximum anxiety. For each minute past the appointment time they were kept waiting, their anxiety climbed until a Mach 1 level of fear was reached. The doctor knew the results of the biopsy. The technicians knew, too. They knew more about his health and future pathway in life than he did. He thought it must be difficult to come into the room and give bad news to someone you'd never met before. This tension, the rising fear factor, was why he insisted on doing all of the medical sessions on his own, sparing Julia. They had discussed this, argued about it, but Rob was firm.

His name was called and he was led to the office of the medical oncologist, but then another twenty minutes waiting for the doctor to arrive. Finally, a light tap on the door and she entered: mid-fifties, short graying hair, serious expression.

"Mr. Barrow, I'm Doctor Stone," she said. An indifferent handshake as she moved to sit down in front of the computer. Silently, she typed a bit and studied the screen.

"So we have some decisions to make," she said, turning away from the screen to look at him.

"I take it the biopsy was positive?" he asked.

She frowned. "I thought you knew."

"So how bad is it?"

She turned back to the screen and studied the numbers. "Gleason of nine."

His heart struck hard in his chest. He had researched the Gleason grading system for prostate cancer and had hoped for a score of six or seven, which indicated slower growing cells. Ray had told him that a Gleason of nine indicated the most aggressive form of the disease. It was disorienting to think that as he sat in this moment in this room with this doctor, the dominant physical reality in his life was that diseased cells had joined forces in his body.

"Watchful waiting a possibility?" he asked, uncertain what else to say.

She frowned. "Not with a Gleason of nine." She glanced down at her watch. Rob wondered about this. Why wasn't she skilled enough to steal a glance at the clock without a patient noticing? Her impatience annoyed him, a man not easily annoyed. There was a trial, she said, a new drug, or more accurately a new series of drugs. He seemed a good fit. She had the consent documents with her, a fat stack of papers, actually. Perhaps he should consider it? But Ray had made it clear to him that a Gleason of eight or nine required surgery. "They are in the business of running trials over there," Ray had said. "They're great, very competent, but sometimes they get over their skis on the trials. If they try to sell you the shiny new model, just decline. Surgery can be very effective. Lot of guys have the operation and never see another cancer cell in their lives."

Rob, Julia, and Ray had talked it through the night before. If the biopsy was positive Rob would go to the office of Dr. Steve Chen, the surgeon and friend of Ray's, and make an appointment for a radical prostatectomy. This involved the surgical removal of his cancerous prostate, which would bring an array of potential side effects. He had read enough to know that a certain percentage of men had no choice but to wear adult diapers.

Chen was around forty, medium height, disheveled dark hair, welcoming smile. He wore an ill-fitting blue suit, button-down blue dress shirt, and a striped tie loose at the neck. He greeted Rob warmly, spoke with fond recollections of having their mutual friend Ray as a teacher in med school.

"You could not have a better guide through all of this," Chen said. "And I want to start by saying that I've been doing this for some years now, and I have seen countless patients like you get through surgery very nicely and go on to live long healthy lives." Chen looked at his computer. "I want you to have a couple of weeks to relax so you are well rested before surgery. At your age, anesthesia can be tough. How about September 16, 6:00 a.m. A Thursday, you'll go home the next day and have a restful weekend. That work?"

"September 16, well, okay," said Rob. "I wondered whether you do it robotically?"

"I am comfortable doing it either way, but the robot allows us to be a bit more precise," said Chen. "So I will be at a console from which I will manipulate the instruments. You'll receive general anesthesia, we have a ventilator breathe for you during surgery, and I would expect it to go well. You're healthy for your age, not overweight, have no underlying medical conditions. You are a very good candidate for surgery. The goal is clean lines, no damage to adjacent nerves."

"What are the chances I will have incontinence?"

"Very low," said Chen.

"Sexual function?"

"Trickier," said Chen. "We will talk that through later."

"What are the chances I die during surgery?"

"About one in ten thousand."

"Because, Dr. Chen," Rob said, "my wife needs me."

3

American Sycamore

In the good weather Rob's preferred location was the secluded garden in the backyard of their home, their "nest" as Julia had called it from the start, way back in 1978 when they purchased the property from a family stuck in a years-long inheritance conflict. It was a two-acre corner lot that had fallen into disrepair. That was back in a time when they were starting out in marriage, in life, in their professions, Julia on her way to becoming a journalist of some note as well as a historian, Rob on a path to teaching law. Thanks to Julia's parents' generous support, the young couple was able to escape the financial strains that were so difficult for most Americans starting out.

Julia fell in love with the property the moment she saw it. She had told Rob that evening: *This is the place. This is where our family life will happen, where our children will be born and grow up, where our grandchildren will come to visit, where you and I will grow old together. This is where everything that matters will happen.*

It was tucked into a secluded area near Radcliffe, easy walking distance to Harvard Square and Rob's office at the law school, and the history department where Julia was enrolled. The house was a 1790 Colonial with good bones, as the architects put it. Real estate agents thought of it as a teardown, but Julia had other plans. The lot itself was overrun with weeds, bushes out of control, trees that had not been trimmed in a generation. But she saw that the house could become a jewel, and she set to hiring an architectural firm that specialized in preserving old homes. It would have cost far less to tear down the existing structure and build a new house, she was told by a contractor, but she would not hear of it. This house had been built by hand by men who were contemporaries of the Founding Fathers. These were the Yankees who settled New England and fought at Washington's side in the Revolutionary War. Julia and Rob would honor these men by restoring what their hands had constructed. There were new beams cut from the same Vermont forests as the originals along with a reconstructed foundation, all new systems without, as Julia put it, "intruding on the character" of the place. Four chimneys were rebuilt from the basement up, but the original stone of the fireplaces themselves was restored. The wide pine floorboards were removed, the foundation resurfaced, and the floorboards reinstalled with nails copied from the originals.

Julia had never taken on a project like this one, but she thrived in doing so. She was there at the jobsite many mornings to greet the workers, sometimes with coffee and doughnuts. She was drawn to the specialty carpenters who appreciated the opportunity to work on an historic property. These were people who understood the value of preservation, of honoring work done centuries ago by the craftsmen of the time. Sometimes the work was painstakingly slow, but she did not mind. When it was all done, the main house had been renovated and a new wing added that looked remarkably like old photos of the original. Upon completion of the work, she hosted a catered dinner for the workers—the construction crews, carpenters, architects—everyone who had contributed to bringing this beauty back to life.

When Rob returned from the hospital, it was early evening. Julia was out running errands, and he was eager for her return. Rob poured a whiskey and went outside to the garden, taking a seat on the flagstone terrace, slightly elevated above the property. For forty years this had been his retreat, a place where the tranquility of nature settled upon him, actually settled *within* him. He glanced around and his eye fell first, as was so often the case, on the American sycamore across the yard. It was estimated by experts to be approximately 350 years old. Rob had often reflected upon the fact that this tree that he was now blessed to gaze upon had been here when Washington and his men had camped in Cambridge. The connection mattered to Rob. The sycamore with its thick, furrowed bark evoked the strength and durability of America. Its massive canopy provided shade for a huge swath of the property, some of its leaves the size of a catcher's mitt. The preening ash in the far corner stole the attention in fall with its green leaves turning a flaming yellow and then, as though choreographed, shedding every last leaf over the course of a few days, leaving a golden carpet on that section of the lawn. Rob loved this patch of nature. Over time, he had come to know the rhythms of the place—the exploding glory of spring, buds bursting, the settled elegance of summer with all of nature in sync, the vibrance of the autumn, and the frigid New England winters, trees mostly bare, frozen ground, shrubs in their protective burlap. Back in the earlier days, when Rob took it upon himself to rake and dispose of the leaves in fall, he had a fondness for the ash tree's efficiency as its leaves seemed to fall in a two-day choreography. The sycamore, though, was a stubborn old fellow who did not easily yield its leaves. Rather, the shedding process would begin in early fall and only very gradually, grudgingly, Rob thought, did the massive tree give way to the cruelty of winter.

Rob was by no means an arborist. When they had first moved into the place, he didn't know one tree from another. But over time he had come to know this place, and he had come to think of the sycamore as having a distinctly American character: individual, proud, steady as she goes. It kept growing and growing, reaching heights well beyond the others, clinging to some of its leaves throughout even the fiercest of winter storms, never reaching a point where, like the ash and others, it was entirely bare against the fronts roaring down from the Canadian provinces. One year, Rob had noticed that there were still leaves clinging to the sycamore when spring came and the new leaves began to emerge, and he was struck by the durability, this determination to hang in there against the natural forces to which all the others had succumbed. Closer to the house was an oak, three black locusts that, in spring, produced a dazzling display of white blossoms that illuminated the yard. A landscape architect had added flowering dogwood, various shrubs, and all along the back of the yard that separated the property from their friend Ray Witter, a dense privet hedge that was maintained by a landscaper and his son who took pride in the precision with which they trimmed the hedge and cut a narrow walkway for Ray's easy entrance to the yard. Toward the back of the property a small, man-made pond attracted wood ducks and, once in a while, a great blue heron.

Rob sipped his whiskey. It was a calm summer evening, the day's heat lifting, the shade of the property protecting the yard from the highest temperatures. Rob sat alone and took a deep breath, looking slowly around and feeling, as he always did, comforted by the serenity of nature, a blessing from God. He read through the pathology report, not understanding everything but getting the gist. On his phone, he tunneled into Google's netherworld of medical information. Surgery was a must. What if the cancer had gotten a running start, metastasized? Who knew where it could go? Actually, he knew. Google told him exactly where it would go if it got loose: into the bones. Yes, the *bones*, the physical foundation upon which the human was constructed. Imagine having cancer cells racing like atoms run amok in the hadron collider within his bone structure. And so he would have surgery. At the moment, he was more concerned with the bladder control issue than lack of sexual function. What if he started randomly peeing his pants? What if he had accidents in bed? During a meeting or teaching a class? God forbid while arguing a case in front of the nine black-robed justices

of the Supreme Court! And the idea of wearing Depends—Jesus H.
Christ. He had never given much thought to aging. He had always kept
himself fit: running, good nutrition, no tobacco, not too much alcohol. But now there were rogue cells, a malevolent force determined to
spread as widely throughout his body as possible.

He thought of the Philip Roth observation that "old age is not a
battle. It's a massacre."

"I have cancer." Rob said it softly. "It is August 27, 2021, and I
have cancer." The wind blew through the trees. Julia would be home
soon and they would talk. When he had learned of his illness, for some
reason he thought of his mother. He really had not thought of her
much in years, largely because she had never figured very much in his
life. He had always preferred to be alone when he was growing up,
and this was the original source of his reserve that bordered on social
awkwardness. He was a bit off, Julia told him, but in being so there was
also something genuine about him. Rob Barrow had zero pretensions
and that, Julia had told him early on, was both rare and admirable.
She had always admired the steadiness and determination that guided
him from what was an unusual upbringing. While Julia had enjoyed
comfortable early years in Manhattan, Rob had been at the other end
of the scale—or off the scale in some ways. He had grown up in a
one-bedroom apartment with his mother, a ghostly presence, and no
father. His mother said he had been killed in the Korean War, but
Rob came to believe she did not know who his father was. There were
men in business suits who came and went from the apartment, walking past Rob at 3:00 a.m. as he feigned sleep on his living room cot.
The apartment was on the main drag in Roslindale Square, a Boston
neighborhood, and the bus and truck traffic moved steadily through
the evening, diesel fumes permeating the place. It was a narrow brick
structure, three stories, two units per floor flanking a staircase. These
had originally been cold-water flats for immigrant laborers in the
1920s and up through the '40s. Rob had been born in the apartment,

older ladies in the building assisting his mother in the birthing process. Rob was tucked into a corner of the twelve-by-twelve-foot living
room next to the one radiator that worked. And there he would remain
into his twenties, from crib to cot. There had been a coal-fired stove
and an icebox in the 1950s, and his mother never saw any need to
modernize. She worked as a waitress at downtown hotels in what she
referred to as the "swanky places." Their schedules rarely overlapped.
Rob would often see her coming in when he was getting up to go to
school. After school and sports Rob usually spent a few hours in the
library, returning to the apartment around six when his mother was
about to head out to work. She rarely made meals for him but made
sure there were cans of soup and boxes of cereal in the green-painted
cabinets. Rob learned to be independent at an early age. His universe
was the apartment, school, the sports field, and the library, all within a
fifteen-minute walk.

One weekend when Rob was fifteen, two police officers arrived
to tell him that his mother had died in a car crash. One of her male
friends had been behind the wheel. The neighbors were supportive,
quite kind in fact. The mothers and grandmothers brought him food,
asked him how he felt, and he said he would be okay because that was
the truth. The landlord, Mr. Farrell, a special friend of his mother's
who owned property throughout the city, had often visited the apartment and sometimes gave Rob a few dollars. After her death he came to
see Rob, a pressed sharkskin suit, white shirt, tie pin, slicked back hair,
intense aftershave, and told Rob he could stay in the apartment as long
as he wanted for no cost.

"She was a fine lady," Mr. Farrell said solemnly, shaking Rob's hand
and giving him three hundred dollars in cash.

Rob realized in retrospect, of course, that his mother suffered from
some sort of mental illness. There were long stretches where she barely
uttered a word. Sometimes she would whisper things that made little
sense and then emit a curious kind of laughter. Occasionally, she would

carry on an animated conversation with herself. As strange as the situation was, Rob never felt lonely. He worked at school to achieve academically and, in the process, was moved up a grade, and then another in high school. When he was not in school or playing ball, he was reading and studying. He read history and science and biography and was captivated late in high school by theology.

But now, here he was decades later in his beloved garden with news that Mr. Reliable, as Julia called him, was having trouble processing. The stillness was interrupted by the ringing of his cell phone. Rob reached for it, fumbled it, and somehow pushed the wrong button, cutting off the caller. For all his brains, the complexity of the phone was daunting to him. A moment later it rang again and he pressed down on various buttons, worried he might miss a call from one of the doctors. Maybe they were going to tell him there was a mix-up, that the biopsy was clean! But it was an undergraduate staff member at the student newspaper, *The Harvard Crimson*.

"Professor Barrow?"

"Speaking."

"Hi, professor, it's Judith Jansen at the *Crimson*, and I wonder if you have just a minute?"

"Ahh, well, Judith, I am a bit distracted at the moment."

"I promise it will be quick, professor," she said. "I'm writing a piece about progress on the *New York Times* 1619 Project. It's the two-year anniversary, and I'm asking faculty members their thoughts about its impact thus far. Any thoughts, professor?"

"I read the article, of course, some time ago, but, to be honest I haven't given it much thought since then," said Rob.

"Is it something, professor, that you have considered integrating into your courses?"

"In constitutional law?" Rob replied. "Well, never say never, I suppose, but I don't think, at least from what I know about it, I don't think it's quite relevant for what I am teaching these days."

At that moment Rob heard Julia pull into the driveway.

"Judith, I apologize, but I have to run," Rob said. "My wife just got home. Sorry I can't be more helpful. Call any time."

Through the years Rob had always been polite and cooperative with *Crimson* reporters, but the last thing on his mind on this particular evening was whether a new theory of history by a *New York Times* reporter related to his courses. When Julia arrived, she dropped her briefcase in the kitchen and headed to the terrace.

Rob rose and kissed her.

"So?" she asked.

"Confirmed cancer in the prostate but not outside it. At least they don't think so, and it's really pretty straightforward," he said. "Surgery very common for this."

She winced. "Rob . . ."

He took her hand and they sat, side by side, in the well-worn Adirondack chairs. He smiled at her and said softly, "You look beautiful," a phrase he had uttered countless times through the years. He had meant every word of it every time he had said it.

"It's okay," he said. "Nothing to worry about. As long as it's contained in the capsule, 99 percent chance they'll cut it out and it'll be right as rain, Jules." He smiled, attempting a look of reassurance. But Julia's face betrayed her fear. It was clear from her expression that she knew the unshakable Rob was shaken. She could see in his sharp hazel eyes a look of uncertainty and confusion that she could only describe as fear and this startled her, for she had seen fear in Rob's eyes only once before, years earlier, and she suddenly started to cry. Rob rose and reached for her, embracing her, standing nearly a foot taller, holding her, protecting her from the universe and its astonishing power to inflict harm. And now he of all people was counted among the vulnerable. She was not crying for herself but for Rob. She wanted him protected, felt that he deserved to be protected from the harms of life. She pulled back a bit, and he responded by loosening his embrace. She wiped her eyes with the backs of her hands and grasped his forearms, holding them tightly.

"I will take care of you," she said. "No matter what happens, we will do this together."

He went inside and poured a glass of red wine, which he brought out to her.

"What should we do to prepare for the surgery?" she asked. Now she was all business. *What is the problem? How do we fix it?*

He shrugged. "Oh, not much," he said. "They gave me a few pages of instructions, which I left on the kitchen counter. There's a prescription for antibacterial soap I'm supposed to shower with for a couple of days before the operation. One night in the hospital, come home with a catheter for a couple weeks, then they take that out and I'm off to the races. Good as gold. Right as rain."

It so happened that at that moment Ray Witter, whose home abutted Rob and Julia's, came through the slight opening in the privet hedge and sauntered across the backyard, past the little pond and the elms and the magnificent sycamore. This was Rob's signal to pour a not-so-wee dram of scotch for Ray. Ray was the dearest of friends, a rural Iowa farm boy whose intellectual gifts had been evident from an early age.

"Such service!" Ray exclaimed as he reached the terrace, accepted the glass, and simultaneously reached out to hug Julia. He patted Rob on the shoulder and sat down. In addition to being dean of the medical school, Ray was an expert in medical safety. He had been a member of the Institute of Medicine committee that wrote the 1999 report *To Err Is Human: Building a Safer Health System*, which estimated that as many as 99,000 preventable deaths occurred annually in American hospitals. He had created a course at the medical school, which he personally taught, called The Patient Is Your Mother 101. The idea was simply to treat each patient as you would have your mother treated.

"I have to ask, Ray, what are the risks of surgery?" Rob asked. "They mentioned a few things at my last appointment."

"Minimal," Ray said. "You are in good shape. These operations are pretty routine now, and Chen is solid. Precise, diligent. The greater risk is being in a hospital at all, where mistakes happen but are systematically concealed. Progress, but we still have these medical black holes, where patients are harmed, then paid off to keep everything secret. It's a sinister practice for the simple reason we need to know about the mistakes to learn from them. They are gold for us because they are teaching opportunities. Are there particular procedures that subject the patient to a potentially deadly septic infection, and, if so, how do we figure out a standard way of preventing it that we can share with the world? No, hospitals duck and cover. It's a fucking scandal. These nondisclosure agreements with patients—bribes to prevent them from talking—are tucked away in secured safes in medical centers. I've been trying for how long now, Rob?"

"Fifteen years at least," Rob said.

"Ray, *seriously*?" said Julia.

"Sorry, can't help myself. I actually did a little checking, and the good news is there have been zero nondisclosure agreements involving Chen or involving patients undergoing a radical prostatectomy for years. The surgeons are good, and they have nailed a standard procedure for this with a high degree of reliability."

Ray reached into his shirt pocket, took out a tightly rolled joint, and lit up. He inhaled deeply and released his breath slowly, then took a modest sip of his scotch.

"The risks, Ray," Rob said, pulling Ray back into the moment.

"Standard postsurgical stuff," he said.

"What they told me," Rob said, "is there is a risk of infection, incontinence, and reactions to general anesthesia, which I have never had. And they said that even weeks or longer after the operation there could be episodic pain from the catheter's scar tissue. That sometimes it lingers."

"What does *quote* reactions to general anesthesia *unquote* mean exactly?" Julia asked.

"I wondered about that," Rob replied, "and they said 'delirium, confusion, memory loss, et cetera.'"

Julia considered this. "Memory loss," she said softly. "Maybe there's a benefit there."

They all fell silent. She was sorry she said it and stared down at her hand for a few moments, a visual offering of contrition.

4

1619

In summer, Rob had agreed to conduct an orientation class for a group of incoming freshmen. Some of these students were the first in their families to attend college, while others had emigrated to the United States with refugee status or had grown up seeming stuck in urban poverty. A few had arrived from Asia just a few years earlier, speaking not a word of English. They were, by any measure, a highly select group of talented young people. The session was scheduled for August 30, a couple of weeks before his operation, and Rob looked forward to it as a welcome distraction. He knew he would enjoy introducing these students, barely out of high school, into the magisterial world of the United States Constitution. Rob stood before the class of thirty-plus gathered in a small lecture hall, fresh-faced kids filling seats in rows rising gradually up from the front of the hall to the rear.

It was a humid morning with temperatures heading into the nineties that day, but Rob nonetheless wore his standard teaching uniform of khaki trousers, tweed sports coat, blue button-down Brooks Brothers shirt, and club tie. He was well over six feet tall, thin, quite fit, with a narrow face and receding hair. The students, bare-legged and in flip-flops and T-shirts, arrived with their coffee and laptops, and it struck Rob as a joyful moment for them. Here they were entering Harvard, plucked from an applicant pool where barely one in ten was admitted. He scanned the class and noticed that about two-thirds of the students were Black, along with a mix of whites and Asians.

"Good morning and welcome," he said, smiling, looking around the room. "My name is Robert Barrow, and I'm a professor of constitutional law, and I want to tell you a story this morning about a man named Clarence Gideon, who was accused of robbing a poolroom in Panama City, Florida. It was alleged that during the early morning hours of June 3, 1961, Clarence got away with several bottles of beer, some wine, and about five dollars. Clarence Gideon had quit school at age fourteen and run away from his home in Hannibal, Missouri. He was a thin, odd-looking boy with glasses who committed a series of petty crimes. He spent several years in prison in the 1930s for property crimes and, later, for crimes in Texas and Kansas. If Clarence did not have bad luck, he would have had no luck at all. He was always broke, had three failed marriages, suffered from tuberculosis, and was forced to give up custody of his children to state authorities for neglect.

"When Clarence was charged with the poolroom break-in, he asked the judge to appoint a lawyer to represent him. In denying his request, the judge said there were few circumstances under which Florida law permitted him to appoint an attorney for an indigent defendant. One of those conditions was if the defendant was in danger of facing the death penalty, so Clarence did not qualify for a court-appointed attorney. He defended himself, making an opening and closing statement, questioning and cross-examining witnesses. His eighth-grade education was no match for a prosecutor. On the charges of breaking and entering and petty larceny, the jury returned verdicts of guilty, and in August of 1961, Clarence was sentenced to five years in prison. And in the vast majority of cases that would have been it. Clarence would have gone and done his time, been released, and gotten on with whatever type of life he had been able to carve out for himself." Rob paused and looked up at the students sitting with their backpacks and laptops in the riser seats.

"But instead, what happened was extraordinary, testament to what is unique in American law and character. Because Clarence was able, from his cell, to study the law and make his case. There's power, even majesty, in the fact that Clarence's prison library enabled him to make a case that he had been unfairly convicted and imprisoned. From inside the prison itself he had the tools to make the case that he did not belong there."

Rob fell silent as he strolled slowly across the front of the classroom. "I long ago promised myself that I would never rush past this part of the story—this part where, as I just noted, this poor convicted criminal in prison was offered the tool to secure his freedom. Were there libraries in Russian gulags? Libraries in the camps where Mao Zedong sent Chinese dissidents to die? It seems a small thing—a library in a prison; a ragged collection of books. But it strikes me as very American to have, in a wretched place of confinement where virtually all of your freedoms are taken away, the freedom to learn and think; the freedom to permit your mind to explore great writing, visionary thinking. In prison, Clarence set to writing a petition to the United States Supreme Court to hear an appeal on his case. Clarence wrote his petition on prison stationery—by hand, in pencil! Here was a drifter, a petty criminal, a man who had failed at virtually everything in life, writing in pencil from prison to the greatest legal minds in the nation. *And they agreed to hear his case!* Not only did the court take Clarence's case, but the justices appointed the distinguished Washington lawyer Abe Fortas to represent him in the matter. During his appearance before the court, Fortas made a powerful case that a defendant without a lawyer could not hope to get justice, and wasn't justice a core value of the American experiment? 'You cannot have a fair trial without counsel,' Fortas told the justices."

Rob paced slowly at the front of the classroom, pausing for a moment before he said, "The Supreme Court ruled 9–0 in favor of

Clarence Gideon. Nine to nothing that every defendant in the country, no matter his or her ability to pay, deserved to be represented by an attorney at trial. The court ordered Clarence's case sent back to state court for retrial, where he was represented by a competent attorney and promptly acquitted by a jury."

Rob was covering familiar ground. For years, he had told such stories to students as a way of encouraging them to share his reverence for the majesty of American constitutional law. For the foundational beauty of the American experiment. But as he started to tell a follow-up story about the *Brown v. Board of Education* ruling in 1954 striking down the notion of separate but equal, a number of students began to stir.

"To be honest, professor, those stories feel kind of outdated," said a Black girl in the front row. Several students around her nodded their assent. "I would be more interested in getting your views on the current situation and, in particular, what your take is on the *New York Times* 1619 Project."

"Yes, professor," said another student. "That's where the issues of race and justice are joined today, not sixty years ago." A couple of students laughed.

"Ancient history," one mumbled.

Rob paced, taking this in. "Fair enough," he said. "I get it. But even today, so many years later, Gideon matters because it demonstrates America's aspirational nature. You see that in *Brown*, in *Roe*. The steps are incremental, it is true. The fact that *Brown v. Board of Education* came as late as 1954 is, to my mind, a scar on the national character."

"1619, professor," said the girl in the front row. "Your thoughts?"

Rob smiled. "Wouldn't you say it's more in the historical or political realms than the legal?" he asked.

"All three," she replied.

"You may be right," he said. "You may very well be right, but I don't see the legal argument in it. It strikes me more as an intellectual provocation, historical provocation, than a legal argument. Maybe I should read more about it and we can talk about it another time, but from what I have read it essentially proffers the notion that the nation was really about slavery all along—forget individual liberty, forget the Enlightenment. But frankly, the assertion that the nation's *reason for being* was to protect the rights of slave owners is tough to defend. Serious historians have made clear that the Founding Fathers, for all their flaws, were intent upon establishing a nation based on freedom and liberty for all. Such an expansive idea of freedoms was unheard of historically. A majestic new idea. America's essence is a belief that all men are created equal and its core aspiration is to make that a reality."

"Of *people*," said one of the students. "The equality of *people*. Not just men, professor."

"Of course, of people, yes," Rob said, with a nod toward the student. "Thank you. That is the aspiration. For a *New York Times* reporter to call this a 'lie' seems intellectually reckless to me. The idea that a journalist or group of journalists—none trained as historians, by the way—would take it upon themselves to reframe the history of our country in a way that declares, *Oh, by the way, what you thought was a pursuit of freedom and the equality of people—forget it. Not true.* To suggest that it was actually a slave owners' protection scheme, it's . . ." Rob shrugged, dismissing the notion. "The *Times* reporter who conceived of the project, Nikole something, initially asserted that 1619 was the nation's true founding and, later on, denied she had said that, despite evidence to the contrary. But, as I said, I am no expert on this, so if you have other thoughts, please fire away."

Students were exchanging glances, and Rob noticed that another half dozen or so Black students had entered the lecture hall and taken seats near the back. Several trained their iPhones on him. The room fell silent, but the air was electric. Students stirred, glancing at one another as though no one knew what to say or do. And then a Black student of medium height and build, in jeans and a sweater, hair pulled back, bright eyes and an air of confidence, asked, "Professor, do you own a mirror?"

Nervous laughter from the students.

"A mirror?" Rob asked.

"A mirror, a looking glass, a thing in which you can see yourself," she said. She was smiling, trying to sound playful, but the edge to her words was obvious. "Do you own one?"

Rob tried to go along. "Of course. I wonder why you ask." He tried to sound light-hearted, but it came off as awkward.

"When you look in the mirror, what do you see?" she asked.

"I see an aging face," he said, forcing a laugh. "A wrinkled older man."

"I say respectfully that what you actually see is white privilege," she said. "White *male* privilege, the most toxic strain. I suggest that you reconsider what you have said here about the project." *The* project, he would later think.

"Professor," said another young woman, "I need to convey to you how uncomfortable I am right now, and I need to ask you, *Am I safe in your classroom?* Is a Black woman safe in your classroom or for that matter on your campus?"

"Or in your *world*," said another student.

Rob frowned. These comments struck him as unserious. Performance pieces. *I will go to Harvard and tell the powers that be the lived reality out on the street.*

"Come on, guys, we are all in this together," he said, spreading his arms wide, a gesture to include everyone. "All of us are here to learn. The answer to the question is, Of course you are safe in my classroom. We're here to explore the law, history, ideas, and if some of those ideas make you uncomfortable, then welcome to the turbulent history of constitutional law in the United States."

The student who had questioned the safety of the classroom was speaking softly but with the fervor of the true believer. "Professor," she said. "Really? You want to go there? Disrespect for its founder—Nikole Hannah-Jones. You said she was Nikole *somebody*."

"I couldn't in the moment recall her last name," he said.

"You stripped her of her dignity," the student replied. "You disrespected her by depriving her of her name. An unfortunate echo from slave culture."

"I—" But Rob caught himself.

"Say her name!" someone in the back demanded.

"My response, based on a consensus of historical scholarship, is that the founding was light years from the greedy small-mindedness portrayed by the 1619 Project. You may choose to believe it or not. My belief is that the Founders saw an opportunity to do something that had rarely if ever been done in civilized society—to create a nation where freedom and liberty prevailed in pursuit of the sacred notion that *all people are created equal.*"

A ripple of laughter.

"Why is it, do you think," Rob asked, "that people from all over the world do whatever they can to find their way to America rather than, say, China or Russia?"

"We were dragged here, sir," said the student. "Hunted down, chained, cast into the holds of slave ships, and delivered on to these shores as cargo to be bought and sold like any other commodity. Did your ancestors suffer such a fate, sir?"

The student in the front row, slender, bright-eyed, spoke up again. "Professor, may I read a short excerpt?"

"Of course," Rob replied.

"This is from the original *Times* article," she said. "It says, 'One critical reason that the colonists declared their independence from Britain was because they wanted to protect the institution of slavery in the colonies, which had produced tremendous wealth. At the time there were growing calls to abolish slavery throughout the British Empire, which would have badly damaged the economies of colonies in both North and South.'" She looked up at Rob. "They had an economic interest in slavery that was so powerful they declared independence from England."

Rob liked her. He liked her manner, her spunky personality, the fact that she wanted to engage on the ideas.

"I recall reading that, and—look, I'm not a historian," Rob said. "I want to emphasize that. But I have read history carefully in connection with my work on constitutional scholarship. I believe that statement you read is inaccurate. Revisionist history and, really, I have to say, a reckless statement."

"Professor," she said, "do you think it's possible that you, like a lot of people, have an overly romantic notion of America's founding?"

Rob laughed. "My wife tells me that all the time," he said, but the students weren't disposed to lighten the mood. "I know that I do to a certain extent. It is a by-product, I guess, of my devotion to the Constitution and the vision of the Founders."

"Do you believe America is an inherently racist nation?" the student asked.

Rob considered this. "When I was in law school a very long time ago, I spent a summer working for the NAACP Legal Defense Fund," he said. "And one of my mentors there told me something I have never forgotten. This was the 1970s. Someone had written a piece saying that in America there is 'racism around every corner.' And I asked this wise older man, a Black lawyer, about that, and he said to me: 'Around *every* corner? No. Around most corners? Yes.' And so I think there were a lot of racist attitudes then, racist laws and practices related to voting, housing, employment. But I think we are in a far better place today. We have made enormous progress. Are there still a lot of people who are biased against Black people? Of course. Is America—the nation as a whole, the government, the laws, the schools, companies, hospitals, the people—a racist nation? No."

As if on cue, a couple of dozen students got up from their seats and began filing out of the classroom. He had crossed a line.

The girl in the front row didn't leave immediately. She stood up and regarded him.

"You don't get it, do you, professor?"

"What, exactly?"

"It's obvious," she said. "America is a fundamentally racist nation. Institutional racism abounds."

She turned and started to leave but not before Rob had the last word.

"I believe in America," he said. "I don't apologize for that, nor do I retreat from it."

5

The Great Squander

Julia Browning Barrow had shifted gears after law school and earned a PhD in American history with a specialization in the twentieth century. She contributed a series of columns to the *New Republic*, sharp-elbowed pieces critical of what she perceived to be the deficiencies of the baby boomer generation. The ideas soon became the germ for her doctoral thesis focused on the boomer legacy: *What had the boomers done to protect and enhance the legacy they were given?* Work on her dissertation took years longer than anticipated, as did a subsequent book project. She was also sidetracked by life, by motherhood, by teaching, by an occasional piece in the *Atlantic* or *New Republic*.

By the second decade of the twenty-first century, however, Julia was locked in. Her book was a scathing indictment of America in the modern age, a dark view of history and its portents. *From Woodstock to Altamont: How the Baby Boomers Squandered the Gifts of the Greatest Generation* was a portrait of America in decline; of epic failure by the haloed generation; of deceit and incompetence throughout the institutions that were supposed to nurture "this fragile thing called democracy," as she wrote in the introduction. She proclaimed that the boomers had "a greater potential for good than any generation in any nation in human history." Rob had suggested she delete this thought as overly sweeping, but Julia stuck with it.

On the Friday before Labor Day, when FedEx delivered the fat package containing corrected page proofs of her book, Rob and Ray greeted her in the garden with a standing ovation. Ray hooted, Rob whistled, and she felt both honored and loved. The men embraced her in turn. Rob offered a toast. "To you, Jules, for all that you have achieved and with all the love I have in my being," Rob said. "Congratulations!" They clinked glasses and sat, the men beaming at her, Julia holding the proofs on her lap, 370 pages she had meticulously, even lovingly, constructed.

"You've got balls, Jules, I will tell you that," said Ray. "To hang in there all the way, through everything, I just . . ." In the moment he was emotional, and Ray was hardly ever outwardly emotional. "I am honored to be here with you, and I consider it one of the great blessings of my life that you and Rob are my friends."

She reached over and squeezed Ray's hand. "We are a little family, the three of us, aren't we?" she said. Julia looked around the garden and felt the sense of security she always experienced here. There was the earthy fragrance, the dark green leaves, the audible creaking of the oaks in a strong breeze. This was their place, their hideaway. It was where they not so much hid from cruel realities as found the sustenance to live with those realities. This was where the healing power of friendship and love came together.

"So a few very early reviews, Jules?" said Ray.

"Small handful in the trades," she said. "My favorite is one where the reviewer said something like, Professor Barrow's thesis is that America's decline is owing to—and the quote goes something like this—'a lack of commitment to a sense of honor and failed leadership in the institutions that matter, including Congress, the presidency, the military, big business, the media, religious institutions, and the educational system.' And then the reviewer adds: 'Perhaps to fill out the extreme negativity of her view, Professor Barrow might have included the Girl Scouts and Little League Baseball on her bill of indictment.'

"The good news about any potential reviews," she joked, "is that the person who dissents from my analysis the most will never write a review, thankfully. At least, I hope you won't, Rob!"

"You have my word on it," Rob replied.

"Honestly, guys, seventy-three million baby boomers and this is the best we can do?" Julia said. "The most highly educated generation in world history, and this is how we honor our forebears?" She thumbed through the proofs and found a particular passage. "LBJ's Great Society would end poverty, bring good jobs for all. Instead, we got fifty years of warmongering: Vietnam, Iraq, Afghanistan. Staggering income inequality, the journalistic pornography that is Fox."

"That said," Ray interjected, "Rob remains America's chief optimist, the final holdout. Rob, you're like the Japanese soldier they found twenty years after the war ended, hunkered in a cave on a remote Pacific island ready to do battle."

"I think DeLillo was *wrong,*" said Julia. "The JFK assassination isn't what 'broke the back of the American Century.' It was the turn *inward*, away from higher purpose and the common good. Fast-forward and our so-called demographic cohort worships at the altar of NASDAQ, reading Paul Krugman to stoke our generational outrage followed by a soothing interval with the *Times* crossword."

"What worries you the most, Jules?" asked Ray.

"The judiciary," she replied, "or I should say the shadow judiciary in the form of the Federalist Society and its right-wing agenda in the hands of its six justices on the Supreme Court. What happens when all these cases come up related to voting, gay rights, not to mention *Roe*?"

"But they can't overturn *Roe* after all these years. Settled law, hands off," Rob said.

"It would be medieval," Julia snapped. "Take away a right that women have had for half a century? But they have 6–3 majority, Rob.

What makes you believe they won't use it? Let me guess—you think Chief Justice Roberts will save the day, phone booth, cape, robes, hold back the tide of tyranny."

"What if the cape gets tangled in those robes?" Ray joked.

Rob laughed. He didn't mind the mocking tone. He had grown accustomed to it through the years.

"He is very conservative, Rob. If he has the votes to overturn, why wouldn't he just go ahead and do it?" Ray asked.

"Because he's an institutionalist who recognizes the importance of guarding the legitimacy of the court with the American people," Rob said. "And he knows that to take away the right of a woman to make her own decision after fifty years would be an overreach."

"Insane is what it would be," said Julia.

"It's who Roberts is," Rob continued. "He is the court's guardian. When the Obamacare issue came before the court he twisted himself into a pretzel and issued an opinion that upheld it because he knew that depriving twenty million people of health insurance would be seen as a draconian act, which it would have been."

Julia went into the house, returning a moment later, face flushed, wine glass refilled. She was heated now, fueled by wine and the adrenaline injection of receiving the page proofs, and angry about the course of history. "The good-hearted liberals cheered the progress of women, Black people, gays," she said, "but forgot about blue-collar workers in Detroit's River Rouge plant, where historic upward mobility became a mirage. In the blink of an historical eye, formerly middle-class working families tumbled from the foundational elements of the American dream to insecurity, confusion, resentment, and just plain fear. Woodstock to Altamont, a portent of things to come. Kennedy morality an alien concept. Mary Jo drowned, forgotten. Joe Sr. nailed half the mothers when Jack was at Choate; Rose in the next room, listening to the banging wall, clutching her rosary beads. And these were the people who carried our hopes? Our aspirations? *Jesus.*" She shook her head slowly. "We inherited something precious, even sacred, from the Greatest Generation, and what do we do but pass along a squalid legacy? The final sentence in my book I really believe is true, and I know you believe it's hyperbole, Rob, but to me, it's the truth: "In a sea of hubris, upon these rocks, the once promising generation crashed, sinking into the depths, a reclamation project for archeologists of a later generation."

6

Irrelevant

The *Harvard Crimson* was housed in a classic New England red brick building tucked in a quaint Harvard Square side street. The paper was published daily during the academic year, and it had produced an impressive number of journalists who had gone on to prominence in the field, including giants of the twentieth century such as Theodore H. White, Joseph Alsop, Walter Lippman, and David Halberstam. Of more recent vintage had been the likes of Ross Douthat at the *Times* and Jim Cramer at CNBC, as well as Michael Kinsley and Mickey Kaus from the *New Republic*. The physical setting in the newsroom was less august than the list of alums. Desks askew, random stacks of papers, bound reports, piles of books, walls lined with framed copies of past front pages: assassinations of the Kennedy brothers and Martin Luther King Jr., Nixon's resignation, withdrawal from Vietnam, and the iconic banner headline after the Harvard football team rallied in the final seconds to tie Yale: HARVARD BEATS YALE 29–29.

Judith Jansen cared not at all for football or the newspaper's history, but she cared very much about making an impact at the *Crimson*. She had returned to Cambridge a couple of weeks early to get a head start on the year. She happened to read that August 2021 was the two-year anniversary of the special *New York Times Magazine* issue devoted to the 1619 Project and thought that could have some bite as a news story. She phoned a couple of dozen faculty members, wrote a piece about their thoughts, and emailed it to the *Crimson* editor, Andy Burns.

"Impressive!" Andy said, greeting Judith in the otherwise empty newspaper office before most staffers had returned to Cambridge for the academic year. "Getting a jump on things—A for effort!"

"Hey," said Judith, pleased to have the editor's attention, "great to see you!"

"And you," said Burns. "*LA Times* summer interesting?"

"LA crime beat in summer not to be missed," she said. "Stayed with my uncle in the Hills. Lots to talk about."

Andrea "Andy" Burns was an impressive physical and intellectual presence. Nearly six feet tall, she had been an all-Ivy volleyball player freshman year before quitting the sport to devote her time to studying and working at the *Crimson*. A native of Indianola, Iowa, she had achieved perfect scores on the college boards, ranked first in her high school class, and had earned top honors in the National Latin Exam for four consecutive years. She had cropped blonde hair and bright blue eyes and had the appearance of an all-American corn-fed young woman. After her sophomore year she had done a summer internship at the *New York Times*. After that experience she had no doubt that her road ahead would be journalism, for she believed it the most effective profession through which to work for justice and equity in American society.

"Nice reporting on 1619," Andy said. "Lots of push and pull. Interesting how adamant some of the historians were about what they perceive as flawed thinking. Also interesting how comically clueless some of the faculty were. Bender not even knowing what it was? 'Never heard of it.' Crazy."

"I explained it to him twice, and he said he didn't know anything about it," Judith said. "He said he had not read a newspaper in twenty years—didn't have time. I guess the physics and math people tend to live in their own little worlds."

"I was disappointed in Barrow's reflexive negativity," said Andy. "*Irrelevant?*" She frowned and shook her head dismissively. "Let's follow up—ask around, see what comes up. Anyway, I sent it back to you with a few edits, questions, nothing heavy. It reads well. We'll run it on page one on—what's our start date this year?" She consulted her computer. "Okay, yeah, September 7, day after Labor Day. Let's get it on the table right away, kind of speaks to the moment I think, and there's a nice array of opinion. Predictable, I guess, but revealing nonetheless."

Judith admired the editor. What struck her about Andy was her self-possession. She had a nice calm steadiness about her that she envied. Judith was physically dwarfed by Andy. She was slope-shouldered, five three, with long dark hair she preferred to wear up, deeply tanned from the summer in LA, having worked the night shift. Judith's face was thin, with bright blue eyes thanks to her Dutch heritage. She had a reluctant smile and an air of intensity. She was from a family of achievers, brought up to be an achiever, and she was now in a place where she was determined to make a mark. Her parents were well-known New Yorkers of Dutch descent: Mia Jansen, a literary agent, and Mees Jansen, managing partner at Cerberus, one of the world's largest investment managers, where his computer-like brain, sharpened with a PhD in applied math from Carnegie-Mellon, fueled part of the firm's investment success. It was noteworthy that the firm was named after the mythological three-headed dog guarding the gates of Hades, preventing the dead from leaving.

The most successful *Crimson* staff members had a sense of reserve about them. Many others, Judith among them, all but vibrated with ambition. When too many students like Judith occupied the venerable old building at 12 Plympton Street, the 103-year-old bricks and mortar were stressed under the seething ambition, which threatened to detonate the structure. It was a tribute to the original architects and the

masons who laid the bricks and hung the plumb lines that the building had remained sturdy enough through the years to contain the egos
within.

Judith would stick close to Andy, for this would be her year to break
through as a top reporter. She had worked diligently over the summer
in LA at a job she had gotten thanks to her parents' connections to a
couple of board members there. Competition at the *Crimson* was fierce.
A staff position burnished students' resumes on the way to the heights
of law or business. The *Crimson* experience was all but mandatory for
students aspiring to future roles at the *Times*, the *Wall Street Journal*, *The
New Yorker*, or *Foreign Affairs*. Judith was focused on the moment, not the
future. Her sophomore year goal was to produce a mix of basic reporting and to break some attention-getting hard news. Her father, whom
she idolized, had made it clear to her that summer that he was highly
suspicious of journalists and thought she was perhaps making a mistake
going in that direction.

"Most journalists, the elites excepted, sit on their asses on the side-
lines," he told her. "They watch. They observe. They don't *do* much
of value. That's why they are paid shit. I have twenty-seven-year-old
kids who work for me making ten times what the editor of the *New York
Times* makes. Think about it, kiddo. Maybe a couple of years on this as
a lark, I get that. But you only get one life—you want to be in the stands
selling popcorn or on the field playing the game? I mean, come on,
Jude, you're too smart for the ink-stained wretch crowd. But as long as
you are doing it, just keep in mind that if people at the university aren't
talking about your work, you're wasting your time. And what is wasting
time for people like us?"

"A crime," she dutifully replied.

Her father laughed. "That's my girl!"

Judith and Andy chatted for a few minutes about other story
ideas, and as Judith got up to leave, Andy asked, "You recorded all the
interviews obviously, yes?" This had become *Crimson* policy: no audio

recording of a quote, no publication. No more the days of trusting scribbled notes from reporters' notebooks.

Judith hesitated but then replied, "Of course."

On September 7, her piece ran on page one with the headline FACULTY MIXED ON 1619 PROJECT. There were numerous quotes from a variety of members of the Faculty of Arts and Sciences and a few from graduate schools. The article found much support for the initiative, but also some strong pushback, especially from faculty members in the history department. Rob was quoted near the tail end of the article: "Professor Robert Barrow was clearly uncomfortable discussing the topic. He dismissed the 1619 initiative as 'irrelevant' and abruptly ended the brief phone interview with the *Crimson*."

7

Happy Birthday, Rob!

On the morning of September 16, 2021, a Thursday, Rob woke at 5:00 a.m., showered with the antibacterial soap, and dressed. Julia was up and waiting for him in the kitchen. She did her best to conceal that she was suffering from a slight anxiety/wine-induced hangover.

"Good morning," she said, clutching his hand, smiling broadly. "Happy birthday!"

"Thank you."

"Ready?"

"I believe I am," he replied brightly. "I believe I am." He forced a smile. Julia knew this was not normal Rob. This was a rare beast known as nervous Rob, and when a person who is very rarely nervous gets nervous, unusual things happen. And so it was in the car, Julia at the wheel, heading to the hospital.

"Did you hear about the girl on the docks in New York?" he asked, as she drove through light early-morning traffic.

"No," she said, assuming he was referring to some sort of news item. "What happened?"

"Well," he said, "see, there was this young woman in her early twenties, and some said she was the most beautiful girl they had ever seen. Stunning. And there she was in all her beauty sobbing as she sat on the dock. It so happened that a young man her age offered a helping hand. She told him that she had to get to Italy, and did he know of any ship where she might stow away? He considered this, and soon enough he had her ensconced in a small room at the engine level of a vessel where he worked. Some weeks passed during which there was intimacy between them. One day the captain happened upon her, having had no knowledge of her presence. He asked what she was doing there. She told the story of the young man and how their relationship had blossomed.

"To be honest with you," she said, blushing, "he's been fucking me."

"I'll say he's been fucking you," replied the captain. "This is the Staten Island ferry."

Julia burst out laughing. "Rob Barrow, my God, *I never* . . ."

Though she laughed not so much at the joke itself as at Rob having told such a joke and using such language.

He nodded, affirming his comedic triumph. "It's a good one."

"Rob, you are a very quick-witted man, funny in your dry-humor way, but I honest to God do not think I have ever heard you *tell a joke* before. I'm not kidding."

"Not my genre," he said as he gazed out the window. His mind had floated off somewhere. The apprehension bees were buzzing furiously in his head.

"But I have to say that as you have gotten older, maybe in the past ten years, you have gotten funnier. You've always had this quick, mischievous wit underneath there somewhere, but you have always been such a serious person that you rarely seemed comfortable letting that side of you be seen."

"Staten Island ferry," he repeated with a smile. "Didn't see that coming, did you?"

She laughed again. "I did not."

They checked into the surgical area, where Ray was already waiting for them. He had been to his medical school office in the very
early morning hours, as was his custom, and walked the few blocks
along Longwood Avenue to the hospital. Rob, Julia, and Ray had been
friends, supporters, rescuers, guides, and intellectual adversaries for
more than forty years. With Ray remaining single after a short, failed
marriage early on, they had found comfort with one another. Ray had
various female partners through the years, but few had lasted save for
a Vietnamese woman nearly his own age whom he saw once a week in
Boston for drinks, dinner, and whatever happened afterward.

Ray greeted Julia and Rob with quick hugs. As usual, he looked
slightly undone: scraggly beard, shaggy hair, a few tangles, graying, and
at the point of exhaustion. He wore a gray suit, the trousers unpressed,
a white dress shirt, and no tie. His face was a bit puffy with dark circles
under his eyes, but more than anything it radiated a sense of kindness.
How can I help? was the phrase he had spoken more than any other
throughout his adult life as a physician, professor of medicine, and dean
of the medical school. Ray was a genius. As a child, he had tested off
the charts on measures of IQ, skipped two grades in primary school,
which had him entering the Naval Academy at Annapolis at age seventeen. Ray completed undergraduate course work in three years and,
in his final year at the academy, completed the science prerequisites for
medical school from which he graduated at age twenty-three. He then
completed a one-year residency and was off to Southeast Asia at age
twenty-five.

He was a man of medicine, a healer with a mission to alleviate
human suffering wherever he found it. In his younger days Julia said
Ray looked like Jim Morrison of the Doors—square jaw, arrestingly
intense dark gaze. But he had the air of an observer, hanging back,
watching, processing it all, the aura of a spy. During the early months
when he and Julia were dating, back when she had been in law school
with Rob, she had found a photograph of him in his naval officer dress

uniform, and it looked like a Hollywood film poster. "James Dean joins the navy," she remarked at the time. That was before she fully appreciated the demons that would prevent Ray from having any sort of normal romantic commitment.

Rob Barrow, by contrast, with a pleasant yet unremarkable appearance, still wore the same uniform from his law school days—khaki trousers, a light blue oxford cloth dress shirt with button-down collar, and a herringbone jacket—with one difference: In school the clothes were secondhand, purchased at an out-of-the-way shop in Cambridge, while now he purchased off the rack from Brooks Brothers. Few people could credibly testify to having seen Rob as an adult dressed in any other fashion. While he was not leading-man handsome by classic definition, he was attractive, with distinctive features— a prominent jaw, the brightest green eyes. He blended in, but on closer look there was something of a rock musician air about him, too. Not lead but a shy backup player, maybe rhythm or bass guitar, a contributor to the show without the need or desire for the spotlight. Cerebral, reflective, a shadow player hitting all the right notes.

As they waited, Rob fixed his gaze on Julia, who was so lovely. No longer the stunning law student who at twenty-three turned heads wherever she went, but she had aged gracefully in a way that left her with beauty and an air of elegance. She was trim, as fit as a teenager, five feet four inches tall, slender, shapely legs, short grayish hair in a cut that framed her pretty face, crystal blue eyes. Much had changed through the years, her face now lined, creases under her eyes whose brightness had dimmed, but the penetrating blue gaze remained.

"Mr. Barrow?" a receptionist mistakenly said to Ray.

"Nope," he said. "She dumped me forty years ago for this gentleman."

"Jeez, Ray," Julia said, having heard his little joke for the hundredth time.

"I'll let you two go ahead," Ray said. "Everything's going to be fine. Give me a buzz when he's in recovery, please."

A nurse led Rob and Julia to a prep area, where Rob changed into a hospital gown, placed his clothes and wristwatch into a plastic bag, and settled comfortably into a bed, where he sat up enjoying the warmth of a freshly laundered blanket. Rob was impressed with the clockwork efficiency of the team. The doctors and nurses came and went, cheerful, expert, prepared for each and every case on the docket for the morning. Julia stood at the side of the bed watching as the nurses worked their way through a presurgical checklist. There were patients in similar beds behind flimsy curtains on both sides of him in the long, exceptionally brightly lit room.

"It's comforting," Rob said softly to Julia.

"They're so professional," she said. "They make it all look so routine, so easy."

Julia sat on the edge of the bed holding his hand. He was calm, confident in the skill of Steve Chen, and grateful to have been guided through by his friend Ray, whom he trusted completely. Soon a freckled nurse inserted the propofol IV and directed Julia to a private family waiting room several floors up.

She leaned over Rob's bed and hugged him.

"Love you," she said.

"Love you, too," he said. "Don't worry. I'll be right as rain."

8

Amnesia

Rob knew from reading the literature in preparation for surgery that his body would be placed into a state of suspended animation. Intravenous propofol began the process in the prep area. In the OR the anesthesiologist administered an inhalation anesthetic called halothane. She worked a tube down through his airway to the lungs to enable him to breathe during surgery. Under anesthesia, Rob's brain would occupy a netherworld where even the body's most acute sensors were rendered unable to respond to stimuli. He was placed into a state that was essentially a reversible coma, where the circuits in the brain were blocked, preventing neurons from communicating with one another. These were the disruptions capable of causing the kinds of troubling side effects he had been warned about. When he had asked Ray about these possibilities, he had said, "It will be fine, Rob."

Even for the most composed individuals, cancer was frightening: the meanest leather-jacketed bully in the neighborhood, patrolling the alleyways, looking to beat the shit out of any unsuspecting nerd on the way home from a night of bowling and ice cream. "Cancer is, as my friend Siddhartha Mukherjee put it, the 'emperor of all maladies,'" Ray had explained to Rob. "It hovers, always there, staking out its own turf in the body and the mind. This is an established phenomenon. People in treatment describe this very experience you describe, Rob, where the cancer, whether you consciously think about it or not, is present in your space, your aura. It distracts the mind, clutches at the emotions, saps energy. The *idea* of cancer is one of the most powerful natural forces, depriving humans of energy, striking terror, the precursor of death."

Everything Rob had accomplished in the law was courtesy of his brain. Without it functioning at a maximum level, he was nowhere. It got him through school, enabled him to make a living—and more than that, to reach a level of distinction within his profession. He'd been retained by cities, states, corporations, and the US Justice Department to participate in litigation related to complex constitutional matters. He had lectured at major law schools, delivered keynote addresses at a variety of conferences through the years, written analyses on obscure constitutional history and questions in law journals, and authored a textbook on the matter of *Gideon v. Wainwright* and the underpinnings of the right of indigent defendants to be provided with counsel. He was also among the leading experts on the historic decision in *Brown v. Board of Education.* But as he lay as still as the dead in a subterranean hospital operating room, wires in his brain crossed. Neurons misfired, and when he awoke in recovery, the consequences of those misfirings began to reveal themselves. Eyes open, he saw a nurse next to his bed pouring ice water into a cup. She covered the cup and slid a straw though a small opening in the top.

"My throat," he said.

"Breathing tube," she said cheerfully. "Sometimes a little scratch in the airway."

She handed him the cup and he drank, his hand shaking. He felt something strange, and when he reached down he remembered that they had told him he would emerge from the surgery with a catheter. He examined it under the covers and saw a reddish thumbprint on the head of his penis. How weird, he thought. During the surgery at some point, someone—a nurse or doctor—had held his penis in place for some reason. Did they make penis jokes in the OR? *Look at this dude!*

Would seem kind of unprofessional, but who knew. He realized that his bladder was emptying urine through the tube and into a plastic bag tucked under the covers without his having to get up and go to the bathroom. How convenient!

The nurse was chattering away: the weather was *mahvelous*, he needed to take it *easy-peasy* for a while. Making small talk, she asked him where he was from.

"Canberra," he said.

"And you came all the way here for your operation," she remarked.

"My wife drove me."

"I got it," she said.

"I feel a little out of it," he said. "Groggy."

"Oh, everybody gets that," she said. "You'll be good as new."

Julia arrived and broke into a smile. She reached out and grasped his hand, holding it tightly and looking into his eyes. There he was, her beloved, in one piece, a survivor of the surgery, and she prayed in that moment that all of the bad cells were gone.

"You must be exhausted," she said.

He nodded, smiling, happy indeed to see her.

"You folks traveled some distance," the nurse remarked to Julia.

"It was pretty quick," Julia said. "We came early—no traffic really."

"I mean from Australia."

"Sorry?" Julia said.

The nurse nodded knowingly and discreetly pulled Julia aside. "Common to have some confusion afterward," she said. "Usually goes away in a couple of hours. Your husband seems to think he's from Australia. Chart says you live in Cambridge."

Julia hesitated, then laughed. "We do," she said. "I think he's in a weirdly playful mood today. He was this morning."

Steve Chen, the surgeon, arrived in scrubs, all business, eager to get to his next case of the day.

"Groggy?" he asked Rob.

"A little."

"It went well," Chen said. "Very clean margins and was able to spare a lot of nerves. Fair amount of bleeding so we'll keep you overnight, monitor blood pressure, et cetera, and send you home in the morning. Catheter comes out in two weeks or so. Could be some pain, chafing. You've got the night bag and a more convenient day bag you strap around your leg and you'll be able to move about pretty much without restriction. Common sense. No heavy lifting, no vigorous exercise, and we'll see you for a follow-up."

"One night," Julia said.

"Yeah, we'll continue to check his vitals, but he should be fine tomorrow."

"Thank you, Doc," Rob said.

"Yes, thank you for everything, Doctor Chen," echoed Julia. She sat down in the chair next to the bed and offered Rob more water, which he drank. She held his hand and smiled.

"A big day," she said softly.

"Oh, yes," he said reflexively.

And it was then that the crazy stuff started.

"Where is this?" he asked Julia.

"Recovery," she said.

"Where?"

"What do you mean? In the hospital."

"Where though?" he asked.

"If this is part of your joke-day routine, it's not that funny, Rob," she said as softly as she could.

This puzzled him.

"Joke day?"

"The joke you told me this morning, Rob. In the car. *I'll say he's effing you. This is the Staten Island ferry.*" And she laughed.

Rob had a puzzled look on his face, glancing around, eyes narrow, forehead creased.

"Where am I?" he asked.

She hesitated.

"Joke, right?" she said.

"A hospital," he said after scanning the room a couple of times.

"Yes," she said.

"Of course," he said, nodding as though he knew exactly what was going on. He was the most agreeable of men—had always been this way, never a complainer. At the law school he remained cool through even the most heated debates. "Mr. Chill," the students called him behind his back. When he learned of this, he laughed. He had never in his life had any sort of nickname, and he kind of liked the feeling of being someone unusual enough or cool enough or weird enough to warrant one.

She was watching him closely, and he didn't seem right.

"Feel okay?" she asked.

Rob took a deep breath. "Fine," he said, which he would have said if someone had hammered a nail into his forehead.

"You don't seem it."

"A little tired," he said.

"You've been through a lot," she said. "Surgery is tough."

He smiled at her reassuringly. "I guess," he said softly.

"Rob, humor me, okay?"

"Sure," he said.

"Tell me why we're here."

"You drove me here," he said.

"Rob, what's going on? Do you not know why we are here?"

"You just said for surgery," he said.

"What kind?" she asked.

"Good question," he said.

"Good lord!" she exclaimed, leaning over, studying his face and eyes more closely.

"Rob, *who am I?*" she demanded, a note of desperation in her voice.

He seemed surprised by the question. "My wife," he said.

"What is my name?"

"Julia."

"Where do we live?"

He considered this. He seemed more embarrassed than confused, but it was obvious he was struggling. Finally, he guessed. "Canberra?"

"Jesus, Rob, you know we don't live in Canberra," she said. "We *visited* Canberra last year when you gave that talk at the law school. Is that what you're thinking of?"

As Rob was considering this, his eyes closed and he fell asleep. Julia slipped out to the waiting area and phoned Ray. "There's something wrong," she said. "He doesn't know where he is."

"Pretty common," said Ray. "Anesthesia drugs pack a punch. He'll be okay."

"But, Ray, this is serious, he thinks we live in Australia, for Chrissakes. Canberra."

Ray burst out laughing.

"It's not funny," she said.

"It kind of is," Ray countered, still laughing. "But I'll come over now—be there in ten minutes."

When Ray arrived, he logged into the room's computer and scanned Ray's chart.

"Looks good," he said to Julia. "Vitals stable."

Later, when Rob woke up, Ray sat at the side of his bed.

"How you feeling, pal?" Ray asked.

Rob looked around. "A little tired," he said.

"So do you know where you are?"

Rob glanced around the room. "Hospital," he said.

"Where, though?"

"Not sure," said Rob.

"Rob, do you know who I am?" Ray asked.

"Of course, Ray."

"What's my full name?"

"Raymond Witter."

"And what do I do?"

"Physician."

"What is my particular job?"

"Dean of the medical school." Rob frowned. "Why the questions?"

"What branch of the military did I serve in?"

"Navy, Vietnam, Phu Bai," said Rob, then he appeared puzzled. "Why didn't I go to Vietnam with you, Ray?"

"You were in school, Rob. Student deferment." Ray continued, "What's the date of your wedding anniversary?"

Rob thought, then shook his head.

"The new dean at the law school, what is her name?" Ray asked.

Rob shook his head.

"Where did you and I used to hang out back in the day? The bar?"

Nothing.

"What was the *Brown* decision?" Julia asked.

"*Brown v. Board of Education*—no separate but equal."

"*Marbury?*"

"Established judicial review." These classic Supreme Court cases were embedded so firmly in his memory nothing could shake them loose.

"Rob, you have had a bit of memory loss," Ray said. "Fairly common after general anesthesia and particularly so for older people, and in case you've forgotten, Rob, you are an older person."

Rob smiled. "You, too," he said. "But not you, Jules."

"Can I get you anything?" Julia asked.

"Water, please."

He sipped through the straw as Julia held the cup in place. He finished and nodded. She sat with him for some time as Ray went out of the room to call a couple of faculty members and get their take on the situation.

"What's it like out?" Rob asked Julia.

"Warm, beautiful," she said.

He fell silent and soon dozed off again. While Rob slept, Ray explained to Julia that patients who suffered memory loss after surgery had temporarily scrambled the hippocampus and the prefrontal cortex. "Propofol plus the gases—nitrous oxide, halothane, a number of others—sent him to never-never land, and he's working his way back. It's okay, Jules. He's seventy years old. These are powerful drugs. Sometimes the body reacts in unpredictable ways."

"He *will* be okay?" she asked.

"Guaranteed," said Ray.

"How long does it take?" she asked.

Ray shrugged. "Couple, few weeks at most."

"*Weeks!*"

"Maybe sooner," said Ray, "but let's be patient. He'll be okay."

Ray put his arm around Julia's shoulder and pulled her close. "He's lost his keys, Jules," Ray said. "They'll turn up. There's a classic case of a magician in the early twentieth century—this was in Vienna—who suffered nearly complete memory loss but remembered with ease every detail of every magic trick he had ever performed. Takes time for the fog to clear."

The following morning Rob had cleared the medical hurdles to be discharged from the hospital, though he seemed detached. He was even quieter and more reflective than usual. The neurology attending physician, a young woman with a warm manner, explained to Julia that about 40 percent of patients over age sixty experienced some level of confusion, delirium, or memory loss after general anesthesia. "If I may suggest," she said, "sometimes memory loss makes people acutely aware of being monitored, which increases their anxiety. Try to create a natural atmosphere, and I think you will soon see signs he is coming out of it." The doctor reached out and gently placed her hand on Julia's arm. "How is his memory normally, would you say?"

"Otherworldly," said Julia. "Amazing."

"The good news is that people with exceptional memories can go for a while in some distress and then, bang, it's like flipping a switch. I'm not saying that will happen with your husband, but it is possible."

The final piece of the discharge process involved a nurse arriving with a wheelchair and guiding the patient down to a waiting vehicle. But Ray hated wheelchairs, and he knew Rob would likely hate them, too.

"He's ambulatory," Ray said to the nurse. "But thank you."

"But, Doctor, we're not supposed to make exceptions."

"He'll be okay."

It seemed a small thing, but Ray did not want his closest friend in the world riding in a wheelchair like some fragile old geezer who couldn't do for himself. Rob Barrow was more fit than most of the people in the hospital, he knew, and he was going to rescue his friend from this indignity.

"You okay there, pal?" Ray said, as he and Julia walked on either side as they moved slowly to the elevator.

"Feels good to move," Rob said.

"You look better already," said Julia, which made Rob smile.

Through the lobby they walked out the main doors, and there was Ray's car, parked directly in front of the entrance.

"How can you just leave your car there?" Julia asked.

"One of the few privileges of being medical school dean," Ray said.

They guided Rob into the front passenger seat, where he could extend his long legs, and Julia sat in the back seat. She noticed a half-smoked joint on the car's console.

"Ray, I mean, *seriously?*"

Noticing it, Ray laughed and placed it inside the center console compartment.

"For later," he said.

They drove carefully through the traffic, making their way out of the congested medical area, across the Charles River and into their familiar leafy neighborhood, home to faculty members, Nobel laureates, scores of members of the American Academies of Arts and Sciences, an aging cohort of intellectuals, academic stars from back in the day now being put out to pasture, moving to Vermont, protesting that they were being pushed out. They were sociologists, linguists, political scientists, mathematicians, biologists, physicists, anthropologists, economists, engineers, computer scientists, and more, a collection of people whose ambitions and credentials were supposed to meld in the last four decades of the twentieth century to achieving the goal of matching the reality of America with her aspirations.

9

I Remember McCann's

Rob's stoicism during the next three and a half weeks was monk-like. He arrived home from the hospital on Friday and remained largely cloistered upstairs in his office. He spent his days reading and writing, saying little, early dinner and then to bed. Julia was alternately alarmed by the stubbornness of the amnesia and encouraged by Ray's unwavering certainty that Rob would soon emerge from it. But Rob's dizziness, confusion, and memory loss persisted through the first full week of October. After two weeks during which Rob did not improve much if at all, Julia and Ray met with the law school dean, and all agreed that Rob should take the rest of the semester off. The younger teachers who had taken over Rob's classes temporarily would continue working through the rest of the term. Julia contacted the legal team Rob was associated with for the First Circuit case, and they were well prepared in Rob's absence.

A week later, Julia could see Rob gradually easing back into his old self when he said he would like to sit with her in the garden that evening. They sat next to one another, ate some scrambled eggs, and Rob spent most of the time quietly gazing around the garden.

"I love this place," he said softly. "Everything that matters happened here." He turned to her and squinted. He started to speak, but could not. His eyes were misty. "I don't care how old you are, please don't give up this house, this garden."

"Rob, I pray we will be here together for many years."

He didn't respond for a moment, then he asked her, "What is the date today?"

"October 15," she said.

"Three hundred and fifty years," he said nodding toward the American sycamore. "Someday human beings might live that long. Cellular repair making big strides."

"I would not want to live that long," Julia said.

"But what if you were healthy the way you are now?" he asked.

"I cannot imagine that would be possible."

"Some of the cell biologists think it may be."

After a while, Rob stood, took her hand, and he embraced her, holding her for a long time.

"Have I told you that I love you?" he said. "I don't remember."

He pulled back, holding her at arm's length. He was smiling.

"You may have mentioned it at some point," she said.

They embraced again. "I love you, too, Rob Barrow."

The next day he continued working in his study, but he came downstairs a couple of times to sit and chat with Julia, and he suggested that they get together that evening in the garden with Ray. She was thrilled. He was definitely coming out of it.

The night was warm, Indian-summerish. Morning rain had left the yard as fecund as it had been all summer, a rich dark green, nature's jewel. "I must say that being in our little sanctuary with the two of you makes me feel as though nothing's wrong," Rob said. He turned and smiled at Julia, then Ray. "It's sort of like fog, at first dense and then, gradually, burning off with the sun. I am remembering more—about college, law school, everything. It's a relief."

"Rob," Julia said, "this is a little crazy maybe, but do you remember the time in law school when, what was his name, the professor who kept his pipe in the side pocket of his tweed sport jacket?"

"Winthrop," Rob said.

"Winthrop, right, a sweet older man, and he would drift off topic every once in a while, but I distinctly recall the time he asked the class whether anyone could name all the men, up to that point, who had served as chief justice and their periods of service. And I remember everyone looking around at one another, and all of a sudden you said you could give it a try. Do you remember that?"

"Wow, Jules," he said. "That was funny, wasn't it, because what I remember was it seemed like such a simple question. I thought, 'Well, anyone focused on con law would certainly know that,' but yeah, I remember it for sure." He seemed to enjoy the memory.

"What happened?" asked Ray.

"Oh, man, he went through the list like it was nothing," said Julia. "The class went nuts after he had finished. It was such a weirdly impressive thing to be able to do. People thought he was a little bit off, bizarre. Freakish memory, which, I guess, is kind of ironic at the moment."

"Rob, take us through the list, please," said Ray. "Or as much of it as you recall."

Julia frowned. "Rob, you certainly don't have—"

"No, I'm feeling more like myself," he said. "Okay, John Jay starts it all off in 1789. President of the Continental Congress in 1778, served as chief until 1795, when he became governor of New York. John Rutledge, kind of an aberration, served as interim chief four months, but then the Senate voted down his confirmation. Oliver Ellsworth, then one of the greats, John Marshall, who served for thirty-four years during which he wrote the opinion in *Marbury* establishing judicial review. Roger Taney, then Salmon Portland Chase, who had been Lincoln's treasury secretary. Morrison Waite, Melville Fuller—interestingly the first associate justice to serve as chief, which now that I think of it seems pretty surprising. Edward Douglass White. Then a really unusual one, President

William Howard Taft became chief thirteen years *after* being elected president and, obviously, is the only person ever to serve as both chief and president." Rob smiled. "Decent resume. Then Charles Hughes, Harlan Stone, Fred Vinson, Earl Warren, Burger, Rehnquist, and now, thank God, since 2005, John Roberts."

"Bravo!" said Ray clapping. "Of course, I have no idea whether you were right or not."

"It was perfect," said Julia, beaming. "One of the doctors told me when you were being discharged that it could take a while to remember, but that some people with good memories could get it back like hitting a switch. I am so, so relieved, Rob."

"Me, too, I have to say," said Rob. "Very unsettling sensation to not know how to navigate your own brain."

"This gives me an idea," said Julia. She went to her study and returned with a silver-framed photograph, holding it in both hands and beaming.

"My God, we were *sooo* young." She handed it to Rob, presenting it with both hands, as though bestowing a gift.

"Wow," said Rob. "Look at this, Ray."

"Oh, yeah," exclaimed Ray.

"McCann's!" said Rob. "The bar on South Huntington. Our Friday night place." And they all stood at once and embraced and Julia cried and laughed at the same time, and Ray laughed, and Rob's sense of relief was palpable.

"It was a narrow storefront with a neon sign above the doorway, rusted. The electrical coils buzzed and flickered, which made it sound like a bug-killing zapper," Rob said.

"I remember that!" said Julia.

"And inside it was clouds of cigarette smoke, everybody smoked back then, and when you walked in, on the left was the bar and stools, half of which were broken. There were tables, and a jukebox."

"And a pool table with worn felt," Julia said.

"And mostly guys, bus drivers from the transit barn next door, you remember that, Ray?"

"I do," said Ray. "And always cabbies, too."

"And cops," said Julia.

"So the sixty-four-thousand-dollar question, Rob," said Ray. "When was that photograph taken, and who took it?"

Rob laughed and shook his head, amazed by the vivid nature of the recollection.

"Friday, July 24, 1974," said Rob. "When the news came on the TV over the bar, we learned that the court ruled against Nixon, requiring him to turn over secret Oval Office tape recordings."

"What was the vote?" Julia asked.

He reached out and grasped her hand.

"Unanimous," he said softly and smiled. "An affirmation of the majesty of the American system of jurisprudence. No man is above the law."

"And we went crazy, the three of us, remember, Rob?" said Julia.

"You went crazy, Jules," he said.

"But you went crazy in your own quiet, stoic, non-crazy, Rob-like way," she needled.

"And the owner took the picture," Ray said.

"Eddie McCann," said Julia. "He called us the brainiacs! 'Hey brainiacs, this calls for a picture.' And he snapped it, and bless his heart, a week later he had a copy for each of us. You remember, Ray."

Ray remembered everything. He had been a very young medical resident at the time, working a few blocks up the street from McCann's at the Veterans Administration hospital, a twelve-story brutalist structure looming in its forbidding government gray over a grim neighborhood. McCann's had been his escape from caring for the hospital overcrowded with men in their twenties and thirties who had suffered horrific wounds in Vietnam. Ray hated that fucking war, hated what it had done to all those boys, hated the tragedy heaped upon the families, sorrows and loss that no one should have to bear. He hated the people who ran the war, directed it, promoted it. He hated everything about it, except his patients. His patients he loved.

"It's where we bonded," Ray said.

"It's where Rob and I could continue our debates from class," Julia said. "With you as referee, Ray."

"I was always on your side, Jules," he said.

"Wow," said Rob. "Those were great days."

"Anything and everything was possible," said Julia. "We wanted to do so much *good*."

Rob handed the photograph to Ray, who shook his head in amusement. "Look at us," he said. "We were so young. And you two haven't really changed that much, but I must be twenty pounds heavier."

"Twenty?" said Julia in mock surprise.

"Maybe twenty-five."

The photograph captured a moment in time when they were at the beginning of what would become—had become—a lifelong friendship, a bond that had been cemented through the years, connected for another half century into the distant future. In the photo Ray was smoking a Gauloise, a habit he had picked up in Vietnam. He wore standard-issue hospital scrubs, sweat stains under his arms, spatters of something—blood?—on his tunic. Ray's eyes were marked by dark circles, attesting to his all but round-the-clock schedule both caring for patients on the hospital wards and working in a research laboratory on matters related to cancer and the human immune system. Rob was a beanpole, thin, angular, with a reserved look on his narrow face, but a shy smile.

And then there was Julia Browning, the kind of girl everyone noticed—a classic American beauty, arrestingly pretty face, full red lips, ice-blue eyes, and a complexion that highlighted the ever-shifting color palette of her cheeks. Her neck was thin, longish, ears small, pressed tightly against the side of her head. Her hair was a rich brown, long in the style of the times. She had small breasts, slender legs, and a notably shapely butt which was accentuated in the snug blue jeans she often wore. There was a sex appeal about her, certainly, but more than that, Julia possessed an old-world elegance. She was, by upbringing and appearance, a product of America's elite. She had declined an opportunity to appear at Manhattan's debutante party during her senior year at Dalton. She and her politically aware friends had received the culture's message that such events, once prestigious, were, by 1967, the antithesis of cool. This act of rebellion had been a hard one for Julia, who was very close with her parents, but she had stood her ground and they grudgingly yielded.

Rob had first noticed her at a law school picnic on the banks of the Charles River, where he happened to be watching her when she cocked her head to one side, turned from the eastern breeze, and brushed the hair out of her face. She looked off toward the river, and as she did so, he caught the softer evening light on the side of her face, her hair pushed back haphazardly, strands catching the light here and there. She was petite. He saw her sit down on the grass with classmates and with her feet tucked under her legs, she seemed childlike. She was one of those girls comfortable in her own skin, able to fit in anywhere with classmates, professors, visiting speakers, everyone. If she was aware of the stolen glances of men as she passed by she did not show it. By the end of first year of law school, the word around was that half a dozen other students had tried to date her, but she was skilled in the art perfected by certain beautiful women of declining such invitations with grace. The mystery of her dating preferences was solved midway through second year when she arrived at a law school social function with her new boyfriend, Ray Witter. A doctor, everyone said. A year later, in the summer of 1974, as they gathered at McCann's, she and Ray were still together, though barely. Ray was six years older than Julia and Rob. His most appealing quality, to Julia, was his instinctive kindness. But she learned in their time together that he was held hostage by the war, by Phu Bai, by the horror of man's inhumanity to man, as he put it. At twenty-eight, he was scarred so deeply she wondered whether he would ever be able to heal. Staying with Ray meant living with the memories that Ray himself was unable to escape. She could not do it, yet she feared that a breakup would mean their trio might break apart. But in the months after Julia and Ray broke it off, the three of them continued spending time together. Movies, beer nights, long contentious discussions about politics, the law, and the health or lack thereof of the American experiment, which was, by far, the subject that fascinated Rob most. And then a sunny spring day in 1975, Julia and Rob were at the Paperback Booksmith on Brattle Street in search of a collection of essays describing the various ways in which historians viewed the decade of the 1950s in America. Rob was along for the walk mostly, to keep her company. After she had paid for the book and they were back outside, she said, "How about a cup of coffee?"

"Sure," he said, and they settled into an outside table at a small shop around the corner. Julia lit a cigarette, but Rob declined.

"Trying to quit," he said.

After a pause, Julia had said, "I have a question for you, Rob. What do you think about going out on a date with me?" She smiled, leaning forward, her eyes wide.

He pulled back, frowning, seeming confused. "What?" he asked.

She laughed. "A *date*," she said. "Dinner, a movie, whatever. Are you unaware of this social custom?" She could barely contain her laughter.

"I mean, Jules . . ."

He fell silent. She had assumed that perhaps this notion had crossed his mind at some point. She would learn that, while it had done so fleetingly, he had dismissed the idea as far-fetched.

"Julia, seriously, though, we're *friends*," he said.

"Well," she said evenly, "maybe we could be more than that."

"I would never do anything to jeopardize our friendship, or my friendship with Ray," he said. "Never."

"Neither would I," she said.

He sipped his coffee and shook his head.

"Crazy," he muttered.

"Why crazy?" she asked.

"Julia, I mean . . . I don't know," he stumbled. This man, as verbally dexterous as anyone she knew, was stumbling in search of a thought or words, or something. She smiled. She loved this reaction. It was so awkwardly authentic. *So Rob.*

"So let me get this straight," she said. "It's crazy because you don't know why. Is it because you don't like me?"

He frowned. "Jules, don't be ridiculous," he said in a scolding tone.

"Oh, so you *do* like me, good," she said. "*Whew,* that's a relief."

He looked away from her at the passersby.

She leaned forward and whispered. "So you do find me attractive, Rob? Because I would like it very much if you did find me attractive. Because I find you quite attractive."

He sat quite still and watched as her face seemed to light up, her eyes bright.

Silence.

"You are way out of my league, Jules," he said finally. His face was flushed.

She laughed out loud. "Rob Barrow, that is the dumbest thing I have ever heard you say. False modesty does not become you."

"I'm not being falsely anything," he said, agitated now. "We are friends, the dearest of friends, and my relationship with you and Ray is everything to me, and I would never do anything to jeopardize it." He was stern now, certain in his belief and in his commitment to the two friends whom he relied upon and loved.

"Christ, Rob! We're having our first fight before we're actually a couple! This is so cool!" And she leaned back and began laughing so uproariously that passersby turned to notice.

When she had calmed, she leaned forward, reaching across the little table and taking his hand in hers. "This *looks* thing, Rob, you've got that on the brain. You are such a handsome man. But that's not even the point. The point is"—she dropped her voice—"I really love the way you *are*. I love *who* you are." She wanted stability, reliability, honesty, modesty—and Rob was all of this and more.

Rob was stunned. He cocked his head as though not certain what he had heard, but in that moment he felt all of the pieces falling into place. At some level, he had long felt that this was the reality. That he was very much in love with her. But now, with her words, Rob realized that he was free to express the reality in his heart. And then he started laughing, too, his laughter growing more joyous by the moment until they stood and embraced and he held her close and they laughed some more and they were in that moment, joined together at the beginning of what would be a lifelong journey as a couple.

"You found a good one," her father had said the morning of their wedding, a simple Roman Catholic ceremony. Ray was best man, of course, and Hank Browning, in tears, gave away the bride. Drinks and dinner followed in a Back Bay restaurant. For Rob Barrow and Julia Browning Barrow life was good.

10

He Is Guilty of Being Who He Is

Judith Jansen had nosed around. She asked a number of junior faculty members about Rob and discovered that he had taught an orientation class for new students that had gone sideways. She was able to reach a few of the students who had been in the class who said they had wanted to talk about the 1619 Project and not, as one put it, "ancient legal rulings." Her initial piece soliciting faculty reactions to the 1619 Project had run September 7, during the first week of school. For multiple weeks thereafter, Judith had been absorbed in schoolwork, finding her way to the library nearly every evening to keep up with her course load. Through September and into October she had picked up indications that Barrow had upset some students in the orientation class. When she dug into it, she was able to interview several of the students who had been in the classroom that day, and by mid-October she had found time to write a follow-up article about Rob with the headline CLASSROOM CHILL, published in the *Crimson* on October 21. She had called to solicit Rob's response to the piece but had been unable to reach him.

The chill in the classroom was palpable. Professor Robert Barrow spent most of an orientation session focused on the history of the Supreme Court, including cases going back six and seven decades. The elephant in the room was what the students described as their "urgent desire to focus not on dust-covered law books but on *the now*," as one freshman put it.

This article comes after speaking with a dozen students who were present when Professor Barrow lectured about the foundations of American constitutional law "absent any references to modern-day ramifications—legal, social, economic, and moral—that have bearing on the lived experience of people of color and others living under the yoke of American oppression," said Sandra Dalton, who said she had grown up in public housing in Detroit.

Students interviewed said Professor Barrow was reluctant to discuss the historical fact that so-called Founding Fathers were slave owners who benefited financially from the legality of slavery in the country. He referred to the original 1619 article as having been written by "Nikole something."

"It was obvious that the professor knows a great deal about Supreme Court rulings from several generations ago, and there is no doubt that some of those marked important progress, especially on school segregation and the right of all defendants to counsel," said Sandra Nguyen, whose family emigrated to the United States from Vietnam. "But he directly contradicted the core principle of the 1619 Project by baldly asserting that America was defined by the pursuit over two hundred years to live up to the founding ideals, and I honestly don't know how you can look around at the lived reality today and believe such a thing."

The article went on from there, quoting several other students echoing one another.

"I guess it's the attitude that bothers me most," Andy said, as she and Judith met at the *Crimson* office. "The hubris, the unwillingness to reexamine old ideas and assumptions. I am wondering whether the attitude isn't embodied in the Barrow quote. He's got classic sixties liberal credentials—worked on *the* causes—Southern Poverty Law Center, NAACP, wrote about questions of constitutional legitimacy of the Vietnam War. But that was a half century ago for Chrissakes!" She shook her head, got up, and turned toward the window. She spread her arms wide, indicating the Cambridge community. "They cling to this notion that what they thought about, wrote about, and did fifty years ago grants them some sort of lifetime intellectual pass. *We changed the world! We fought the war! We were Chaney, Goodman, Schwerner! We died fighting racism and the war!*"

"And now they discredit 1619 and dismiss antiracism," said Judith.

"It offends his sense of ownership of the historical narrative. *Nobody tells us what the founding of the nation was about. We tell you.* It's so striking," Andy continued, "how protective these men are about the raison d'être of the founding. The Founders were slaveholders mostly, but if you sell the founding as inspired by the Enlightenment, you get away with it. But what if the whole enterprise was to protect slavery for the economic benefit of the elites?"

Andy mulled it over for a few days before writing a brief but pointed editorial headlined ATTITUDE, published October 28.

Behind the faculty pushback against 1619 is an attitude mixing a sense of entitlement, even, dare we say it, *ownership* of the subject matter. Professor Barrow's comment that the *New York Times* journalism related to 1619 is "irrelevant" embodies this attitude. He and other faculty members are saying implicitly, "If you want to redefine anything having to do with the founding and the intent of the founding, you damn well better submit to our inspection first and we will judge. We, the intellectual elite, will make judgments about the relationship between the founding of the nation and the enslavement of a race of people."

What could be more relevant to the law and the so-called justice system than the treatment of Black people? What does it say about our faculty that a constitutional scholar of Barrow's standing deems the most urgent issue of our time *irrelevant?* Add to that the recent *Crimson* reporting revealing that during an orientation class in late August, Barrow was dismissive of students pressing him on the significance of the *New York Times* 1619 Project. In that class, students told the *Crimson*, Barrow dismissively referred to the 1619 author, Nikole Hannah-Jones, as "Nikole something." Disrespect, arrogance, condescension—it's quite an attitude.

Journalistic rigor was built into the *Crimson's* process, and in this case a copy editor by the name of Rafik Hassan went to Andy with his concerns. Rafik was a senior who worked on the *Crimson* because it forced him to spend a bit of time each day outside the biology lab. He was of medium height, slim, a former cross-country athlete who invariably wore jeans, an ill-fitting sports T-shirt, backward ball cap, and sneakers.

"Andy, got a minute?" Rafik asked, as Andy was about to head out the door.

"Of course, Rafik, what's up?"

"Well, a couple of things," he said. "So you know what I trip on here, Andy? I trip on the 'irrelevant' quote that the piece hangs on. Irrelevant to *what?* When people say something isn't relevant, they're typically talking about a subject matter that is specific. Easy fix would be to use the whole quote. Creates context and helps the reader gain a better understanding of what we're saying. Sometimes we speak in shorthand because the issues are so familiar to us, but not everybody is fluent in our shorthand." He smiled.

"Sure," she said. "I'll get the full quote from Judith and insert." As they talked, Judith entered the newsroom. "Hey, Jude, perfect timing," said Andy. "Rafik had a thought about strengthening the piece here," and Judith pointed to the relevant section. "So let's use the full quote from Barrow."

"It will clarify exactly what is not relevant to what," Rafik said. "Okay?"

Judith hesitated. "Oh, okay," she said.

"And one other point that's a little less precise," said Rafik. "So the offense here by Barrow is saying that the 1619 Project isn't relevant to something—and you'll pull up the full quote so we have it. But even with that, his offense isn't exactly clear to me. I mean, isn't it possible that a magazine article about slavery might not be relevant to what a faculty member is teaching at any given moment?"

"Sure," Andy said, "but we're talking about an *attitude* here as much as anything else."

Rafik seemed amused by this.

"So his offense is his *attitude*?" Rafik said. "So that's what he has done wrong, have a certain attitude? *Really*, Andy?"

"Rafik, the attitude speaks to privilege," said Andy. "Intangible, but telling. It's dismissive, arrogant, condescending. It excludes those who disagree as the *other*. When you first came here from Iran did you feel, here in America, that there was a particular attitude toward you? I mean outside the university community."

Rafik considered this. "Of course, but that was because I am from what many Americans consider a weird, dangerous country and an Islamic one at that. This is about *ideas*. You are saying they are guilty of an attitude toward certain ideas—"

"Ideas that are focused on people from another *quote* weird *unquote* country, foreign place, who are different and deemed inferior," said Andy.

"If I may, Rafik, there's another, equally valid way to look at it, I think," said Judith. "Barrow maybe is not guilty of *a thing*. He is emblematic of what needs changing; the ultimate privileged white male with money, a position of authority granted to him by other privileged white males, with the inherent power and prestige that the American patriarchy bestows upon such people. His offense is an attitude toward the 1619 Project, but more broadly his offense is that *he is who he is*."

11

This Is Not How
I Imagined It Ending

Rob fielded phone calls from numerous friends and colleagues, but he valued his privacy and put off allowing anyone to come by for a visit during his recovery. He missed teaching, but he would be back in the classroom in January and that excited him. In the meantime, he found joy in immersing himself in the 4,440 words of the living, breathing document to which he had devoted his professional life. Of all those seeking to visit, his old friend and colleague Jerry Katz was the most persistent, so he called and invited him to drop by on a pleasantly cool evening in early November, the chill a portent of more assertive fall weather ahead.

Jerry arrived with a fancy bottle of wine and a bear hug for Rob. They had been on the faculty together forever, it seemed, and Rob had long admired Jerry's warm sense of humor and understanding of the world. Jerry was former chair of the international relations department, a China scholar who had worked in the State Department and the National Security Council during the Clinton administration and as an advisor in the State Department under President Obama. Jerry's scholarship on China was widely respected, and his articles in *Foreign*

Affairs were read closely from Washington to Beijing. After an undergraduate degree at City College of New York, Jerry earned a PhD at Harvard. He spoke with a thick New York accent from his Brooklyn upbringing. He was a hearty man of medium height, barrel-chested, with a huge, squarish head, the hands of a longshoreman, unkempt beard, and an affable manner.

"You survived!" Jerry exclaimed, stepping back to take a good look at him.

"Thank you, Jerry, I'm so pleased to see you too."

"I see the *Crimson* is on your case."

"Yeah," said Rob. "I don't really care what they write, to be honest. I mean at this stage of the game."

"I hear you," said Jerry as he took in the garden, the flowers, trees, shrubs, the little pond.

"I never get tired of this place, Rob, no matter how many times through the years you and Jules have been kind enough to invite us over," said Jerry. "Never ceases to amaze me."

"Peaceful," Rob said, nodding in agreement.

"Peace is good, peace is good," Jerry said. "Hey, we're getting up there. Seventh, eighth inning, who knows, maybe ninth, we don't know. Better that we don't, I suppose. Tell me, how are you feeling and no bullshit, Rob, be honest with your old pal."

"Much better," said Rob. "A little fatigued but ready to get back to work. Ready for the January semester."

"As you return, I shall depart," said Jerry. "I'm hanging it up. I told you I was considering it, and it's time."

Rob was taken aback. "Come on, Jerry," he said. "Are you serious?"

"You know when you're not wanted," Jerry said. "You go from being, if I may say quite immodestly, a star in the field to *being the old guy who reshaped the department, how long ago was it? Reshaped* was the word the dean, in her infinite wisdom at age thirty-nine, used to describe what I did with the department. You know me, Rob, I am known to be direct. Some people say blunt, some say obnoxious, some say crude, but"—Jerry leaned forward and smiled broadly—"I know this shit cold. I sound like a blowhard right now, but I've logged a half million miles. And she says to me, this brilliant young dean we have now with her PhD in gender studies. *Gender studies*, Rob? Gender fucking studies and now the dean? What is this, a sitcom? She says she appreciates how I *reshaped* the department. Reshaped, I said to her. Was Lazarus *reshaped*? I raised that department from the dead, and it did take breaking a few eggs to make the omelet, yes, it did—you see, Lazarus had an omelet for breakfast that morning! If they had someone who was ready to take over and guide the department into the future, I would be all in, no ifs, ands, or buts about it, absolutely, Rob. But they *do not*." Jerry continued, laughing out loud. "I'm a big, fat, hairy, opinionated guy who scares the ladies!"

Jerry sat back and inhaled deeply. It was as though he had just competed in the hundred-yard dash and needed a break. He frowned, deep furrows in his weathered face. He scratched his beard.

"Self-pity is not an attractive characteristic in guys our age, but honestly, I'm drowning in it," Jerry continued. "Intellectually, I get it. Hey, it's their time now, not mine. And really, in my mind, I accept that. In my heart, it's harder."

Jerry smiled. He tugged gently on his beard, the mask he had worn all these years to conceal the soft, sensitive man underneath the faux-gruff exterior. They sat silently for a moment. Rob went inside and brought out two bottles of beer, handing one to Jerry.

"I do love the kids, Rob," Jerry continued. "Wonderfully active minds, desire to change the world." He sipped his beer, then smiled. "Collaborated with two of our doctoral candidates on a recent paper, comes out next month. Gifted kids, rural Chinese girl, bad teeth, perfect English. Plus a young guy from India who may be the brightest student we have ever had. Math, physics genius, but focusing on world affairs. Amazing. Short little fat guy, absent-minded professor. Wore the same clothes every day the first few weeks of term. I had to pull him aside, gave him money for new clothes. Didn't have a penny to his name." Jerry took a deep, heaving breath that took on an asthma-like wheeze.

"You okay?" Rob asked.

"Never better!" Jerry exclaimed. "The better question, my friend, is are you okay? Jesus, Rob, what you have been through. I just . . ." Jerry looked down at the ground and shook his head. The breeze picked up out of the west along with the distant sounds of thunder. Rob had checked the forecast earlier and knew thunderstorms were coming. After a moment, Jerry reached over and grasped Rob's arm, holding it tightly for a moment.

"There are no straight lines in life," Jerry said. "And dear God, you know that better than anyone."

Rob gazed off into the garden, taking in the birds he couldn't name and the shrubs and the barely rippling pond and at the sycamore, and he had the sense that he was doing the only thing that could be done, which was to continue on as best he could. He thought, *It's not easy*, and he was about to say this to Jerry, but those words hardly began to describe the reality of the endurance contest that was his life. And besides, Jerry knew. Jerry understood. His sense of empathy fairly glowed from his bearishness. They sat in silence for several minutes listening to the low rumble of distant thunder, somehow comforting to Rob. Jerry felt the need to lighten the tone and said, "I heard our pal Ray may have a significant other. Can this possibly be true?"

"These rumors pop up every now and again," said Rob. "But you know Ray. He says he's not suited for a normal relationship, and I believe him. Since the war, he's been pretty stubborn about trusting anyone—or any institution, for that matter. Through the years, Jules has set up dinner with various women she knew, and some of those encounters lasted a few months, never longer. But now he has a friend, a lady he sees pretty regularly, retired Vietnamese diplomat. She's at the Kennedy School. He doesn't talk about it much. They have dinner."

"I love the man," said Jerry. "My God, he's helped me and my family through every conceivable type of medical issue. Ray lives to help others, no question in my mind, Rob. It's his purpose in life. Look at the lot of us now, cancer, bum tickers, bad knees, hips. So many of us who didn't measure up, not to the expectations of others but to our own vision of ourselves, where we hoped to be. I hear it all the time. You recall what Isaiah Berlin said about the hedgehog and the fox—the hedgehog knows a lot about one thing while the fox knows something about many things. Too many hedgehogs. It's the nature of the beast in a way, isn't it? We're all experts in one thing, or at least we're supposed to be. But I think over time either that narrow focus allows one to thrive—you're an example of that, Rob—or it leaves you alone in a dusty corner of the library stacks struggling to find meaning in *Beowulf*."

"This is the micro to Julia's macro view," Rob said. "And while I acknowledge that there are a lot of disappointed people, from my hedgehog perspective the system holds. I'm a believer, Jerry. The Enlightenment, the Founders, the Constitution, the Supreme Court's ability through the years to find its way toward justice. Imperfectly. But we find our way."

Jerry reached over and grasped Rob's hand in his huge paw. "You are a good man, Rob, and I am so happy you came through that damn operation with flying colors."

Tears welled in Jerry's eyes.

"You okay, my friend?" Rob asked.

Jerry took a deep breath and pulled out a handkerchief to wipe his eyes. Then he managed a bit of rough laughter. "*Reshaped* the department *my ass*."

12

Oppressed People
on *This* Campus?

Rob donned heavy corduroy pants and a down jacket, pulled his Boston Bruins ski hat down over his ears, and took his coffee out into the garden. He sat down in his Adirondack chair and regarded his garden. Wind from the east whipped all the trees bare with the exception of the sycamore. How could those few remaining leaves hang on in such weather? The temperature was in the upper thirties but felt icy, and within a few minutes his coffee was cold. He headed back into the house, then set out for campus. He plunged his hands deep into the jacket pockets and walked at a comfortable pace, turning toward the square by the Loeb Theater. Students in zipped-up jackets, some with scarves wrapped tightly, hurried through the wind. He made his way into the square and cut through Harvard Yard, where it was clear that some students had already headed out of town for the Thanksgiving break. The dean's office was located in Longfellow Hall, a two-story clapboard building that served as George Washington's headquarters for a time during the Revolutionary War. Rob entered the historic structure with a sort of reverence, even as he wondered why he had been summoned to the office of the dean of the Faculty of

Arts and Sciences. Pauline Scott-Norton, a well-respected administrator and scholar of gender studies, was a tall woman in robust health, early forties, well dressed, and cordial upon Rob's arrival. She led him into the office with lovely views out onto the Yard. As he took a seat, Rob noticed that a sculpture of Washington was covered over with a trash bag, duct tape securing the bag at the neck. Rob stood staring at it in astonishment. America's first great military leader and president, the man who led the infant nation through the Revolutionary War, was now a victim of cancel culture.

"Rob, I appreciate you coming in," she said. "I know you've been going through challenging times. How are you doing?"

"Well, Pauline," he said with as much cheer as he could muster. "All is well, thank you. How about you and your family?"

"Everyone is good. Please," she said, indicating an old-fashioned brass coat hanger. Rob hung up his jacket and hat and took a chair opposite the dean, who sat down behind her rather imposing desk.

"To the business at hand," she said. "I assume you are aware that a number of students have come to me expressing concern about your approach in an introductory session at the start of the year."

"I am not aware of that," he said.

She seemed surprised. "You saw the piece in the *Crimson?*"

"I did. But I was not aware they came to you."

"A group of students from your orientation session came to me a month or so ago," she said. "They told me that they had been thinking more and more about the class, the orientation session, and they had decided that it had, as they put it, crossed a line." She leaned forward and picked up a yellow legal pad from her desk. "These students were quite thoughtful, Rob, and we had a productive conversation. There was concern among the students about what they consider, as several of them put it to me, the overtly racist way in which you responded during a discussion related to the 1619 Project. You apparently referred to Nikole Hannah-Jones, a very distinguished journalist, as 'Nikole somebody.'"

Rob shrugged. "I forgot her name," he said with a sheepish grin. "A senior moment."

She frowned. "That interaction, in addition to your comment to the *Crimson* earlier this year that the project is *quote* irrelevant *unquote*, is, well, the two taken together are troubling, Rob. Certainly you can understand that. We're trying to move forward at Harvard, and if we don't set a standard, who will? So, I wanted to talk with you and get your thoughts on these matters and share my own."

"I wonder, Pauline, do you think I did something that was inappropriate or somehow a violation of student rights or proper conduct? What, exactly, is the offense you seem to believe I committed?"

The dean nodded and thought a moment. "I would say this. The students felt that you deliberately, or inadvertently, created an unsafe atmosphere for people of color by focusing on history purely from the perspective of the white male patriarchy. Their view, expressed to me, was that the essence of that white patriarchy is the belief—apparently enunciated by you during class—that America was founded in pursuit of liberty, justice, freedom for all, that sort of thing."

Rob took in her words. *That sort of thing*, he thought. The majesty of the founding principles of American democracy was *that sort of thing*? He glanced over at the hooded and duct-taped bust of poor old George and replied, "I believe those *are* the principles upon which the nation was founded, yes, I do believe that. It's interesting you raise this, because after that class I did some additional reading and in that reading I found a quotation from the *Times* that, to me, is striking. It said, 'Our democracy's founding ideals were false when they were written.'"

Rob took a deep breath and exhaled slowly. He shrugged, and though he said nothing, his shrug said it all.

She pursed her lips, her eyes narrowed. She appeared puzzled. "I understand that, Rob, but there are two sides to the story. There is much new scholarship, as you are undoubtedly aware. This is not a settled matter. The students would argue, and many scholars as well, I believe, that there is a very different way to look at it. When a student calmly pointed out that most of the Founders were slave owners, you evidently grew angry, which was clearly a non-antiracist reaction. And you made a point of saying that the *New York Times* 1619 Project creates a portrait of an America you do not recognize, which is puzzling to me, because one would think that by now you would strive to see the world not only through your eyes as a privileged white man but also through the eyes of oppressed peoples here on campus."

As he sat absorbing what she said, he couldn't help but wonder how much of what she was saying stemmed from beliefs and how much was a product of the times and a need by someone in her position to conform. "A 'non-antiracist reaction,' I . . ." Rob shook his head. "As for oppressed people on this campus," he said. He was about to continue, but he looked again at old George, trash bag over his head. What had happened? Rob wondered. What was going on? Here was this talented young woman in one of the most prestigious academic positions in the country speaking in tongues. Rob suddenly felt weary. He liked Pauline, and he wanted her to like him. He would make a bit of a joke, needle her a bit.

"The 'oppressed people here on campus,' Pauline?" Rob said, smiling. "Those shivering refugees in Eliot House?"

But he didn't exactly stick the landing. His tone wasn't joke-like, more tart. Pauline looked displeased. But Rob would rescue the joke with sincerity, or actually with faux sincerity that would convey his fine sense of humor. He added, "I do a fair amount of pro bono legal work, and if there is an oppressed segment of our population here on this campus, I hereby offer counsel." He smiled. She grimaced.

"You tried to be funny with Pauline?" Ray said later. "Brilliant idea, Rob."

Pauline took a deep breath and exhaled, an annoyed parent dealing with a rambunctious child. "Rob, I was hoping you would take seriously what the students had to say to me," she said. "Sarcasm doesn't help matters. Juvenile attempts at humor don't really help us." This was not how he had hoped the meeting with the dean would go, but as he thought about it in the moment, he wasn't surprised. Nothing he could say would impede the acceleration of the express barreling down the track at him.

"Why did you tell the *Crimson* reporter you thought that the 1619 Project was *quote* irrelevant *unquote*?"

"I didn't," he said.

"Then why did the reporter write that you did?"

"Beats me."

She made a note on her legal pad. "One of the students specifically told you during the orientation class that she felt unsafe in the classroom and in your presence, and you did nothing to make her safety a priority."

"Pauline," Rob said. "Dean Scott-Norton. *Please.* Listen to what you are saying. You are an accomplished person. You know beyond any doubt that that girl—"

"Woman," said the dean.

"That that *woman* would be hard-pressed to find a safer place on Planet Earth than my classroom. May I say with all due respect to you and the position you hold that any suggestion that the student was in any way, shape, or form unsafe in my classroom is light years, *many* light years, beyond the distant boundaries of what, by any reasonable definition, could be regarded as preposterous. She was *acting*, Pauline. She was performing. She wanted a scene the kids could laugh about later that night."

Rob sat up in the comfortably padded chair. He hadn't realized he had been in a sort of slouch. Maybe that was it. Maybe his body language conveyed to her an I-do-not-give-a-shit attitude. He sat up, good posture.

"Let's reset a bit here. The students came to my class to get a taste of the basics of constitutional law. I walked them through some of

the historic cases, with emphasis on *Gideon* and *Brown*. I thought these
would capture their attention not only because they are iconic rulings
but also because they are great stories. You know the significance of
these cases in American law. But these students evinced little interest in
the cases or in the evolution of constitutional law. This is my field, not
history or polemics or race or the latest controversy. When I was asked
for my thoughts about the *Times* initiative, I said it was my opinion that
America is by no means defined by the pursuit of slavery but rather by
the pursuit of liberty and freedom and justice for all. An aspiration, I
emphasized. And I would be more than willing to engage in that debate
with anyone on this campus, student or faculty."

She stiffened.

"I was hoping you would come in here with at least a modest effort
at contrition, Rob," she said. "The reality is that the students were not
comfortable in your classroom. The reality is that you were quoted in
the *Crimson* as dismissing an important new work of scholarship as *quote*
irrelevant *unquote*."

The dean stood and gazed down at him. Was it a look of pity? "I
see no alternative other than to take this up with the faculty disciplinary
board. You will be notified."

Rob remained seated. "*Notified?*" he said with a tone of incredulity.
"*Notified?* About what? That I am guilty of having a different intellectual
view than a classroom of kids barely out of high school? Notified that I
failed to pledge full faith and allegiance to the new orthodoxy?"

Rob stood up. He wanted to say something calm, collegial.
Instead, purely on instinct, he walked the few steps over to the bust of
Washington.

"Pauline, I have to say that it really bothers me to see old George
this way," he said. "Would you mind if I removed the trash bag?"

"The students who came to me with concerns about your behavior
chose to do that. They were exercising their constitutional right of free
speech. Touch it and I will call security."

13

Memories 1979–1980

September 10, 1979

My dearest Thomas, I felt your first kick today, and I want to note the date, September 10, 1979, so that many decades from now when I am old and gray, a grandmother doting on your precious children, we will be able to recall your very first sign of life. I was lying on the sofa in the living room reading a novel by a wonderful writer named Joseph Heller. It's called Something Happened, *and I am not at all sure where the plot is headed, but I feel a sense of connection with the characters. As I was reading, suddenly, a kick in my stomach. It was shocking! Thrilling! And I said, Hey, you little guy, I think it is the happiest day of my life because you've sent me a message! I'm here! you said with that kick, and man, oh man, do I know you are there. It is very bizarre in a way to be writing something to someone who will not even be able to read for, what, another five or six years, something like that (how bad am I that I am about to be a mother and I actually am not sure when kids start to read!!!). Yikes.*

As I was lying there, in walks your dad—yes, Rob is about to become a father! Your dad came in from work (it was 8:15 p.m.!!). When I told him about the kick, he let out a whoop like an Indian on the Plains, and believe me, buster, your dad is not one to typically show that kind of exuberant emotion! He knelt down next to the couch, pulled up the massively baggy shirt I am wearing, and he kissed my tummy. He kissed me and you at the same time!

I think it goes without saying that I have never been so happy. Did I mention that already, wink-wink! Your dad is an amazing person in so many ways. He is, and I am not exaggerating at all, literally one of the leading scholars of constitutional law in the United States. Crazy, I know. In fact, soon after we found out I was pregnant with you, he became a tenured faculty member at the law school! Much more important than his sheer brilliance is his love for you and me. We are so blessed.

There is so much I want to teach you—really, I should say that we, your dad and I, want to teach you, and at the top of the list is gratitude. I have learned in life to take time every day to reflect on how fortunate I am to have health, a happy marriage, an interesting profession, and, most of all, you. Gratitude centers me. It places the world into perspective. I realize that so much can go wrong so quickly. Tragedy abounds. I think of the mothers whose children are shot and killed in the streets of Boston every other night, it seems. It happened again today, a teenager, seventeen, I think, shot coming out of a convenience store. The heartache—I cannot even imagine. I pray for the mothers. They interviewed the boy's mother on the local news, and she was catatonic, broken. Obscene that they stick a microphone in that mother's face in such a moment. I recognize that there are perils out there that we will have to navigate together in the years to come. Teenagers drinking! And, worse, driving. I have confidence we will make thoughtful choices. We can only worry about the things over which we have control. The other forces in the universe, especially the malign ones, are entirely unpredictable, and when they strike, we are entirely at their mercy. Some things make me very afraid for you. I have seen firsthand how drugs and alcohol have the power to ruin peoples' lives. It is a horrible thing to witness when someone—friend, college classmate, neighbor's mother—takes the one life granted to them by God and wastes it under such a scourge. I pray each day for you, and one of my prayers is that you will always choose health and emotional well-being.

I rarely thought about such things before, but now that I am about to be a mother, I think differently. I am a wife, of course, and a lawyer and a *student, etc., but above all else,* a mother. *And I have realized in reflecting* *upon it that I have never wanted anything more in my life than to be a mother.* *Strip it all away—marriage, work, the pursuit of ideas, understanding how* *the world works, friends, family, etc.—rip it all away from me, and I would* *still remain my essential self as your mother. There is no doubt in my mind* *that my defining purpose is to be a mother. It is an instinct, a desire more* *powerful than anything I have ever felt.*

When I told your dad the other night that I felt an urge to communicate *with you, he said, "What's stopping you?" (He's extremely practical, your* *dad!) Write him a note or two, he said. And so here we are. A correspondence* *is born with the kick of the tiniest of feet inside me. And here I am respond-* *ing in writing, and it feels absolutely natural! That we will be together for* *so many years to come is amazing to me. I sit here thinking you will arrive* *in two to three months, and you will begin your individual life journey, but* *you will always have us, your father and me, there to guide in whatever way* *is helpful to you.*

We have hopes for you, of course. We will certainly make sure you have *the finest education possible, but then whatever you choose to do profession-* *ally, we will support you one thousand percent. I have asked myself what do* *I most want in life for you, and I have a lot of thoughts, but I keep coming* *back to the idea of a life where you have love, of course, but also inner peace,* *the kind that calms the mind and spirit. Much harder to achieve than it* *sounds—for many if not most people it is elusive.*

Thomas Browning Barrow made his way out into the world in the early evening hours of January 15, 1980. He was as bald as a cue ball with what looked to Julia like an enormous head on a tiny little body, but she was assured by the delivery doctor that he was "perfect." And, of course, to Julia and Rob, that was exactly what he was.

He had his mother's small ears and his dad's slightly elongated face. Julia cradled him in her arms in the hospital bed as she and Rob huddled over him, marveling at the tiny hands and feet, at his dark eyes looking this way and that, at his delicate lips and the way he moved his moistened pink tongue around in his mouth. They were a family now, the three of them, and they were joined in the hospital by Ray Witter, who was an unofficial member of their family, godfather to little Thomas.

Her body reacted to the birth in ways she had never experienced. There was a sharp, pungent odor that accompanied the birth and a dark red vaginal discharge that a nurse explained was called "lochia." Her tiny breasts became quite large ("Check these babies out, Rob"), engorged with milk. They felt hard and quite heavy, and she wondered how women with unusually large breasts tolerated the weight. At night, she sweated in bed, soaking her nightgown and the sheets. Her hormones had gone a bit haywire.

Thomas was a calm baby who adapted to a predictable feeding schedule—at several intervals during the day and then twice during the night. She would sometimes wake to the sound of his crying at 2:00 a.m. and find that she was wet from sweat and have to discard what she was wearing and quickly don dry pajamas and an old wool sweater to keep warm. She sat in a wooden rocker her parents had given them—it was the chair in which her mother had breastfed Julia—and fed him while Rob snored quietly on the far side of the bed, so deeply asleep that he would have no recollection in the morning of her having arisen during the night not once but twice. Within weeks she was exhausted in a way she had never experienced.

"I'm so tired it's painful and funny at the same time," she told Rob.

But in midmorning when the baby napped, Julia did the same and was restored. Her parents drove up from Southampton and visited for a week, bearing gifts and a sense of awe at the life cycle that only the aging fully appreciate.

"Something like 70 billion people have lived on the earth," Julia told Rob at dinner one evening. They were seated at the kitchen table,

Julia nursing Thomas while Rob broiled chicken breasts and boiled broccoli and rice.

"My point is that all of those parents were right," she said. "All of those billion babies were the most precious because every child born to every parent is by definition the most precious ever. How could it possibly be otherwise? You go through your life, as we have, and you love your husband or your wife or your siblings or parents or whomever, and then this child is born and, instantly, and I mean *instantly*, it is by an order of magnitude the most important thing in your life." She smiled, a look of wonder on her face. "It's a kind of miracle in a way, I think."

"I guess I think the whole thing is a miracle," he said. "The sperm, the egg, gestation, and then a human being. I know it's all basic biology, but it still feels spiritual to me."

She considered this. "I find it inexplicable in one sense," she said. "But in another, it could not be simpler. Of course, your child is more precious than any other. It is literally part of you. It's definitely got a spiritual component. And I thank God for him every day."

Thomas, as I pushed you in the stroller today along the banks of the Charles, I thought about how precious life is and how fragile, as well. As we walk, I wonder about the people I see, especially those of advanced age, who, it is clear, will not live much longer. Before you were born, I very rarely thought about such matters other than concern for my own parents. The idea of mortality was not something that I considered more than briefly every now and then. But now, for the first time in my life, I am responsible for the survival of another living human being! It is the greatest responsibility one can have, and I embrace it with all my heart.

After our morning walk today, when we got home, I fed you and put you in for your nap—your sleep schedule has become like clockwork!—and I knelt by your crib, and I prayed to give thanks for all that we have in our little family. I thanked God first and foremost for you; for the miracle that is your existence. I thanked him for your health, and I prayed for the health of myself and your dad and my parents and Uncle Ray. I thanked him for the bliss with which our household has been blessed. And as I prayed, I could not help but think of those lines from Wordsworth that I read in college. I don't recall it precisely, but it was something like—

Bliss was it in that dawn to be alive,
But to be young was very heaven!

In the kitchen, with my cup of tea, I felt very heaven! *This is life, I thought. This is what existence as a human being is at its core. It is love, it is gratitude, it is love of another greater than love for one's self. This, for me, defines life's spiritual and human essence. It's odd. I have never been much of a crier, but now I tear up at the slightest emotional cue. I cry out of joy at you being here with me.*

14

Wash the Oxycodone
Down with Scotch

The day after Thanksgiving, the pain was intense. Chen had mentioned that some patients developed scar tissue after surgery that could persist even after removal of the catheter. Rob didn't say anything about it that morning at breakfast when Julia was about to drive up to Maine to visit a friend for the day. He wanted her to enjoy herself, not worry about him. She needed the break from him and the cancer-related stress. Ray, he knew, was in an all-day conference at the medical school for international students, and he didn't want to interrupt something so important. But as the day progressed, it worsened. After surgery, he had taken the prescribed pain medication, oxycodone, as directed. He had a few caplets left and took one that morning, but its effect was minimal. He called Chen's office and asked whether he should up the dosage but was cautioned by the nurse not to do so.

"But I'm in a considerable amount of pain," he said.

"It's best to follow the doctor's recommendation especially with an opiate," she said. She was condescending, talking to him as though he was an idiot, a nuisance in her day.

"Could you ask Dr. Chen to call me, please?" Rob said.

"Dr. Chen is in surgery back-to-back all day," she said.

"Oh, okay," Rob said. "How about one of the other doctors in the department? Could you have one of them give me a call? I seem not to be conveying properly the degree of pain I'm experiencing. I really do need to consult with a doctor."

"Well, Dr. Woods is away at a conference," she replied wearily. "I could have him call you next week."

"Is someone covering for Dr. Woods?"

"Dr. Gillespie."

"Do you think you might impose upon Dr. Gillespie to call me for two minutes so I can get this dosage increased?" He was failing to conceal his irritation.

No return call came from Dr. Gillespie or anyone else throughout that day. *These fucking doctors*, Rob thought. They always said it was about the patient or patient-centered or other PR phrases, but that was bullshit. It was about *them* and what worked for their schedule and what was convenient for them. Ray had told him this a million times, and now Rob understood. He felt powerless, standing alone outside the castle, the gates shut, drawbridge up, alligators patrolling the moat. He couldn't penetrate the system, and it made a man who was rarely angry quite angry. Rob had experienced anger so infrequently in his life that it nearly always came as a surprise, and he found himself inept at handling it.

At 5:00 p.m. Rob called Ray and explained the situation. Forty-five minutes later Ray came through the privet with a single malt and a pocket full of painkillers. "It's all about the metrics," Ray said. "All the hospitals want to be the one to prescribe the fewest opioids. It's cowardice. They claim they're patient-centered, and then when the patient is suffering, do they relieve the suffering or do they worry about their own opioid count for the year? Imagine doctors being perfectly content to let patients suffer. I got a call from a patient whose wife had a knee replaced and she was in a lot of pain, which obviously is common, and they told her to take Tylenol. She was crying with pain. Fucking *Tylenol* when she's at nine on the pain scale."

"So what did you do?" Rob asked.

"Same thing I'm going to do for you, Rob," said Ray. He handed Rob a prescription container with sixty oxycodone pills.

"Take as much as you need to make the pain go away," Ray said. "You'll figure it out. Stay ahead of the pain. Take the dose that works for you at regular four-to-six-hour intervals. Stay on that dose, whatever it is, for the next few days, and then, only if you feel relatively pain-free, you can experiment with a lower dose. You'll know if you've taken too much—you'll feel really shitty, and you might vomit. You will get very constipated, so I also brought the laxative that works well. Make sure you take it."

"Could I get addicted?" Rob asked.

Ray laughed. "I don't see that happening. But if it does, I tell you what, we'll send you to rehab."

"I'm curious where you get these drugs," Rob asked. "Wouldn't the pharmacy people get suspicious if you're prescribing all these pills for yourself?"

"Oh, of course," he said. "I would never do that. I get them straight from the pharma sales reps. They give me whatever I want."

"Wow," said Rob. "Is that kosher?"

Ray laughed heartily. "Of course not. You just sit and relax." He went into the kitchen and returned with two glass tumblers. He poured a few fingers of scotch into each glass.

"Wash the oxycodone down with scotch," Ray said. "Gives you a jump-start."

"Really?" Rob said skeptically.

"Christ, when I have bad insomnia it's my go-to."

They chatted for about an hour until their drinks were finished.

"Feels better, doesn't it?" Ray asked.

"Wow," Rob said. "I feel so much better. Thank you."

"Mission accomplished," said Ray. "I have to get back to school for a reception for the international kids so I'll see you tomorrow. Any issues, call me."

After Ray walked back through the yard and the privet to his home, Rob remained sitting in the garden. Light from the house illuminated the terrace, but most of the yard was in shadows or darkness by now, and though the temperature was falling, he didn't want to go inside. This was where he belonged, where he was destined to be. He was feeling quite pleasantly pain-free, but his mind was troubled by the idea of cancer. What a terrible word. The doctors said that they had removed all of the bad cells, that they had caught it early, that prostate was one of the slowest growers, that they had excellent treatments even in the event that the cancer should reappear, which the doctors believed unlikely, and on and on. And yet, he couldn't help but wonder what it would be like to find that the disease had accelerated, made its way to the bones and through them to his major organs, and then there would be nothing that could be done.

His fears receded within the embrace of the drugs and alcohol. He recalled the propofol from surgery, and soaring over Fenway and the Emerald Necklace. He felt a bit like that now. His gaze fell upon the thorny, brownish stems of the rosebushes in full retreat from the cold. But Rob could see the roses now as they had been in summer, clutches of roses climbing the trellis, and he felt he could see how deeply red they were, a color that seemed aggressive, even martial, given to drama and violence. He liked roses very much, but he preferred peonies and the richness of their shade of white, something out of a painting by John Singer Sargent. He summoned an image of the oak leaves, dark green, nature's signature. He liked the fact that there were thousands of them replicated almost exactly alike throughout the tree. Maybe tens of thousands. He marveled, as he so often had, at the longevity of the trees. That particular oak, just beyond the sycamore, had flourished in this very place for at least a century, perhaps longer. How sturdy these

mighty trees were against the intrusion of winter. The oak and sycamore had been rooted here during World War I, the Great Depression,
World War II, the sixties, Vietnam, 9/11. It seemed kind of amazing,
but in Rob's condition, almost everything at that moment seemed kind
of amazing. What a marvelous sensation to be shielded from pain or
discomfort. Earlier in the day he had been feeling sorry for himself, and
he didn't much like that. He thought of all those people on the second
floor at the Cancer Center awaiting their blood work. He thought of
Rita B and wondered how she was faring. There were people in there
with cancers of the brain, cancers of the pancreas, diseases that had a
kamikaze aspect to them—kill the host at any and all cost and do so as
quickly as possible. He, on the other hand, had a more controllable, less
lethal cancer. At least in theory.

15

The Chief

On the first day of December, Rob and Julia settled into comfortable chairs to listen to a radio broadcast of the day's argument in the United States Supreme Court in the case of *Dobbs v. Jackson Women's Health*, more colloquially known as the latest *Roe v. Wade* case. Rob had read the briefs from the petitioners and the government, and he had read a number of the amicus briefs as well. In fact, he had edited and revised one such brief submitted by a women's health organization in Cambridge. The issue at hand was whether it was constitutionally permissible for the state of Mississippi to prohibit abortion after fifteen weeks, the "gestational age," in the Mississippi law, with no exception for rape, incest, or the life of the mother. The fear among many constitutional scholars was that the court's conservative majority could use the case to go further than deciding that question. That, in fact, the conservative justices might use the case as a way to overturn *Roe*. Rob said very little during the course of the two hours of argument before the court. Justice Kagan summarized the liberal position succinctly: How could the court now consider "fifty years of decisions saying that this is part of our law, that this is part of the fabric of women's existence in this country"? Julie Rikelman, an attorney representing the Mississippi abortion clinic, told the justices that the central issue was the right of a woman to control decisions about her own body. "For a state to take control of a woman's body and demand that she go through pregnancy and childbirth, with all the physical risks and life-altering consequences that brings, is a fundamental deprivation of her liberty," Rikelman said.

But the conservative justices were having none of it. One after another expressed comfort with the Mississippi law. More than that, it was clear that the consensus among them was to use the case to over-turn *Roe*.

"There's only one hope," Rob remarked toward the end of the argument. "The chief has to persuade them to answer the simple question in the case: Is the Mississippi law constitutional? Period. Don't answer unasked questions."

"And the question of *Roe* is not asked?" Julia asked.

"It is not asked in the original filings by Mississippi," he said.

As if on cue, Roberts said, "The thing that is at issue before us today is fifteen weeks," making it clear that his preferred option was to uphold Mississippi's law and stop there.

"Why answer a question that is not explicitly present in the case?" Rob asked.

When Roberts accused the Mississippi attorney general of a bait-and-switch tactic, Rob was heartened. In the state's petition seeking Supreme Court review, the Mississippi attorney said that "the questions presented in this petition do not require the court to overturn *Roe*." But the state changed tactics once the court agreed to hear the matter and mounted a full-on assault to overturn *Roe*.

"The chief doesn't like that kind of tactic," Rob said.

Rob had predicted months earlier that Roberts would seek a compromise position—precisely as he was now doing. This thrilled Julia. "Rob!" she exclaimed when the chief said the court should allow Mississippi to set a fifteen-week limit on abortion but not decide *Roe*. The way in which the chief calmly laid out this option seemed reasonable. It would solve the Mississippi case, stop well short of overturning *Roe*, and avoid an all-out culture war.

"Do you think they'll do it, Rob?" Julia asked.

"What the chief is suggesting?"

"Yes."

Rob nodded. "I do."

16

"My Dad, Doc . . .
I'm All He's Got"

On the first Saturday in December, under a cold mist, Ray and Rob set out for a walk through the Mount Auburn Cemetery, a sprawling landscape serving as the afterlife residence for Winslow Homer, Longfellow, and others in the intellectual elite. This acreage by the Charles River was a sanctuary for Ray, a place for reflection and a good walk that got the heart beating faster. Once within the cemetery, they followed a perimeter road past carved granite memorials more than a century old. The narrow internal roadways were lined with oak and elm, ancient trees that had remained sturdy as many thousands of humans had been buried beneath their shade.

"In here I can feel the quiet," Ray said as they walked along, past one grave marker more ornate than the next. "I get a sense in here of peace that we think of as beyond the grave, but it is also here, the aura of this place. I wonder whether it could be a hint of the peace you feel on the other side." Ray turned to Rob and could not help but laugh. "These are the deep thoughts one has in a cemetery," he observed sarcastically.

Ray had his binoculars strapped around his neck, even though the

conditions for spotting birds was less than ideal. Then, suddenly, he
hoisted the glasses and studied a bird in the distance. "American gold-
finch," he said. They walked on and without the aid of the binoculars
Ray spotted a northern cardinal as well. He turned to the side, moving
past the first row of headstones to the second, where a large monument
occupied a patch of ground where B. F. Skinner lay. "After he retired, he
was still around here," said Ray, "and I had an idea when I was a junior
faculty member to solicit his support for a grant proposal I was writing
that integrated some behavioral issues into a study of people with complex chronic conditions. So I get all my material together, work through
other faculty to get an audience with the great man. I go over there—he
kept an office just off the square—and we meet and I explain my idea,
and I will admit in retrospect that it wasn't one of the great intellectual
breakthroughs of all time, but it wasn't nothing either." Ray laughed at
the memory. "He thought that my approach to the grant was the stu-
pidest thing he had ever heard! He belittled me—though he did it in a
very quiet, restrained voice. I left there and the only thought I had was,
I hope I have just had the worst meeting I will ever experience."

"Was it?" Rob asked.

Ray shot Rob a look of incredulity. "You know what faculty meetings are like. They're painful enough to merely attend. I have to *preside*.
It's getting a tooth drilled without novocaine."

"No different at the law school," Rob said. "Maybe worse."

"Worse than senior physicians at Harvard teaching hospitals?"

They walked in silence for some distance until Ray pointed out the
impressive marker for the grave of Felix Frankfurter. Rob, of course,
knew the justice was at rest here; in fact, had visited the grave on a
couple of occasions.

"What a mind," Rob remarked.

"Here, too," said Ray as they next approached the marker bearing
the name Winslow Homer. They circled down toward where the cemetery abutted the river, then made their way up the steepest part of the

property to a stone chapel, elegant in its English lines, something out of a Cotswold village. From the top of the hill they started down a gently descending pathway.

"So let's talk about the elephant in the room, Rob," said Ray. "Cancer is the one word that can derail anybody. It's the malevolent response of the universe for the creation of life. But we have to look at the bright side. If it was pancreatic, you'd be dead in ninety days. Unless they trapped you in a trial and tortured you with rat poison, which is the current standard treatment. I have complete confidence that you will get through this."

They continued on, both zipping up their jackets against the cold, the mist having turned to rain.

"I want to show you something," Ray said, turning to a remote section of the property. They moved along until they came upon a flat piece of stone on the ground with the inscription:

McGeorge Bundy
Born March 30, 1919
Died September 16, 1996
Boston, Massachusetts

Ray stood quite still, head slightly bent, gazing at the grave marker. "He hides here," Ray said. "He hides here, Rob, so no one will notice. So no one will stop to consider what he did. He was one of Halberstam's best and brightest. Gifted intellect but, like so many of that ilk, his self-belief outstripped the reality of his capabilities. He pushed Kennedy on the Bay of Pigs, was in the room for the Cuban missile crisis. But most of all he was there to convince Kennedy, then Johnson, to go all in on Vietnam. More troops, then more still. More nineteen-year-old marines. In America we had an inexhaustible supply. Bomb the north, then bomb them some more."

Ray shook his head slowly, as though he was unable to fathom what

Bundy had wrought. "He and the others were raised to believe in their own destiny as the elite among the elite who would make decisions others lacked the intellect and moral authority to make. Hubris was the disease of that era, and he was infected. Terminal case. I wonder whether he ever came to understand the harm he had done. I wonder whether he ever visited the wall, read the names. If you don't read the names and think about their young lives and their promise, then you can't understand the tragedy of it. Fifty-eight thousand. Average age twenty-one. What kind of people send their young men to such a fate?"

After Vietnam Ray had tried to "get well," as he had once put it to Rob and Julia. He had married, but seven months later he begged his young wife for forgiveness for, as he put it, "the way I am." She knew he was right. How could you live your life with such a tortured soul? He tried therapy, meditation, acupuncture, hallucinogenic drugs, and religion, and found that faith, a focus on God's grace and the afterlife, helped more than anything. He believed in eternal peace. He came to believe that a just God would have a place where peace was the nourishment for his marines and their families. But the war haunted him.

In 1971, Ray Witter was assigned to a medical-surgical hospital unit in Phu Bai, forty miles south of Hue. Lieutenant Witter landed in Saigon on a blistering day in May looking splendid in his bleached white uniform and gung-ho to contribute to the war effort. He seemed during that time to resemble a character out of central casting—tall, lean, fresh haircut—with the easy manner common to the confident, to those with an intellect that simplifies the cognitive side of life. He was a young man ready for the world, destined for important work in the field of medicine, comfortable in his skin.

And then Phu Bai, where the medevac helicopters' rotors kicked up a fine, talcum-like dust that would soon turn to mud in the rainy season. Until then it was blinding dust, baking heat, quiet times, and then *bang*—mayhem when the two sides clashed somewhere out there on the paddies, in a village, a valley, or on a hill that would be taken one day with the loss of a few dozen teenagers and then lost a week later with no one seeming to notice. The hardest thing was keeping track of time. The only rhythm was when they were overwhelmed and when they were not. He marveled at the team's ability to triage a dozen new arrivals in mere minutes. The trick was to determine as quickly as possible who would certainly make it and who would certainly not, then focus on those cases where the question of life or death hung in the air, up there lost in the dust and the glare and the deafening sound of the helicopters that patrolled the skies like another avian species native to Southeast Asia. The cloudless skies made for oppressive heat, and that was bad enough. Worse, for Ray, anyway, was the glare that laid bare the reality of it all. The truth was right there, as though under some sort of spotlight, and you could not fail to see it; you could not look away. The glare hurt your eyes, but looking away, well, when you did that, there was something lost inside. Ray could not look away.

One day when the choppers arrived, Ray was in the latrine with another bout of the runs that seemed to have gone through the base every other week. He had arrived in Vietnam a trim, fit young man of 175 pounds, but was now barely 155. The way his cheekbones protruded made him look scary or ill or both. The children have arrived, he thought. It was his cue to himself to use whatever skill he possessed to try to save a life. That was how he had tried to get through it. Inside, as the months and casualties passed, Ray built an internal sense of rage against the dying light in so many boys who had lain there on the gurneys, under his care, and slipped away, never again to see their mother or father or girlfriend or high school buddies. Never again. It would take some time for news of this tragedy to reach the modest home in Chula Vista or farm in Indianola or apartment in the Bronx. But soon enough word would arrive, and it would turn another family inside out, send the mother plunging into a dark, dark grief, the father to drinking and fury and bitter tears. And then from that one family word would go

out to cousins and grandparents and teachers and coaches and teammates and throughout that network that was attached to one degree or
another to the life of that one lance corporal, the grief would take hold
and there would be another hole in the fabric of the universe.

Near the end of his twelve-month tour of duty, after he had witnessed the deaths of innocents on an epic scale, Ray wrote a letter to
Secretary of Defense Robert McNamara, inviting him to come to the
base and spend a few days shadowing him to see what the leaders of
the United States had wrought. Death on a vast scale. The letter did not
get past the censors.

But he would be leaving soon enough, and he would put his life
together and he would take the only possession that really mattered
to him—the hand-scrawled notebook listing the soldiers and marines
he had cared for. To young Dr. Witter the list was a sacred text, for it
included only the names of the boys he had cared for who had not
made it. When Ray had returned to the states from Vietnam, he carried his list with him and was so afraid of losing it that he had made a
Xerox copy and mailed it to his parents in Iowa for safekeeping. Back in
the states he used all of his savings to travel each weekend, working his
way down the list. Flights from his base in Washington at Walter Reed
to Arkansas, New Jersey, California, Florida, Missouri, Maine, Kansas.
With information from navy files, he would find the addresses and he
would show up. He never called in advance. If the family was not at
home he would wait. He once perched on the front porch of a home in
rural Georgia for twenty-three hours before the family returned home.
He told the parents who he was and that he had taken care of their
boy and though he had tried his best to save him, he had been unable
to do so. But he wanted the parents and siblings to know that he and
the other doctors and nurses had tried the best they could. He told
them they had cared for him as though he were their own son. And the
parents and sometimes siblings and grandparents and occasionally a
girlfriend or wife would fall into a stunned silence and then one of them

would be crying and then they would cry together and embrace. And they would ask questions—sometimes just a few, sometimes dozens. *Did he say anything? Was he in pain? Did he suffer? Did he look afraid? Did he pray?* Ray answered the questions patiently, as honestly as he could without revealing the nature of their child's wounds. He would never do that. He believed that if he described in detail what had happened to their boy, what he had seen happen to hundreds of boys, the nightmarish images would haunt them all their days. He did not want the families to suffer any more than they already did, and so he collected all the images in his own mind and he carried them with him so the mothers and fathers did not have to.

He always told the family that the boy had said to him, "Tell my family I love them." This was not real, not in a literal sense, but Ray felt it was true that the dying boys had communicated a spiritual message to him.

There had been one kid who, as much as any other, had stayed with Ray. The medic carrying the front end of a stretcher with a marine carrying the back end shouted to Ray, the first physician he saw, as they emerged from the helicopter.

"Doc, let's go on this kid!" The medic set the stretcher in the triage area where the fate of so many was determined. Ray ran inside and leaned over the wounded marine.

"JJ," the medic said, breathing hard from the exertion. "I know the kid."

Ray examined JJ's wounds, the holes where shrapnel had shredded his filthy T-shirt and blasted through the chest wall. He could only imagine the clumps of metal now in his lungs, liver, kidneys. JJ was white from loss of blood. He was alive, though he would not be much longer.

"Doc," JJ said in a barely audible whisper. "Doc, *please*. Don't let me die."

Ray began the process of cleaning his wounds, but even as he did so he knew the reality.

"My dad, I'm all he's got. It'll kill him, Doc, *please.*"

Ray kept working. The medic stood by, watching Ray imploringly.

"Where you from, JJ?" Ray asked.

"Kansas, sir," the boy struggled to say.

"We're gonna try and get you back there, JJ," Ray said, a repeat of what he had said to dozens of boys.

Suddenly, JJ cried out in pain. "God, Doc!" JJ was struggling for breath, fighting. He grasped Ray's hand with surprising strength, and Ray knew it was the last bit of energy this boy would ever use.

"*My dad—*"

And he was gone.

Ray thought of Oppenheimer quoting the Bhagavad Gita: *Now I am become Death, the destroyer of worlds.*

Back in the states, JJ added to his list, Ray had flown from DC to Chicago, Chicago to Salina Municipal Airport, then driven 123 miles to the town of Lebanon, Kansas, which happened to be the precise geographic center of America. Ray arrived in the early evening and found JJ's father on the porch, rocking in his chair, looking out over the cornfields. He was a compact man, full head of white hair, longish out of neglect rather than style preference. He wore denim overalls, bleached over time.

"You military?" Edgar Smith asked as Ray approached.

Ray smiled. "How could you tell?" he asked.

"Bearing," the man replied. "JJ send you?"

"I'm Ray," he said, extending his hand and feeling the strength of JJ's hand in the father's. "Ray Witter. I treated your son."

"Military doctor?" Edgar asked.

Ray nodded.

"Sit here," Edgar said, gesturing to the rocker beside him. "Pull it 'round so's I can see you. Like that.

"They came out to the house, two marines in their uniforms. I look up. They get out of the government vehicle, full uniforms, no finer-looking young men. They talked to me, but I couldn't listen. All I could think was did my boy ask for me at the end."

JJ's father fell silent. Ray waited. He had come to learn through his travels that these parents needed a moment to reflect, to gather themselves, but mostly to remember the child they had loved so completely. Tears made their way slowly down the father's weathered cheeks. He blinked, and more tears came, pushing the ones ahead to move more forcefully along until they dripped on his shirt.

Ray waited another moment, then said, "Yes, he did. He held my hand, and he said to me, 'Tell my dad I love him. Tell him I will wait for him in heaven.'"

Edgar stared hard at Ray, then shifted his glance back out over the never-ending cornfields. Minutes went by.

"My boy say that?"

"Exactly that," Ray said.

Edgar nodded. "Wife passed six years ago. Just JJ and me since then. He wanted the marines. Always did, so what could I say? I didn't want him to go, but . . ."

Edgar stopped rocking and turned to Ray. "Was JJ hurt bad?" he asked.

"He had serious wounds."

"In his head?"

"Chest."

"Bullets?"

"Shrapnel."

"Where'd he die?"

"A place called Phu Bai," Ray said. "We had a medical facility there. He was brought in by helicopter. We tried our best."

"Good lord, I know *that*, I don't doubt *that*. . . . What'd you say your name was?"

"Ray."

"Dr. Ray, I know you did, the military, I know you did."

"He's in heaven," Ray said. "JJ is in heaven now. At peace."

Edgar's eyes narrowed. "You believe that, Dr. Ray?"

"I do," Ray said. "With all my heart."

Edgar nodded vigorously. "I'm damn glad to hear that, because that's what I believe. Have to."

Ray rose from his chair. "He's there," Ray said. "He is one of the heavenly souls. I know he is."

"Stay for supper?"

"I have a late flight back," Ray said.

"Where you headed?"

"Washington."

"Washington, DC?"

"Yes sir."

Another long pause.

"You come all the way from Washington, DC, to tell me about my boy?"

"Yes, sir."

JJ's dad nodded for a bit, then he stood and shook Ray's hand.

"I thank God you came here today. I knew JJ sent you when I saw you. I knew it. God bless you, Dr. Ray."

Ray stayed at the economy hotel near the airport and caught a dawn flight out the next morning. He connected in Chicago for his flight to National Airport. All his trips concluded the same way: the aircraft on a glide path over the Virginia countryside and then lower over suburbia and then lower still with a clear view below of Arlington National Cemetery and all those grave markers, well-ordered from the sky, concealing the terrible reality that lay beneath. And each time he would look out from his window seat—always a window seat home— his heart would break yet again for all of them and for his boys and for the country he loved that had lost its way.

17

This Is the Moment

Ray was in the lab early on a Friday evening a couple of weeks before Christmas when he received an unannounced visit from Michael Dwyer, chairman of the medical center board. Dwyer was a hearty fellow of Irish descent, the map of Ireland on his ruddy face. He sauntered into Ray's tiny office at the far end of the lab and said, "Love what you've done with the place," then burst out laughing as he extended his hand.

"Hey, Mike," said Ray. "Slumming it, huh?"

"Once in a while," he said.

"Don't you usually sit home weekends counting your money?" Ray needled.

"Takes too long," Dwyer replied.

Ray had known Mike Dwyer since his early days on the medical school faculty. Mike was chairman of the board of the group that owned the biggest hospitals in Boston along with hundreds of ambulatory care sites in eastern Massachusetts. He had donated tens of millions to the hospitals. Together, Ray and Mike had also raised tens of millions for the medical school and its research initiatives. Ray, in fact, had proved a persuasive, even charming, presenter with potential donors. The office was narrow, windowless, bookshelves lining one wall. There was a desk

chair and nowhere else to sit. Ray led Mike out into the main part of
the lab, where there were several folding chairs by the far wall.

"Does this place always smell like this?" Dwyer asked.

Ray laughed, nodding toward the cages of rats and mice. "You get
used to it."

Ray was dressed, as was his custom, in plain slacks, dress shirt, no
tie. Mike Dwyer wore tailored trousers and an English-made dress shirt,
his standard capitalist board-meeting uniform.

"That was quite an article you had in the *New England Journal*,"
Dwyer said. "I understood about one tenth of it, to be honest, but I got
the bottom line about immunotherapy. Exciting."

"Lot of potential."

Dwyer looked around the lab, swiveling in his chair. "It's the
damnedest thing what you people do," he said. "I don't have a scientific
bone in my body. I can't pronounce half the words in your article."

"You didn't come here to compliment my article," Ray said.
"What's up?"

"I need you," Dwyer said. "There's a report coming from RAND.
Executive committee of the board commissioned almost a year ago. It's
ugly. If we handle it the wrong way—which is what the instinct of the
C-suite will be, I am sorry to say— it will be a lost opportunity. But if we
have the balls to handle it well, it could be something special."

"What does it say?" Ray asked.

"The truth," said Dwyer. "That my hospital system is great at many
things but not nearly good enough. And I believe that our patients
deserve better, so in the interest of those patients out there who come
to us and place their health and their lives in our hands, I need you to
take on a role as special advisor to the board on safety. You bring the
credibility we need."

"Who else knows about the report?"

"Executive committee members got it last night and, of course,
Walter and Dickie. They're livid."

"I have a lot going on, Mike," Ray said. "We're at an important juncture in the lab with our research, we've got grants to write, I've got a medical school to run, and I'm a practicing physician. And at this stage of the game I don't have much interest in dealing with the bureaucracy. And not to be rude, but haven't we been over this ground before? Until your organization can muster the balls to deal with the nondisclosure agreements and be honest with patients and the public, I'm just not interested in being involved. The medical school has been a wholly independent entity for a hundred years, and thank God it is. Happy to cooperate on fundraising to the mutual benefit of our organizations, but for Christ's sake, Mike, your people are too self-satisfied for me. You know this. When something goes wrong with a patient, we have two obligations. One, to reveal the entire truth to the patient, fix the problem, and cover any costs involved in doing so—"

"We do that," Mike interrupted.

"And our second obligation," Ray continued, "is to reveal the error to the medical world as a way to honor our mission to teach and improve. If we hide and refuse to share things that have gone wrong and share with the world how to prevent the mistake in the future, we're neglecting our obligations."

Ray was sweating and wiped his forehead with the back of his sleeve. His beard had gotten a bit out of control, his hair was tangled.

"You know what they call you behind your back at the hospital?" Mike asked.

"I don't give a shit what they call me, Mike."

"The 'Mad Russian,'" Mike said, smiling. "They call you that because they think you're out of control. You're intense, Ray. You've always been intense, but the past couple years, wow. They love you, but they're afraid of you."

"Good."

"I know you're not out of control," Mike said. "I know there's something inside you driving you. And I remember very well one of those dinners with donors when you and I had a drink afterward. A few drinks. And I said, 'Ray, what drives you?' And you were slouched there in the cocktail lounge, jacket off, necktie loose, and you looked at me like I was clueless. And you said, 'To reduce suffering in human beings.' I believed you. I could see it in you, I could *feel* it. It was visceral. I know you don't have much trust in authority, Ray. I get it. That is why I have come to you and why you are the right person for this role I am creating, medical advisor to the executive committee, which I control. I *need* you, Ray. You and I are the right team to do this. We've been around an awfully long time. We both realize—and I confess it took me much longer to come to this realization than it should have—that in our hospitals we have spent more time congratulating ourselves on safety improvements than getting them done."

Mike paused. He fixed his gaze on Ray's tired eyes. "This is the moment. We can do something special here. But I cannot do it without you. At least read the RAND document before you say no."

Ray nodded.

Mike Dwyer took out his cell phone and tapped a few keys, emailing the report to Ray. "I warn you," Mike said. "You will be unsurprised and angry."

"NDAs?"

"Nondisclosure agreements and more."

"Jesus, Mike, what have I been saying now for—?"

"This is no time for I-told-you-so," Dwyer replied edgily. "You can piss on me afterward all you like. This is an *opportunity*. This is RAND-grade, A+ analysis. This is data. And with you and me together, I think we can get the board to see clearly."

Ray frowned. He emitted a harsh laugh. "Mike, your fucking board cares about one thing and one thing only, and that is being able to pick up the phone and see the world's *quote* best *unquote* any time they want for themselves, friends, and family. Do they know anything about quality? Safety? Other than the bullshit the department heads feed them about how fucking great they're doing? Of course not. The board members give and stay on the board so they can *strut*. So if you think that I give one shit about what your board members think, you are very wrong, my friend."

"Your contempt for my board is well-known," said Dwyer. "You have assiduously maintained the academic integrity of the medical school by keeping them away—except of course when you need an extra fifty million here or there. Your anger's getting the better of you, Ray. Work with me here. It has taken me longer than it should have to see the reality. It took one of my dearest friends, a BC classmate, getting a central line infection in *my hospital* that killed him to open my eyes. I thought a lot about it, and I grieved, and I essentially forced the executive committee to retain RAND—in the absolute strictest confidence—to do a deep dive. The board members came along kicking and screaming. *What could possibly be gained? Our department chiefs know the story. Our frontline people report the facts to us etc., etc.* But I forced the issue, and now we have the report, and if you and I join forces we can quite possibly build a place that might even become almost as good as our reputation."

18

The Injection Goes Directly into Your Penis

As Christmas approached, both Rob and Julia were well into preparations for the classes they would be teaching in the upcoming semester. Rob was eager to get back in the classroom, feeling as though missing a semester had thrown him out of sync. Julia was gearing up to teach an introductory history course called The Sixties in which she was guided by themes from her book. It helped that several newspapers and magazines with which students were familiar had published reviews of the book, all of which quoted the same sentences: "No generation in American history has ever treated its generational inheritance—cultural norms, rules, and a measured sense of discipline—with such unmitigated rage. Government? Blow it up! Business world? Burn it down! Academia? Shut it down! Religion? The Buddha knows best!" The book had sparked a thoughtful conversation in certain intellectual circles and that, she felt, was something of an accomplishment. The notion that rethinking the boomers' overreaction to their parents' generation was something worth doing gave her a sense that perhaps the book had accomplished something worthwhile.

"So you have *the* appointment coming up," Julia said one evening, smiling broadly.

"*The* appointment," Rob repeated with a laugh.

She reached over and took his hand. "It's a very good thing," she said. "I'm really looking forward to getting us back on track. And I think I should go with you."

"Jesus, Jules," he exclaimed. "Thanks, but I'll be okay on my own."

There always seemed to be postsurgical issues. Now he was told during an appointment that if he wanted to have an erection ever again, he would have to take a hypodermic needle, fill it with some magic potion from a compounding pharmacy in California, and inject that potion directly into the side of his penis halfway between the tip and base. His appointment on this particular day was with a nurse who would instruct him on how to perform this procedure. It was a strange intrusion into his life—the appearance of this lifeless, flaccid thing, this thing that for decades was ready for the call of duty the moment his eyes opened in the morning. It was there, springing to attention at even the slightest stimulation. He was a man, and this was how men were for most of their lives. It was a biological fact that the overwhelming majority of men awoke on most mornings with an erection. The balance was off, Rob thought. There had been countless times throughout his life when he had experienced some level of stimulation, visual or otherwise, without ever putting the ensuing erection to use. Wasted. Too bad, he thought. Too bad there wasn't an erection savings bank from which to make withdrawals later in life; *Fidelity Erection 401k.*

Rob arrived for the appointment with some trepidation. The waiting area was quiet, nearly empty save for a couple about his age, the husband quite fit, even robust in appearance, the wife slender with prominent, gravity-defying breasts. Implants? Who cared? She looked good. He was guided to a sterile exam room, stainless steel, harsh lighting, frigid air conditioning. He sat alone for a few minutes, and then a rapid knock on the door and in came a woman, early fifties, compact build, cropped reddish hair, an air of enthusiasm.

"Okay, Robert—may I call you Robert?"

"Rob," he said.

"Got it, Rob. I'm Brenda, and I'm here to help you get some of your life back," she said. "We are going to talk about very private, sensitive matters, and I am going to be *very* direct with you—no beeswax. You good with that?"

"Definitely."

"So here is what we're going to do," she continued. "I am going to teach you how to inject bimix, so hang up your pants on the hook and let's get started."

Rob hesitated. "Hang them up . . ."

"On the hook there."

He slipped out of his khakis and hung them up by a belt loop.

"Underwear, too," she said as she went to a cabinet for supplies.

"Oh, so, you . . . so underwear also?" His heartbeat accelerated. He removed his blue cotton boxers and held them in front of his private parts. She turned, noticed what he was doing, and smiled.

"No secrets in here, hon. Hang 'em up."

He could feel the chilled air shrinking the subject of the visit. *This is nuts*, he thought. He sat there, naked from the waist down, his penis looking rather pathetic. At that moment came a knock at the door and the chief resident, a woman in her late twenties, stepped into the room.

"Sorry guys, but Brenda, are we about to run out of trimix?" she asked as she glanced down at Rob.

"New shipment came late yesterday. It's in the back."

"Great, thanks." She turned to Rob. "Sorry to interrupt. Good luck."

What was that supposed to mean? Rob wondered. Was she really saying good luck *with that thing*?

"Honey, pay attention now," said Brenda as the resident departed.

"I know you're nervous, but I promise you this is going to help restore your sex life. It gives back what the surgery took away. Is it perfect? No. But this injection"—she held up a small vial of clear liquid—"is going to restore your ability to have sex. So let's rock."

She instructed him to sit on the end of the exam bed, and she swiveled into position directly in front of him, looking closely at his penis. "Okay, so all you need are these three things. First, two sanitary wipes. With one you wipe the side of your penis where the injection will go. You do that very thoroughly to prevent infection. The second wipe you use to sanitize the top of the vial. The syringe is used to draw the medicine from the vial." She instructed him to wipe the top of the container, and he did so. "Now take the wipe and sterilize the side of your penis about midway between tip and the base. Don't be afraid to rub firmly to sanitize."

Rob did so.

"So you're right-handed?"

He nodded.

"So take the tip of your penis in your left hand," she ordered, "between thumb and forefinger, and stretch it over to the left so the entire right side is visible."

Rob did so.

"Okay, so watch how I do this," she said. "I'm going to insert the needle into the vial like so"—she turned the vial upside down, held the syringe up vertically, and began to draw the liquid. "So I'm drawing about 40 milligrams, which should be plenty. Over time you'll play with the amount that works for you. Just be careful not to overdo it, or you end up with a four-plus-hour erection, painful as hell, and that means a trip to the ER."

She handed him the syringe.

"Listen, this is a lot easier than you think it is, and after you do it a few times it will be a piece of cake, but right now, you need a steady hand. Pick a spot in the middle of the right side and ease the needle in. You'll feel a prick."

He slowly pushed the needle in, and for one moment it hurt like hell, but then it went in without pain.

"Now the injection should be very slow, so press the plunger slowly, more slowly even," she said as he did so. A few seconds later all of the liquid was out of the syringe.

"Now with a nice, careful motion, pull the needle straight out. Straight."

He did so. She took the syringe and deposited it in the sharps container on the wall. She disposed of the vial, nearly empty, and the wipes.

"Okay, Rob," she said. "Here comes the payoff. It will take a few minutes for the medicine to work, but in the meantime, it needs stimulation."

He could feel a sudden and welcome warmth, the rush of blood.

"You mean *here*? *Now*?" he asked.

"I mean, as soon as I walk out that door you got to do your thing with your thing," she said. "And I know it's not an ideal circumstance with the situation in this room and people going up and down the hallway right outside, and no, we do not have old issues of *Playboy* to assist you. We used to, but some of the girls complained. So it's up to you. And all I can tell you, and I have been doing this for quite a few years and I've gotten feedback from a lot of the guys about what works, my only suggestion is this: You remember when you were in your twenties before you were married and you had a fling with *that girl*? You know the one. You think about it more often than you admit to anyone. The one who you couldn't believe did what she did *the way she did it*."

He hesitated.

"You rascal, of course you remember her!" she said with a sense of triumph. "Summon her image, and things will work very nicely. You cannot be embarrassed, or this won't work. You have to let it rip. Oh, you remember that girl, I can tell. Whoa. I'll bet she was *something*!"

Yes, she was, Rob thought. Yes, she certainly was. At Sears, Rob got into the habit of taking the overnight shipping report up to the office where, in the early morning before office staff arrived at eight, he and the young overnight clerk would retreat to her hiding place in a back office. There in the fumbling darkness, anything was possible. He was a naïve eighteen-year-old college sophomore when he met her and had never seen a naked female breast, much less had sex. But she was a few years older, knew what she was doing, and brought him along. As he aged, Rob thought about her now and then and thought how fortunate he had been at that stage of his life to meet a girl with her patience and enthusiasm. He remembered it all, every detail, and it turned out Nurse Brenda was right.

19

Memories 1980s–1991

Thomas Browning Barrow had been born on a frigid winter morning, January 15, 1980, as a howling winter blizzard swept through from the Great Lakes leaving a foot of dry, powdery snow on the Boston area. Julia's labor was long and complex. Doctors discovered during the process that she was afflicted with an extremely rare uterine condition that required a hysterectomy. Their sorrow at not being able to have more children was overwhelmed by the sheer bliss of Thomas's arrival, seven pounds of joy. Julia remained in the hospital for several nights recovering from the ordeal, appearing alarmingly pale and weak.

Julia's parents arrived later that day and set up camp in the guest room, where they remained for several weeks, helping the new parents. Soon enough, Julia regained her strength, her generous parents returned to New York, and the three Barrows settled into life together in the place that, it turned out, they would always call home.

As a little boy Thomas was sports-mad, eager to play every sport available. He loved the Saturday morning town soccer league, where clusters of five-year-olds buzzed together, chasing the ball. He loved baseball season and learning to oil and shape his new glove, which was kept securely under the bedcovers with him each night. But he found his sports passion in the Friday night learn-to-skate sessions at the local public rink, which led at age six to Mighty Mite youth hockey. With his new skates, shin pads, hockey pants, shoulder pads, helmet, and stick, he was so joyful he could barely contain himself. He was soon barreling up and down the ice, often employing a dive to the ice surface and crash into the end boards as a means of stopping, having not yet mastered the ability to stop while remaining upright on his blades.

He was his mother's son socially. Whenever he and one of his parents would arrive at a playground, even one where Thomas knew none of the other children, he would loudly announce upon arrival: "Hello friends!"

But he was a boy, after all, and the cracks began to show when he was nine years old and a student at Bumbry, a Quaker-inspired primary school where many university faculty members sent their children. Though he was generally very happy there, during the final months of fourth grade he began acting out. He would resist his parents' effort to get him into a bath and bed at the right time, and one night he became quite sour about the book he and his mom were reading together.

"I don't know who that little boy is up there, Rob," Julia said when she came downstairs. "But he is an ornery little thing at the moment."

Rob went upstairs to say goodnight.

"How are you doing there, kiddo?" Rob asked.

"Did Mum tell you to talk to me?" Thomas asked. He wore his Boston Bruins pajamas and was tucked into his bed in a small room adjacent to his parents' bedroom. His room was adorned with pennants from various sports teams as well as photographs of star players.

"And why would she do that, I wonder?" Rob asked, as he sat down on the edge of the bed.

"Well, maybe she's cross with me?"

"Hmmm," said Rob. "Why would your mother be cross with you, a boy who never, ever, ever is out of line?"

Thomas laughed hard at this, loving the way his father would joke with him.

"Well, Dad, sometimes people disagree, like you and Mum have your arguments—"

"Discussions," Rob interjected.

"Okay, discussions about law cases, court stuff, and you don't agree. So people disagree sometimes." Thomas shrugged.

"And you and your mom have a disagreement?"

"Well, I mean, she's making me read this book that—"

"Your mom," Rob interjected, "doesn't *make* you read anything with her. If you remember, you and Mom pick out your books together, and you were part of choosing this book."

"I know," Thomas said. And with that he threw back the covers. "I'll be right back, Dad," he said as he raced out of his room, down the stairs, and into the kitchen where he threw his arms around his mother.

"I am sorry, Mum, I wasn't very nice," he said. "I love you!" he shouted over his shoulder as he was racing back up the stairs, until he literally jumped in the air and landed in his bed, tugging the covers up.

"Whooaaa," Rob said laughing. "You some kind of monkey?"

"Baboon," Thomas replied.

They were silent, Rob leaning over his son, Thomas cozy in his bed, infused with a sense of security and love.

"Good night, monkey," Rob said.

"Good night, Dad."

"Love you, kiddo."

"Love you, too, Dad."

And they hugged.

It turned out there had been something on the young monkey's mind after all. The following day a call came from school, summoning Julia to the headmaster's office.

"Your son faces disciplinary action," the headmaster said tersely.

Julia phoned Rob, and they met at the school a half hour later. The school was housed in an old Cambridge mansion from the mid-1800s, a sprawling Georgian-style residence formerly owned by an old New England family that had made multiple fortunes, initially in the China trade and later in oil. The residence was 20,000 square feet in the main three-story structure with half as much again that size in a modern adjacent building that also housed a gymnasium and swimming pool.

Grayson "Chip" Fulham, headmaster, was a doltish man scheduled for retirement at the conclusion of the school year. But he had also been a prodigious fundraiser and thus had served as head of school for twenty-three years. He was balding, with owlish eyes and a thin nose, and he spoke in a low tone, slowly, choosing his words with care. He ushered Julia and Rob into his simply furnished office, whose major feature was an expansive view of a gradual bend in the Charles River as the water turned southwest before correcting its westerly course.

"Mr. and Mrs. Barrow, thank you, I am sorry to call you to school in this abrupt manner, but we had an incident today that involved your son," he said.

"What happened?" Julia asked anxiously.

"Well, it seems boys will be boys after all, eh?" he said. "Yes. It's always been the case, and though it is rare here at Bumbry, we take any act of violence seriously."

"Violence? He's nine years old!" Julia said.

"A fistfight," said the headmaster.

"What!" Julia exclaimed. "A fistfight. That's ridiculous. He's a little boy."

"What happened exactly?" Rob asked.

It was not a particularly pretty story. "Thomas, and a boy one grade older, started fighting at recess," said Mr. Fulham. "They were instructed to stop by two teachers who were immediately upon the scene. They did not, in fact, stop fighting as instructed, but continued bashing one another with fists and rolling around on the ground. And there was some very bad language used by both boys."

"Where is he?" Julia demanded as she rose from her seat.

The headmaster rose with her. "He is in the nurse's office," said Mr. Fulham. And with that, Julia was gone, Rob following behind. She ran through the hallway, heels loudly clicking on the old pine floorboards, and ran down a flight of stairs, arriving in the nurse's office in time to see her son laughing in quite a jolly fashion with Mrs. Quinn, the school nurse.

"And so I smacked him again," Thomas said, laughing some more.

"Thomas Barrow!" his mother said in a hushed tone. "Look at you."

"Mum!" he said. "I was in a fight, but he started it."

It was such a jarring sight. Here was her little boy, whom she had sent off to the school bus with pressed chino pants, crisply pressed dress shirt, and a navy blue sweater bearing the Bumbry logo. The sweater was not in evidence. The shirt was ripped at the collar, the top two buttons missing, while the stitching from the sleeve to the shoulder had come mostly undone. The shirt was fully untucked, pants grass-stained, and he had a purple bruise below his left eye.

"I've checked him out carefully, Mrs. Barrow, and Thomas is fine," said the nurse. "We've been icing the bruise, and the swelling has calmed down. I suggest more icing this evening at home."

"Does this happen often at school?" Julia asked.

"Oh, once in a while," said the nurse. "Boys will be boys!"

To Rob, Thomas looked quite pleased with himself. He was beaming, and Rob suspected that the adrenaline rush from the fight left him feeling a new kind of excitement that men through the ages had experienced, the sheer excitement of violence. The story, as it turned out, was an age-old one. A boy in the class ahead of Thomas's, the lunkish Roger somebody, had been picking on younger boys for some time. The younger boys were sick of it but afraid.

"I was afraid, too," Thomas told his parents on the car ride home, "but he said we were all cowards, and that made me really mad."

"When you say that Roger had been picking on kids, Thomas, in what way?" Julia asked.

"He took Steven's milk carton at lunch and poured it into his backpack. Then Steve was crying, and Roger and his friends laughed at him and called him a baby."

"That's not very nice," said Rob. "Why would Roger do something mean like that?"

Thomas shrugged. "Plus," he said. "Listen to this, Mum and Dad. In the playground the other day Roger—" Here Thomas interrupted himself. "Do I have permission to say what Roger said?"

"Depends on what he said," Julia replied.

"He called Steve a little prick," Thomas said, his eyes wide, thrilled to be able to say such a word.

"That, my friend," said Rob, "is what is known as an assumed grant of permission for this one instance."

"So I can't repeat little prick again?" Thomas said as he burst out laughing, and his mother joined in, not certain why it sounded so funny but entirely certain that she loved this impish little boy more than anything in God's universe.

"I'm sorry. I should not have laughed," she said.

"It's funny, though, don't you think, Dad?" Thomas said.

"I don't think it's funny when a kid is mean, and calling him a name is mean, so no, Mr. Monkey, I do not think it is funny."

"Not that, Dad, you know what I mean," Thomas said. "The way I said it the second time and got Mum to laugh."

"But Thomas, no more of that, really, you know that kind of language is really inappropriate," Julia said.

"Uncle Ray uses bad words all the time."

"Uncle Ray is a grown-up, and when you are grown up you can use all the bad words you want, but you are a child and children may not use those words," said Julia.

"Who made that rule?" Thomas asked.

"The United States Supreme Court," said Rob. Because of his father's job, Thomas knew that the United States Supreme Court was just about the biggest deal there was.

"Really?" he asked.

"No," said Rob. "Your parents made that rule, and we expect you to respect it."

"You haven't told us what happened with Roger," Julia said.

"I'm not allowed to tell you," he said.

"Why not?" she asked.

He smiled and his eyes were bright. "Because I am supposed to respect the rule that a child cannot use bad language."

"Jesus, you really are going to be a lawyer, aren't you?" she asked.

"Yes, and by the way you just swore," he said.

"I am an adult."

"In the context of telling your mother and me what happened at school today," Rob said, "and why you violated the school rule against fighting and got a disciplinary mark against you, then you may say what was said."

Thomas nodded with satisfaction. "We were in the playground, and I was with some kids in my class, Steven, Ira, Mike, and a few others, and Roger came over to where we were. We were way over in the corner, the far corner away from school. And Roger comes over, and he says something to Steven, I didn't even hear what it was, and I turned around and I said, 'What did you say?' And Roger says to me, 'It's none of your fucking business.'"

"Jesus," said Julia. "His mouth should be washed out with soap."

"So I said, 'Why are you such a little prick, Roger,' and that got him really mad and he punched me and I fell down but I got back up and punched him in the stomach and he bent over like it really hurt so I punched him again but it hit the side of his head and that hurt my hand and we were on the ground wrestling and Miss Flynn came running over yelling at us to stop and when I got on top of him and pinned him down and she was grabbing me and trying to pull me off, but I didn't want to let go because I thought he might hit me, but then he started crying so I let him up. Do I have permission to say what Steve said afterward when it was over?"

"Definitely not," said Rob.

There was a pause. They all looked at one another. Thomas had that impish grin firmly in place.

"You sure?" he said to Rob.

"Positive."

At bedtime, when Julia and Thomas were finished reading their book together, Rob joined them and sat on the edge of the bed next to Julia.

"So what did you learn today?" Rob asked.

"Don't be mean to other people," he said.

"But you already knew *that*," Julia said. "Did you learn anything new?"

Thomas thought about it. "It's a bad feeling to be picked on," he said. "Even though I was afraid, I learned that I am glad I fought him. My friends were all, like, it was a really cool thing to do. That made me feel good."

By the time he turned ten, Thomas was still small for his age, though the pediatrician assured them that he would have a growth spurt in the years ahead. His size did not seem to hurt him in athletics, where he had established a special bond with his teammates. At Bumbry, children were required to participate in a sport each season and Thomas's choices included football in the fall, hockey in winter, and lacrosse in the spring. The joy these athletics brought him was hard to overstate. He would finish a hockey practice, hop into his mother's car with his schoolbooks in his backpack and hockey bag in the trunk, and talk non-stop with boundless enthusiasm.

"Coach put me on the second line for part of practice," Thomas said as he rode home with Julia. He was still sweating profusely from practice, his blondish hair dampened, stuck to his head in disarray.

"I thought he said you were too small to be on the second line?" she said.

"He did, but I think he changed his mind. I mean, we're all in the same grade."

"Some boys have growth spurts earlier than others, like those kids on the first line," she said. "They look like giants out there compared to everybody else."

He laughed. "They're big, but they're not all fast, Mum. Coach says, 'Speed kills.'"

"What does that mean?"

"That if you're faster than your opponent, you'll beat him to the puck," Thomas said. "There are a lot of really good players who are smaller even in the pros, but look how fast they are. 'Shifty,' coach says."

"Are you shifty?"

He shrugged. "Kind of."

"Matty is very shifty, probably the best skater on the team, and you know what he said to me today? He said that if he was put on the second line, he would quit the team."

"Wow," Julia said. "What did you think about that?"

She glanced over at her boy as he was gazing out the window, seemingly thinking this over.

"I will never be as good as Matty," Thomas said. "I may never be the best player on any team, but you know what? I want to be the best teammate on every team."

Why this comment from her son pierced her heart in the way it did, she was not sure, not in that moment at least. She smiled at him and said, "That makes me very proud of you, Thomas. It's who you are, and your dad and I are so proud that you think that way."

"Thanks, Mum."

"So, math test tomorrow, right?" she asked.

"Yes."

"Are you prepared?"

"Yes."

"But are you *well* prepared?" she asked with a laugh.

"You're stealing Dad's question, Mum."

"But are you?"

"I think so. Can I just say something, Mum, that maybe won't sound very nice, but, you know, between you and me?"

"You can say anything to me, honey, you know that."

"I know," he said in a quiet voice, even though it was just the two of them in the car. "I was with Jonah today before practice and he was asking me about the math homework. He said his dad gets really mad when he gets any bad grade."

"Does he try hard?"

"Definitely," Thomas said. "Almost every day before practice now we do our math homework together, and I kind of explain one step following another, but he gets confused, so we go over it again and then sometimes again. I feel bad."

"Well, maybe Jonah has intellectual strengths in other areas that do not come as easily to other people."

"Maybe," he said.

"Dad will be home for dinner," she said as they pulled into their driveway.

"Yay!" he shouted, getting out of the car and hauling his hockey bag into the mudroom, where he removed all of his equipment and set it out neatly on the carpet to dry—skates, hockey stockings, shin pads, padded hocky pants, elbow pads, shoulder pads, helmet, hockey gloves, and jersey.

"Thomas, my God, that stuff reeks!" said Julia.

"I know! Crazy, huh? The gloves are the worst."

He had confided in her earlier in the season that the bigger kids who had had growth spurts had equipment that was so rank the coach made them dress in a separate locker room. Thomas wanted the same level of horrible odor to demonstrate his physical maturity, which was virtually nonexistent. While he still looked childlike, his intellect had the agility of a young adult, so much so that there had been a discussion with the academic dean that Thomas skip a grade. But Thomas hated the idea. He wanted to be with his friends and teammates.

"I'm not doing it," he had told his parents when the subject had been raised.

"Thomas, this is a family discussion, and I'm not sure you have the final say," Rob had said.

"I'll run away and join the circus."

"And do what?"

"Trapeze."

"Dangerous," Julia had said.

"I'd have a net."

"Well, you do not have permission to run away and join the circus, just so you know," Rob said.

"Come on, Dad, when you run away to join the circus you *run away*," Thomas said. "You don't need permission."

"Fair enough," said Rob. "So we'll revisit moving up a grade this weekend."

Thomas was quite serious now. "Dad, I would *hate* it," he said. "I am trying to tell you guys that I would really hate it. I don't want to leave my friends and teammates. We've been together since first grade. We're a unit, a team, and we rely on each other. How would it look if I jump ship on them?" He shook his head vigorously. "I am begging you to listen to me on this."

"We're listening," said Julia. "We just want to do what is best for you."

"So have some faith in me," he said. "I know what's best for me in this case, and it's to stay with my class. Who would take my place in hockey? Who will take face-offs in lacrosse? Who will help Jonah get his math homework done? You've gotta trust me. I am not a child anymore."

No, he was not. And as he grew, he sought to know and understand more about a variety of subjects, his family included. He was very close with his maternal grandfather. They spent hours out on Long Island Sound in summers fishing and identifying seabirds.

He often expressed disappointment that he had never been able to meet his paternal grandparents. Since an early age Thomas had asked Rob about his mother and father, and Rob had shared details about his mother—how she was very kind and worked as a waitress at downtown hotels. But the only thing Rob ever said about his father was that he had gone off to war months before Rob was born and had died in Korea.

One Saturday afternoon, after Rob had taken him to hockey practice, the family was seated at the kitchen table having sandwiches Julia had made for lunch.

"Dad, what do you think your dad was like?" Thomas asked. "If you had to guess, what would you say?"

Rob stopped eating and looked over at Julia. She nodded. They had discussed this and the time had come. Thomas deserved the truth about his family.

"Well, I have to say, kiddo, that I cannot answer that question," Rob said. "And I want to make a confession, because while you were little I wasn't completely truthful with you . . ."

"He *didn't* die in the war?"

"The truth is that I do not know whether he died in the war or not, son, because I do not know who my father was. And the reason I do not know is because my mother did not know. Or, if she did, she never told me."

Thomas fell silent for a moment. "I'm confused," he said. "You think your mother didn't know who your father was or that she knew and wouldn't tell you?"

"I don't think she knew."

"Didn't you ask her?"

"I did, but she never told me anything concrete," Rob said. "She always evaded the issue."

Suddenly, Thomas was agitated. "Dad!" he exclaimed, his face flushing. "How could you not know who your own dad was? Dad!" Thomas got up from the table and ran into the living room, crying, and flopped face down on the sofa. Rob and Julia followed quickly. Rob sat on the carpet next to the sofa and rubbed his boy's back. Thomas was sobbing.

"That's so horrible, Dad," he said. And with that Thomas sat up and threw his arms around his father's neck. "I love you, Dad, and I'm really sad they did that to you. You are the best dad in the world, and you don't deserve that."

"I love you, too, kiddo, but it's okay. It was a very long time ago. And look at my life now. Look how lucky I am. I have you and your mom, and that is all I need in this world to be happy. I promise you."

"I know, Dad, but it's not fair. It's not."

"But what matters now is we have each other," Rob said. "We are together, and we are going to stick together no matter what. Okay?"

Julia moved onto the sofa and held her very sensitive little boy. It was only a few weeks later that Thomas returned home from summer hockey practice with the flu. After midnight, when Julia checked on him, he was burning up, a fever of 106 degrees.

"That can't be," said Rob.

"Let's go," she said, wrapping the boy in his blanket and driving to the emergency room.

20

Positron Image Tomography

Rob made his way to the Cancer Center through the beginnings of a blizzard that would bury the city for a week. He thought it too risky to drive in such weather and chose instead to take the Red Line from Harvard Square to Park Street and change to the Green Line to Longwood, where the stop was three blocks from the hospital. He wore his trusty Bean boots, heavy wool socks, a warm jacket, and his Bruins ski hat. This was a routine follow-up visit, yet Rob felt a familiar anxiety. There was something in his DNA—he had grown convinced of this—that prevented him from properly navigating his way from the Cancer Center lobby to the second floor for his blood draw. He boarded an elevator in the lobby, moved to the back of the space, and was hemmed in by a dozen others, including an older gentleman in a wheelchair. When the doors opened on two, Rob expected the throng to disembark. He waited a beat too long, and before he could excuse his way out of the elevator, past the gentleman in the wheelchair, the doors had closed. He got off on the next stop, seven, and decided to take the stairs, but when he reached the second floor, the stairway door included a red bar to be pressed in emergencies only. He kept going down and found himself in the subbasement.

When he finally made it to the second floor, the receptionist asked

for his name and date of birth and whether he was suffering from a
cold or fever and whether he had a port. She made his wrist band and
strapped it on, sending him into the by now familiar waiting area, where
another eighty or so people had gathered to have their blood drawn
and analyzed. He was feeling confident. There were people here whose
hair had been eliminated by chemo, others with oxygen tanks alongside their wheelchairs, and still others who, on the outside, appeared
the picture of health. For this last group, the body's betrayal was all
internal, and the signs of illness for some would never make their way
to the outside of the body. Some would be cured, others linger and be
treated for a persistent chronic condition for years to come; still others
would be doomed in a matter of weeks. Then he saw her. He caught
sight of the wheelchair out of the corner of his eye, a young woman in
her thirties huddled with a patient slumped in the chair, gown slipping
off her shoulder on one side and down her arm. His perspective was
from thirty feet away and from the rear, but his heart beat faster and he
felt a surge of adrenaline. Rita B was alive! He rushed over and said,
"Excuse me, Rita?" But the woman who turned around and faced him
had a blank expression, glassy-eyed, defeated.

"Oh," he said, "I'm sorry . . . I mistook you for a friend."

He moved to the far side of the room and found a chair in an area with
soft lighting and a series of prints depicting classic scenes of Boston—
Beacon Hill, the Charles, a row of townhouses on Marlborough Street.
He was disappointed. He had thought for a moment that Rita B had
survived, but as he contemplated it, he wondered how likely that was.
She had seemed so close to the end that she could well be on the other
side by now, and in that case she would know more about the afterlife
than all of the most intelligent humans who had ever lived. He envied
her that knowledge.

Not even an hour after he had the blood work done he received
an automated email indicating he had a new test result. When he
clicked, the news stunned him: a sharp PSA spike. After Rob's surgery

the expectation was that the PSA would register zero. But cancer is a funny thing. It scans the world seeking out the hubris of rude health and attacks with unpredictability and sinister intent, and it is immensely clever at avoiding detection. Suddenly, Rob's head was spinning. The appointment with the oncologist was all business, no cheery encouragement, just next steps, and the first was to be a positron emission tomography (PET) scan to locate the offending cells. Life changes came in varying units of time, and Rob felt that with cancer those units could be seconds, even nanoseconds. One moment you believed you were out of the woods only to learn you were traveling ever deeper into a dark forest.

"Possible bump in the road," he said to Julia, back home in the kitchen.

"What? Rob, what do you mean, what did they say?"

"PSA spike," he said. "They're hoping it's a technical glitch, but I go in next week for a PET scan just in case."

She drew back, hands to her mouth, eyes wide. "But Rob, they said . . ."

He nodded. "I know, but . . ." He shrugged.

"Rob, I don't get it."

"They said it happens sometimes."

She straightened up and reached out, embracing him.

On the following Thursday, the first week of the new year, Rob made his way in the early morning back to the hospital subbasement, where cheerful techs instructed him to change into a hospital gown. He was injected with a substance that spread through his body and highlighted prostate cancer cells. It seemed remarkable to Rob, as he lay on the table that would soon slide inside the tube, that scientists had figured out a way to send a few ounces of chemicals through the body that would light up a particular type of cell. While he lay there, he wondered what was happening within his body. How could it be that a sinister, potentially deadly force could be active within his cells without him feeling a thing? The next morning, a call came from the medical oncologist with the results. Rob reached for a pen and took a few notes, with Julia looking over his shoulder. He fixed on a few words and phrases, not fully absorbing the entire narrative, but getting the gist that mattered. He got off the phone, his heart beating too fast, throat tight, sweat on his forehead and neck, and looked at his notes:

Metastasis
Hip area
Opaque image on bone
Clinical trial?

One week later, Rob took a couple of oxycodone pills before leaving the house to loosen things up for his appointment with a radiation oncologist. That the cancer cells had escaped the capsule and made their way into the body was either concerning or, depending upon his mood, frightening. He was relieved that it was the hip area and not his major organs. That was some consolation. The opaque image on bone. Well, yeah, he thought. The bones were the superhighway the cancer cells were trying to reach, struggling to find the on-ramp. Inside the bone structure they were free to barrel though the marrow and blood cells and spread their poison anywhere in the skeletal structure. He was afraid of this; he was also, but for a different reason, worried about being trapped in a clinical trial where half the participants would be treated with a miraculous new, possibly life-saving medicine and the other half would be in a control group with a placebo that would mean an open door to the advance of bad cells. What if he was on the wrong side of the trial?

As was his custom, Rob arrived for his appointment early and met with a team member he did not know, Dr. Vin Lee, an upbeat young man wearing a colorful tie—a way to cheer up his patients, Rob guessed. But Rob's mind was all over the place. His ability to focus, which had come so naturally to him throughout his life, eluded him. He listened to what Dr. Lee said, but the storm in his mind kept crashing into well-ordered thoughts, one gust after another, shifting this way and that, leaving chaos in its wake. In the moment Rob thought: I think I don't want to hear any of this stuff from the doctor because it frightens me, so I will deal with it by stepping back and allowing chaos to reign in my mind. Not just allowing it, but inviting it. Dr. Lee did not say, *Look, your case is outside the normal parameters*, which it was. He did not say, *Holy shit, I can't believe the surgery didn't work or that the PSA took a flying Wallenda much sooner than in ninety-nine out of a hundred patients*. Instead, Dr. Lee said, "We see this sometimes where surgery does not do the full trick. Fortunately, we have other arrows in our quiver." *Robin Hood!* was all Rob could think of when Dr. Lee used this phrase. As a boy he would read stories at the library about Robin Hood and his band of merry men. They had arrows and quivers, but now cutting-edge medicine was enamored with this analogy. Ray used it, everybody used it. Rob liked that. He had enjoyed the books as a boy, liked Robin Hood stealing from the rich to give to the poor. He took a deep breath and was pleased to feel it come easily, without tension-induced struggle, a full intake of air, then an easy exhale. He half smiled. This felt good and was a sure sign that the oxy was working. He did, indeed, like the sensation. It took the edge off of things, made the world move a bit more slowly, enriched the colors around him. He noticed that Dr. Lee possessed a radiant smile. He must have had his teeth whitened, he thought, as he watched the gleaming choppers while the doctor was talking about hormone treatment and radiation. He knew he could read the details of this appointment in the after-visit summary, so he felt comfortable hiding from reality for the moment and allowing his attention to wander, to free-associate. Sometimes during medical appointments Rob was laser-focused, absorbing all of the material and processing it in real time. But cancer does strange things to people, and he was finding that his normal intellectual approach to life was too harsh to deal with the situation.

"A treatment we like and that is very common for patients like you is a combination of radiation and hormone therapy," said Dr. Lee. "We recommend beginning the hormone treatments today."

"Oh," Rob said, surprised.

"The sooner the better in these cases," Dr. Lee explained. "A Lupron injection today, then another about every ninety days. We'll fill your enzalutamide prescription today and you can start taking the pills tonight. If your schedule permits, we recommend starting radiation therapy next week or so. Preparation for the radiation requires some fairly complex calculations to get the right doses. A radiation dosime-trist handles that. Actually, let's start in two weeks to give them time to do the calculations and to allow the radiation techs to do a trial session with you. No radiation, just measurement. So let's say we have the kick-off January 24, that's a Monday. Then you would complete your forty radiation sessions on"—once again he consulted his computer—"let's see. March 18. A Friday."

"Sounds like a long time," Rob said.

"It will be over before you know it," said Dr. Lee. "And the best part is you have weekends off! Radiation on weekdays only because cancer doesn't grow on weekends!"

Rob couldn't help it—he laughed out loud and said, "Dr. Lee, you should be a comedian!"

Lee beamed. "Thank you!"

As Dr. Lee explained these treatments working in concert, Rob imagined a war of sorts: Invasion of cancer cells, we counter by deploying a massive force of ground troops to outmaneuver and over-power the body's testosterone, driving the cancer into full retreat. Then precision air strikes, laser-guided missiles from offshore destroy-ers and F18s in a precise, coordinated attack on the enemy position. Dr. Lee explained that the team would draw up a battle plan. The team included a radiation dosimetrist whose job was to work through the math to get the dose right, and a medical physicist, whose role was explained to Rob, though he wasn't listening at the time, and a radiation oncologist/comedian (Dr. Lee). Rob received the first Lupron injection that afternoon and filled his prescription for enzalutamide that day as well. He began taking the pills that evening, two at night, two in the morning.

A week later, the prep session with the radiation team. Rob traveled again to the subbasement of the hospital, where the narrow hallways and low ceilings lined with pipes struck him as what he imagined it would be like in a nuclear submarine. There was a persistent hum in the air, like a vibration. These machines down here, Rob thought, might shake the structure's foundation, vibrating the pilings sunk a hundred feet into bedrock. But the young techs eased his mind. They explained that this session was a test run—no actual radiation, just measurement of precisely where the rays of energy would be targeted. The cheerful kids positioned Rob just so on the bed of the linear accelerator, a machine designed to deliver electrons to kill tumor cells. He would lie on a narrow bed while a proton beam machine, a huge, rotating monster's head that took up half the room, rotated around him in starts and stops, making a hellacious racket.

As he lay there, Rob reflected on his history in the realm of cancer. *So let me get this straight,* Rob thought, *a bit of an increase in a marker within my blood had indicated a higher risk for cancer. That number had been double-checked and confirmed. Then the biopsy—quite painful, actually—yielded tissue samples that did, in fact, contain cancer cells. No problem, we'll have our best guy—Oh, absolutely, Chen's the top man!—remove the prostate and cancer within—all while you remain in flight, weightless, effortless, gazing down upon the meandering sailboats on the Charles and the chemical-induced greenery of the Fenway outfield where Ted Williams himself, who took time off from baseball to train as a Marine Corps pilot in Pensacola, Florida, had once roamed. And then three or so months later they say, Hold on there, Rob, old boy, sorry about this, but the surgery we were quite sure would capture all those cancer cells didn't actually work. Now there is evidence of those little rascals having escaped, so we sent in our ground forces and now our air power. But just so you know, Rob, the air power will fire super intense energy rays that bore deep into the body to kill cancer cells only, but FYI, the distances between diseased cells and healthy cells are infinitesimal and there is the possibility of collateral damage. Sometimes when we try to blow up the bad guy's house we kill everybody else in the neighborhood minding their own business.*

On the way out he remembered to ask whether there could be any side effects. Could be, he was told, and they might include diarrhea, bladder irritation, frequent urination, sexual dysfunction, fatigue, some confusion, hot flashes, etc., etc., etc.

A few weeks on the enzalutamide and the hot flashes started—a total-body sweat two or three times each day—while he was in the midst of teaching a class, during a conference with a student, in the middle of lunch. At his law school office, a clean shirt, underwear, and suit jacket would be soaked. No warning. This brought a wonderful sense of schadenfreude from female friends and colleagues who had endured menopause. Rob was happy to be of service.

Testosterone defined maleness—at least physically and perhaps even mentally in some respects—and Rob experienced the oddest feelings, the most noticeable being that he lost any and all interest in sex. Like the vast majority of straight men, Rob had always noticed women. No, he did not wear animal skins, grunt, drag his knuckles, or lug a carved wooden club with him, but while all those things had evolved through the ages, the male sex drive remained what it was. For his entire adult life he had noticed women, noticed attractive females and their shapely bodies and pretty faces. He felt, on some occasions, a distinctly sexual attraction. Now, with the Lupron, that was gone. It was difficult to believe in a way, but he didn't care. He would see beautiful women and think, *You're convinced you know what I'm thinking because every man who sees you has the same thought, but no, not me!* What freedom from the power of female sexuality!

*

Julia had caught a nasty cold and was heading to bed early these days, which afforded Rob an opportunity to down a couple of Xanax with a large whiskey as he watched television. Blissful! He switched the channels, found nothing interesting, and shut it off. He began to read, but it was not long before the image of Rita B broke through the drug/alcohol haze, and he wondered what had become of her. After the second whiskey, he felt a compulsion to reach out to her and provide words of encouragement. It would be good for her to hear from a fellow patient. *Do you remember me from that day in the waiting area? The tissue box fell on the floor? Do you recall, maybe not, but I picked it up and handed it to you? Yeah, that was me. And I wished you good luck, I wasn't sure whether you heard me or not but, anyway . . . I just wanted to check in and see how you are doing and whether . . .*

It was quite late when Rob dialed the main number at the Cancer Center. He waded through the options until he heard a live operator.

"Yes, hi, this is Rob Barrow, and I am a patient and I was hoping you could connect me to another patient?"

"The patient name, please?"

"Rita B, I only know the first initial of her last name, and I was hoping—"

"Last name, please," the operator said.

"No, but that's, you see, that's what I'm saying, but if you could look at your list, maybe we can start with—do you have any patients with the first name Rita and last name starting with a *b*—*b* as in 'bravo'?"

Pause.

"I'm sorry, but no patient by the name of Bravo."

"No, no," he said, a nervous laugh. "No, you see I met her in the waiting area quite a few months ago, her first name is Rita, so do you have any patients with the first name of Rita?"

"Sir, I need a last name."

"*B*—begins with *b*."

"I'm sorry, sir, call back when you have the full name and I would be happy to help you."

Click.

He looked around his library and felt comforted by his books and the familiarity of the place, tucked away in a corner of the house over-looking a portion of the garden. He thought maybe he should eat some-thing, but he wasn't that hungry and anyway, he really wanted to try to contact Rita B because he felt he might be able to help her. He had a sense, recalling Rita and the daughter, that there could be financial issues there. Maybe he and Julia could make some sort of anonymous donation, get them on their feet.

He dialed Ray.

"Rob? You okay?"

"How did you know it was me?" Rob asked.

"Scientific advancement known as Caller ID," Ray replied.

Silence.

"You okay, Rob?"

"Yeah, yeah, very good."

"Rob?"

"Yes, Ray?"

"You wanted to talk about something?"

"How did you know that?"

"Well, I mean, you called me, so . . ."

"You called me," Rob insisted.

Pause. "I have an idea, Rob," said Ray. "How about we chat in the morning? That okay with you?"

"You know where to find me," said Rob.

But as soon as he was off the phone Rob remembered that he had meant to ask Ray what happens in the afterlife.

PART
TWO

21

Griswold News

During the period he was receiving radiation treatments, Rob jotted thoughts into a small spiral notebook. Impressions, initially, and then, as the side effects began to take hold, just words or phrases.

The doctors tell me that photon beams can penetrate deeply into the body and that when they hit the tumor they keep going. Seems like potential for damage to a lot of healthy cells, *I say to Dr. Lee. Is that correct? Well, some, yes, he tells me, so that's a great note to start on! Collateral damage all around! The kids, I say kids because they are all in their twenties, run the radiation machine with a sure hand. They greet me warmly each morning, provide full weather updates for the days ahead as well as recommendations for movies they have seen. They have let me into their little social circle here in this subterranean world. I like them! Upon arrival for each session I go to a changing area and don one of those hospital gowns that ties in the back. These are the only things from eighteenth-century medicine that are still used today. If I were entrepreneurial, I would go to a clothing designer and start a company selling comfortable, user-friendly gowns to hospitals. I would make a mint, no doubt. The first week goes quickly, and I am surprised at how unobtrusive the whole process is. I am positioned each day in the exact place the techs want me, so that the beams target a tiny freckle—tattooed on my body (I have a tattoo!). I lie very still as the massive head of the machine rotates around me in fits and starts and no discernible pattern, at least not to me. The sessions take about twenty minutes, and I find myself wishing they would go longer. There is something calming about lying here in this hospital where the most miraculous sorts of things happen to human beings. I think of this not as a place where medicine is practiced but rather as a location where stories play out. On every floor throughout the massive building above me there are three-act plays in various stages of development. The worst are not those at the very end of a journey but those who are at the start for they are the men and women who, only recently, received unwelcome news from their doctor. I think about these people, especially those who are going along happily in life and then are told that the discomfort in their side is not a pulled muscle but pancreatic cancer that will kill them in ninety days. I wonder about the atoms moving through my system and try to imagine the size of a single atom and the size of a single cell, and I marvel at the ability of Ray and my other friends on the medical faculty who understand these things. But let's cut the baloney: all of these random thoughts are distractions, a trick played by my mind to steer me away from thinking about what comes next. I hope for a longer life with Julia and Ray, but, and this is a major but that I have never shared and never will: If the treatment fails and I am loaded onto a ferry with regularly scheduled trips across the River Styx, then, well, I am okay with that. I really am. Why? Peace. Freedom from grief.*

I visit with Dr. Lee at the end of the week's sessions and tell him I'm feeling well. He cautions that side effects take some time to present. I wonder whether they overstate the side effect thing? Maybe some people who are not very healthy are more susceptible. I am hardly in perfect shape, but I think I am fit for my age and expect I will be able to handle this pretty well. He smiles and says that I'm lucky because I have weekends off. He cautions that there may be bumpy days ahead in light of the fact that some of the beams go through part of my stomach and not far from my bladder.

By midweek I was pretty fried. Thursday I went home and crashed for a while. Friday same. Strange to experience a sudden change in the ability of your body to function. Tiredness has always in my experience been a result of physical or sometimes intense mental exertion. This is different. Feels more disease-like.

It all seems to come on pretty quickly. Headaches bad. Nausea worse. All of a sudden, in just a month's time, I am sick with what I consider radiation poisoning. Three weeks ago I was productive up in my office, drafting a journal article. Now I am unable to write anything. Cannot concentrate. Can't read much, in fact. Julia signed me up for an Audible account so I am able to listen to audio books, and I like them—starting with my favorite Le Carré, Tinker Tailor—*but I fall asleep and then have to go back and find my place.*

Don't ever recall feeling this bad. No energy, headache unyielding, constant nausea. Lots of popsicles. Dr. Lee reports good news at week's end: the radiation is hitting its target. It's working? I ask. It is hitting the target, and in that sense, it is working, he tells me. But is it working *working? I ask. We will know more later, he tells me.*

Hanging on by a thread. Home from treatment to bed, sleep, maybe three, four hours. Eggs, mashed potatoes, popsicles. Weird green concoctions Julia makes me drink.

Now grasp what people mean when they say cure worse than disease. Cannot do this anymore.

Difficulty peeing, along with what they term unanticipated discharge—*bladder damage? Nausea permanent state? Cannot deal with the headaches anymore.*

Radiation—never again.

It was a chilly early morning in April, but the sun's rays were breaking through and nature was asserting itself in the great magic act of transitioning from cold and dark to warmth and light, the spring thaw and the coming to life of all that Rob's vision had encompassed every spring for so, so many years now. He was coming back to life as well. Three weeks after the completion of radiation treatments he regained some energy, and for the most part the headaches had abated. Nausea still present but much less so. He was thrilled to be out of the house, back in the garden, in this place where he had been able to reflect upon and process so much of life's unexpected turns. He wore a heavy sweater against the morning chill, but the temperature was already climbing and he knew that within an hour or so he would be able to set it aside. He sipped his coffee as he watched his garden awaken from its winter slumber. What an extraordinary thing nature was! The grass remained thin and brown in spots, but there were also rich patches of green. The perimeter areas were bursting with yellow from hundreds of daffodils, with forsythia supercharging the yellow hues. And then there were those shrubs that seemed on the verge of blooming—what were they called? The thorny ones with a rich reddish hue? He could remember the name of every United States chief justice, but he had trouble recalling the name of this bush that had been among the earliest arrivals every spring. Ah, now he remembered: quince. Yes, something quince. He liked the name. He noticed the leafy ash tree, but his attention was drawn to the American sycamore, whose leaves seemed even larger than in past years. They must be a foot long, some of them, Rob thought. There was a grandeur to this sturdy natural guardian, and he felt a surge of gratitude that it was here and as healthy as ever. How remarkable. The massive canopy was within a few weeks of its full grandeur. He couldn't help but smile that a new spring-summer season was blooming. He set his coffee cup aside and walked down the few steps, feeling the soft, wet earth beneath his feet. He looked around as he walked slowly toward the back of the yard and felt surrounded by life! *How amazing.* He had long thought that this part of the year was at once both the most predictable and most surprising. Everyone knew spring was coming, but when it arrived it did so with a kind of grace and joy that seemed almost human in its emotion. Such blessings, Rob thought. The sycamore, the pond, the quince, the daffodils, the sun's warmth.

"You have a visitor, Rob," Julia said as he entered the kitchen. Sitting at the kitchen table with a cup of coffee was his friend Jerry Katz.

"Jerry, great to see you," Rob said. "To what do I owe this pleasure?"

Jerry rose from the chair and held his friend in a tight embrace. "Rob," he said. "I—" but emotion caught in Jerry's voice, and he had to stop for a moment. Julia stood off to the side, beaming.

"Jerry, you okay, my friend?" Rob asked.

Jerry nodded as he wept quietly. Julia handed him a tissue with which he wiped his eyes, and he took a deep breath. "OK," he said, breaking into a smile. "Rob—" His voice caught again for a moment. "Rob, I have been tasked by the committee to convey to you the news that you have been selected as this year's recipient of the Griswold." Jerry removed an index card from his pocket and read: "In recognition of your contribution to the cornerstone nature of law in a civil society and in further recognition of your enlightening teaching and writing and of your fair-minded and determined efforts in litigation in defense of the rule of law."

Jerry, weeping joyously, bear-hugged Rob again, then kissed him on both cheeks. "I am so happy for you, Rob."

Rob frowned as though momentarily confused. "My God, Jerry," he said. "I'm so honored, it's . . ." The Griswold, which commemorated the esteemed former dean of the law school and Supreme Court justice, Erwin Griswold, was the single most prestigious Harvard faculty prize. The thought that Rob might one day be the recipient had never crossed his mind. Suddenly, Julia was hugging him, too.

In that moment, quite unexpectedly, Rob thought of his mother. He recalled the apartment where he was raised and the traffic noise outside his window and receiving the news that she had lost her life in a car crash. He thought that, had she lived, she would be proud of him.

But his thoughts were interrupted by a reminder from his calendar that he had to get himself to the hospital for a Lupron injection at noon.

22

Memories 1991

Their memories of that time—the day itself and the weeks and months following—were true enough as flashes, slashing images or narrow slivers of time, but as historians of the moment Julia and Rob were unreliable witnesses. Trauma does many things, but one of its downstream impacts is selective memory. For parents, the brain was a tender editor of traumatic recollections. But this wasn't quite right. It was more that the physiological shock enveloping them dispatched a molecular messenger to perform an emergency edit on their DNA, fundamentally changing their nature and who they were and would become in the years ahead.

Decades later, scientists would develop a technique to edit DNA, to trim the helix strands where genetic markers produced cancer or some other dread disease. But the process within the traumatized brain is hardwired and fully automated. The brain contains its own instructions, its own instinct in a way, to do what it can to protect itself from traumatic injury. Another way to describe it is to suggest that a select group of sentries from among the 100 billion brain cells had surrounded and attacked images, language, colors, voices, faces—memories of all sorts—that conjured the emotions of that time and eliminated them with uneven precision. They recalled the date, of course: August 15, 1991.

At the hospital later that night Julia and Rob had been led down the hallway and seated in a claustrophobic, windowless space to wait. It was now 4:30 a.m., three-plus hours since an emergency medical team had been summoned to where their child lay in distress. They watched from the corner of their child's room, staying out of the way of the seven doctors and nurses working frantically, collectively conveying an unmistakable sense that this was a life-or-death moment. Julia retched, then vomited into a stainless-steel sink.

Rob picked up bits of the conversation. *Febrile. Seizure. Unresponsive.* From the side, Rob could see a young doctor mounted astride Thomas, rhythmically applying vigorous chest compressions. Abruptly, she slid aside as another doctor, a young man, placed paddles on Thomas's chest. The electrical shock was so powerful he could see part of Thomas's body elevated off the bed. There was the odor of something burned.

He's gone, Rob thought in that moment. *My baby boy is gone.*

Suddenly, Rob pushed through the crowd of medical professionals. He said in a tone of incredulity, a whisper, pleadingly: "How could this happen?" The doctors and nurses, all falling silent, cleared a pathway as Rob led Julia to the bedside of their son, who lay still, lifeless.

"Tom-Tom, honey, it's Mum," Julia said. "Please say something, Thomas." She sobbed as she reached down, taking her son in her arms and clutching him, using whatever strength she could muster to pull him back from the other side. But the horrific stillness of the child conveyed the reality. Julia gasped for breath and moaned: "No, no, no, please God no."

Ray arrived in that moment, and Julia started to say, "Ray, you have to—" but she stopped in mid-sentence as Ray extended his arms, gathering Julia and Rob, bringing them to him, holding them, knowing in that moment that his sacred duty would be to care for them in the years ahead. He understood loss and grief. He had a sense of what lay ahead. Rob cried on Ray's shoulder, Julia wept on his chest. They cried together, all three of them sobbing. Their lives had been joined together initially in friendship and then in love, and they had helped support and guide one another and the most important thing in their lives, the thing that had bound them together like nothing else, was now gone. This beautiful, gifted, vibrant child was no more.

Ray drove them home. Rob guided Julia upstairs, where she went into Thomas's room and lay on his bed. She soon reached a level of hysteria that required Ray to inject her with a powerful sedative that sent her off to sleep. Rob and Ray retreated to the backyard, where the night's darkness was beginning to yield to the earliest rays of sunlight. They were enveloped in silence, the trees still, leaves unmoving on a windless predawn.

A seizure? A fever-induced seizure had killed their child? How could that be? That could not be true. That could not be real. Rob's voice was choked. He had difficulty getting the words out when he asked Ray, "What did he experience, Ray? Please, Ray. Was he afraid? Was he saying he wanted me with him? To *save* him? Please tell me. Did he know he was dying?" Rob rose from his seat, placed his hands on his head, and began meandering through the yard, Ray quickly by his side.

"What did he want to say?" Rob looked at his friend with an expression that Ray would never forget, for his friend was asking questions to which there were no answers.

"Did he try to call for me? 'Dad, Daddy, please, don't let this happen to me. Daddy, I'm scared! Please I need you and Mum. Please, please do not let me die!'"

Ray gave Rob a pill and urged him to take it. Rob did so and within a half hour or so he felt calmer, almost numbed. "We have to take care of her," Rob said. "That's number one."

"Yes," said Ray. "We will."

They sat in the yard, silent for the most part, Rob staring off into the trees. He cried intermittently. He cursed under his breath. He prayed aloud in the harsh light of the day, a new day, a new life, a pathway forward the likes of which he could never possibly have imagined.

Rob remembered the neighborhood mothers arriving, crisp in their summer shorts and skirts. These women, friends and acquaintances, knew instinctively what to do and how to do it. They were reserved and bore the weight of the moment with quiet grace. They were trim, athletic women, MBAs and physicians with unmistakable Ivy League confidence, practiced in their coordinated efficiency. Rob thanked them over and over again for the coffee, tea, and wine, for the loaves of lemon cake and imported tins of English biscuits. By five o'clock that afternoon several dozen cars lined their narrow street, and the living room and kitchen were crowded with visitors. Rob remembered hugs and handshakes, people perspiring heavily in the heat. Condolences at once sincere and awkward. Rob wore pressed chinos, a blue oxford cloth shirt, and sweated profusely. By late afternoon the downstairs of the house was crowded, the humidity thick, dampening bodies, wilting crackers on plates.

"So sorry for your loss, Rob," was the mantra, and surely everyone uttering those words knew in the moment how insufficient the language was to the reality of the occasion. But that was understandable, for these friends and coworkers were themselves traumatized by the loss. The truest sentiment perhaps came from one of his faculty colleagues, a young woman, a new mother, who had just gained tenure. "Rob, there are no words," and with that eternal truth she hugged him with a determined ferocity. And then there were close friends for whom there were, literally, no words; those so stunned by it all they were incapable of speaking to him. They hugged him, held him, their damp shirts leaving perspiration on his. Some of the women cried. Men, too, especially his closest colleagues on the faculty. People arrived in shorts and sneakers, some having interrupted vacations on the Cape and the Maine islands. It was not long before the muggy air inside gave way to a ripe smell of humanity, people huddled in small groups whispering, breaking off conversation when Julia or Rob approached to thank them for being there.

Visitors moved in an informal procession from one photograph to another, some on walls in the kitchen, living room, and study. Many more in tasteful silver frames were arranged on end tables and bookshelves. Here was Julia in the moments after the birth, baby Thomas swaddled in blankets, Julia appearing exhausted, face flushed, hair disheveled, an air of peace settled upon her. Here was Rob, awkwardly holding baby Thomas, Rob's face serious, stern even, a man who understood his responsibility to this most precious of beings. Here was Thomas in a series of pictures in his blue-and-white-striped pajamas—being rocked to sleep, crawling—and in a shallow bath tended to by Julia. Here they all were, mother, father, and child, wearing silly hats and huddled over a birthday cake bearing a single candle. Here were crayon scratches with no discernible patterns on manila paper.

The photographs told something of a life. First day of school, a class picture, Thomas in the back row, beaming, a happy little boy at ease among his classmates. He was blessed with his mother's features. Here was Thomas at the beach, his bathing suit seeming a size too big, hanging low on his little belly, shovel in one hand, pail in the other, and a look of all business. It was a look that Rob and Julia often laughed about, for it came across as a frown, a wrinkled brow, virtually identical to the look on Rob's face when he paused to consider a complex question. Here was Thomas at age eight, sweaty hair matted down, helmet off at the conclusion of a hockey game, his blue-and-white uniform worn with pride, his hockey stick raised in triumph.

Rob's handshakes were firm, his hugs sincere. Few people stayed long, and everyone, upon leaving, did so with relief. You could see the sense of shock on their faces, the pale, dull-eyed glances, almost a sense of embarrassment at having themselves avoided such an unspeakable event in their own lives. Some of the mourners seemed eager to convey their condolences and retreat from the house in the same breath. It was as though remaining too long in this place risked incurring the wrath of the gods who had decided that on a particular day tragedy would be visited not upon the Abbotts down the block or the Ralstons across town, but rather upon the now broken lives of Rob and Julia Barrow.

More visitors came in the following days. One evening a pathway was cleared through the living room as Thomas's fellow hockey team members from school filed in, each boy wearing his jersey, coaches bringing up the rear. Julia beamed at these beloved boys who were so much a part of her son's life. Half the boys were themselves crying, and she sobbed as she hugged each boy in turn. Julia had reached a point of exhaustion and retreated upstairs into Thomas's room, Rob trailing behind her. She fell to her knees, pressing her face into his pillow on the bed, smelling her boy, clutching the pillow, wrapping it around her face. Rob held her with a sense of desperation.

"I cannot," she whispered to him. "*I. Can. Not.*" He had no doubt that in this moment she meant it. Why go on? Rob wondered. How could you live life when your entire being, your body, mind, and soul, when everything that mattered had burst into flames?

Three days later, the night before the funeral, Rob and Ray were sitting outside on the terrace, a black night, clouds obstructing the moon. Suddenly the screen door slammed, and when they looked up there was a figure emerging from the kitchen, backlit, ghost-like, moving slowly, arms extended, hands in front of her as though feeling her way. Julia walked toward them very slowly, her face drained of color.

"Where is he?" she asked, her voice soft, an air of confusion.

Rob moved quickly, placing his arm around her shoulder and guiding her gently back into the house. "I don't know where he is," she said, and she stopped, pulling away from him. Silence and then a look of shock on her face, half hidden in the light.

"What happened?" she asked, looking around. *"What happened?"* she demanded, and then the realization struck her and she shrieked, crying out, *"Please God, no!"* And she repeated it over and over and over again as he embraced her, holding her tight, not letting her get away. He held her, and they had no choice but to confront the waves of grief that washed over them, waves that would, like the tides, never cease.

Four days after the death of eleven-year-old Thomas Barrow, many hundreds of mourners gathered in the church of Saint Ignatius Loyola on the campus of Boston College, where Jesuits presided. It was all a blur to Julia and Rob. They were driven that morning to the Brighton funeral home, prayers were offered, and the small casket bearing their child was loaded onto a hearse. From there, a black Cadillac limousine carried Julia, Rob, and Ray to the church. Undertakers in gray morning suits led a solemn procession down the main aisle, the casket on a wheeled trolley, Julia and Rob, attired in black—a simple dress for Julia, a suit for Rob—each with a hand on the casket as it rolled steadily toward the altar for blessings and a send-off to the afterlife.

They had asked the hockey coach from school, who also happened to be Thomas's academic advisor, to say a few words, and the young man spoke of what a fine bright boy Thomas was, but how, most importantly, he had been the best of teammates. "There are the great players and then there are the great teammates, and the latter are, by far, the more precious commodity," he said. And at this Julia and Rob cried and held each other, for they could hear their son's voice telling them that his ambition was to be the very best teammate possible.

A reception in the church hall left them exhausted. They went through the motions of receiving mourners, many friends, colleagues, acquaintances. Back at home, they discussed the day's events, talked of how pleased they were with the coach's brief eulogy and how kind it had been for so many people to make the effort to be there. Ray and Rob drank scotch. Julia had some wine, which fueled the calming power of the sedatives Ray had given her.

In the days and weeks after the loss of their boy, Julia and Rob were helped by neighbors, colleagues, and friends. Ray was their anchor. He had moved into the guest room and was the first person in the house up each morning and the last to bed. There he was in the morning, coffee all made, sitting outside on the kitchen terrace, scanning the yard, quiet, thinking. Late at night, when Rob would head up, there was Ray in the chintz-covered chair by the fireplace, tumbler of scotch in hand, thumbing through papers related to his patients or research.

The exact nature of trauma is something of a mystery. The shock it produces is marvelously protective, as it activates cells that rally in moments of extreme tragedy. This shielding response was an evolutionary advantage against the savagery of early primitive human life. This was a coping mechanism, entirely involuntary and common in the midst of military combat or the immediate aftermath of horrific accidents. And, of course, in the sudden loss of a loved one, especially someone many decades shy of what could conceivably be termed a timely death.

A week after the funeral, Rob and Ray were on the terrace early in the morning having coffee when Julia, coffee cup in hand, came outside.

"How did you sleep?" Rob asked her.

"Okay," she said. "Whatever you gave me, Ray, wow."

She was dressed in Thomas's hockey team sweatpants and sweatshirt, navy blue with the school logo in maroon and white. Number 11.

"He really loved the gear," she said.

Rob smiled. "He wore it with such pride," he said.

"Boys love all that team stuff," Ray said.

Julia had not brushed her hair, and it had tangled a bit. She pushed it aside.

"I think for him it was about belonging, you know what I mean?"

she said. "For all those boys being part of the team was so important. They really were all so close, and when the whole team came through the door that night, coaches, as well . . ."

Rob cried softly. Julia reached over and took his hand. A combination of shock and the medication that Ray had administered had had a salutary effect on Julia. In a sense, it lifted her out of reality, dulling her emotions. This was the state in which she would function for months to come. She would sleep restfully each night thanks to the liberal doses of narcotic sleep aids. During daylight hours, several milligrams of lorazepam every six hours calmed her mind. The combination of the therapeutics and her system's natural response to shock steadied her. She cried many times each day, and she raged at times, as well, but the drugs blunted the sharpest edges.

Ray went into the kitchen and refilled their coffee cups, and they sat silently for a period of time. It was a silence in which only the closest of friends find comfort. Julia broke that silence with a comment that surprised both Rob and Ray.

"He will not suffer," she said in a calm voice. She looked at Rob for a long moment. "This is important," she said to him. "I realized this last night. We have to see this for what it is, Rob. He will never suffer. He will never have cancer or face a situation where his child has some terrible disease. He will never have to see us age and wither and die. He will be spared that."

She paused, studying the coffee in her cup.

"He will never lose a child of his own," she continued. "He will not experience the terrible cruelty that exists in so much of the world. In so much of life."

Later, when Rob asked Ray what he thought of her comments, Ray said it seemed a result of the natural shock response. "People say things under extreme stress that they don't realize they're saying and do not actually remember saying. There's some literature suggesting that an aspect of shock is a subconscious effort to counterbalance the tragedy.

I suppose the subconscious mind goes into overdrive to try to offer protection, a kind of rebalancing. *He won't have cancer, won't lose a child.* I can
only guess it's the psyche grasping for anything that in any slight way
counters the horror." He paused. "But I'm just guessing, really. That's
where the shock is so important in that initial stage of loss. And she is
definitely in shock and will be for a while. Same with you, Rob, even
though you may not realize it right now. But it's the shock that enables
you to go on in a semi-normal way. It enables you to try to feel your way
as close toward normalcy as possible."

The inevitable conflict flared in the third week of life after the loss
of their son. Ray had returned to living in his own home and was back
at work in the medical school. It had been said many times that Rob
and Julia were a classic example of opposites attracting and that had
been as amusing as it was true. Now Rob was stoic in a way that grated
on Julia.

"You never *cry!*" she said one day after sobbing herself into exhaustion. Rob embraced her, but she pulled away, wanting only the affection
she could no longer have from her son.

"Why don't you cry?" she demanded. She was glaring at him. Her
hair was undone, her face pale. She was acting like someone other than
herself. Rob had devoted himself every waking moment since Thomas's
death to caring for and supporting his wife, and this suggestion from
her—the implication was clearly that somehow he had not loved his
son sufficiently—offended him. It hurt him. The truth was that in the
shower each morning he cried and cried some more. And then he
pulled himself together to try to bring stability and peace to their lives.

Later that afternoon Rob came downstairs and found Julia curled
up on the floor in the corner, half under the kitchen table, face wet with
tears, eyes hollow. She was very still, breathing shallow, eyes cold and
even hollow as she stared at some spot along the floor. Her teeth were
clenched, and as he sat watching her, he realized what was so unsettling: Her eyes seemed full of hate. And he knew her loathing was not

really aimed at him but rather at existence; at the new nature of life that had been inflicted upon them.

"It is too vile," she said. "This reality. I don't know if I can do it, Rob."

She felt as though the structure of her brain had been altered, that her mind was now a labyrinth with hallways wide and narrow, harshly lit and heavily shadowed. The spaces bent, curved, and rolled this way and that, a spiral staircase here going down somewhere, a fraying rope ladder ascending through a cloud-like opening. She imagined herself roaming through this space, opening doors and cabinets, climbing steps, then descending through an opening and tumbling down into something like a hedgerow maze in the English countryside.

23

Survival

The day after the news from Jerry about the Griswold, Rob and Julia went out for a walk along the Charles. Through the years, they found that walking together was one of the best forms of therapy for them. Slow, contemplative walks following the same route along the river where Julia had pushed Thomas in the stroller so many years ago. We will survive, they would tell one another. We will survive. That is how he would want it.

"I remember one year after we lost him," Rob said. "We were walking along this same path, probably pretty close to this point where the river turns, and I think that was the moment when we realized we had survived for a year and we *would* survive, and more than survive: that we would make a go at living as full a life as possible."

"I remember that walk even though there is so much from that first year that is a blur," Julia said. "I remember when you focused on *What would Thomas want us to do? Would he want us living in misery and despair all our lives, or would he want us to try to be strong, to live a rich, rewarding life and to try to do some good?* And you had said it to me before that, I know, but for some reason that was the moment I was really ready to hear it and hold on to it and make it real in my life. And it's given us our North Star, Rob. That's what has made all the difference."

Listening to Julia and thinking about all of that time they had gone without their boy triggered a flood of emotions, and he brushed back tears as they kept moving forward. Not everybody was able to do that, he knew. The therapists waved bright red caution signals that the terrain after such loss was hazardous with threats of marital and professional peril, depression, despair, black-hole-strength darkness from which some were unable to escape.

"But we have been guided by his spirit," Rob said, "and we have stuck together, and we have hung in there."

"And we've listened to each other," said Julia. "And we've been able to understand that in some ways we are very different people and that we have grieved and do grieve in very different ways. I remember volunteering at school, thinking that being in the place he loved around people who loved him would help, but everywhere I turned there were his friends, his teachers, the hockey bags lined up at the end of the hallway and I realized it was just hurting, not helping."

"We had help," Rob said. "We had Ray."

24

Benzodiazepines, SSRIs

On a day in mid-April, the arborist arrived for the annual tests of bark and leaf health. He drilled core samples, suggested trimming here and there, and fed nutrients "that will make your trees happy."

That evening, Rob, Julia, and Ray gathered in an aura of spring's fecundity, soft, warm air, the scent of rich earth, a mix of flowers, a festive evening to toast Rob for the Griswold. Julia wore dark slacks and a long-sleeved cotton top, sweater nearby just in case. Her thick silvery-white hair was short and well cut, and she still presented to the world as an attractive woman; the rare older lady noticed by other women who could clearly tell that in her earlier days she was a classic beauty. But her once-bright eyes had dimmed. Aging had taken a toll. They all had suffered this to a certain extent, but Julia more than the others. Her eyes, once such a striking ice blue, had clouded. Rob looked much as he had through the years, thin, fit, the rumpled professor with wrinkled trousers, though on this evening he wore a freshly laundered and pressed dress shirt. His hair had thinned out over time, receded a bit, a mix of gray and white. His face was wrinkled, eyes sunken by the stresses of life. Ray's Mad Russian appearance was even more pronounced, with his hair longer and more unkempt even than usual, his beard wilder than ever.

"Thomas would be proud of you," Julia said as she reached out to take Rob's hand. She held it and shifted her chair a bit closer to his on the terrace so she could comfortably hang on without reaching. "And I am proud of you, Rob," she said. "What a career!"

"Amen," added Ray.

"Thank you both. Obviously, it means the world to me," Rob said. This was just what he needed. The support from the two people in his life who mattered most had sustained him even through the worst. To have the great blessing of Julia's love and Ray's friendship through all the years gave him strength. And Ray's dispensing various medications had been essential in getting them through the journey. Early on, Julia had been heavily sedated, needing a shield between herself and reality. With the help of Ray and one of his faculty members in psychiatry, she had gone through a period of trial and error, finally settling upon a daily dose of Zoloft along with supplemental doses of lorazepam as needed. Her internist had warned her that this could lead to memory loss, a risk of falls, and other potential dangers, but she had come to the belief that she understood how to maintain not just her sanity, but a relative level of comfort, as well. For Julia, the difficult issue was alcohol. On most nights she stuck to her two-glass limit, but sometimes she exceeded it, and when she did it was unpleasant for all concerned—slurred words, hiccups, sudden tears, extreme emotionalism—and little if any recollection of anything in the morning. Whenever Rob raised the subject she thanked him and said she was working on it.

Now Rob, too, had come to depend upon the intervention of pharmaceuticals. He, who had never touched a drug in his life until his prostate surgery, enjoyed the fruits of Ray's highly questionable commerce with the pharmaceutical reps. He had come to rely perhaps a bit too much on an opioid now and again for the release from pain, both physical and psychic. And Ray, well, Ray was the master. He had perfected the art of self-medication while maintaining an ability to function at a high level. And, to the chagrin of Rob and occasional fury of Julia, Ray still smoked the occasional cigarette.

"What will you do if you get lung cancer?" Julia had demanded of him.

Ray laughed and said, "Have surgery, of course."

This was the educated class in America—dependent on substances shielding them from reality. For most it was evening cocktails, but for millions of others the gold lay within the effect on the central nervous system of the benzodiazepines, including Ativan (lorazepam), Valium (diazepam), Klonopin (clonazepam), Xanax (alprazolam), and a dozen others, all FDA approved, including the selective serotonin reuptake inhibitors that not only lifted the spirits and calmed the mind but also sharpened the world's natural colors: Celexa (citalopram), Lexapro (escitalopram), Prozac (fluoxetine), Paxil and Pexeva (paroxetine), and Zoloft (sertraline).

"Rob, can you imagine," Julia said, "if someone had said when we were all first together in the seventies that this would be the road ahead? Can you imagine if someone told us back then that we would be sitting here, in the presence of a sycamore from Washington's day, with the crutch of pharmaceuticals that would do nothing less than reroute the chemicals in the brain?"

"It's nothing compared with what's ahead," said Ray. "Implants will block negative emotions, depression, anxiety, and fuel us with good feelings at all times. Those are coming. Can you imagine the market for such things?"

"I would never want that," Julia said. "You have to experience life as it comes no matter what. We know firsthand that the body and the mind have the capability to release a protective response. I remember some things with great clarity, but I also forget most of what happened then for what, Rob, six months?"

"Oh, I would say at least."

"And it was the best thing that could have happened. It allowed

me to place some of my emotions and memory in a kind of coma,
allowed me to emerge from that coma only gradually, reintroducing me
to reality. Otherwise . . ." She thought for a moment and chose not to
complete the sentence.

25

"We Cover Up. We Conceal."

On Friday evening, Dr. Raymond Witter arrived at the hospital CEO's suite of offices, sumptuously appointed with walnut cabinets, designer sofas, easy chairs, and a thick coffee-colored carpet with thin gold threads woven throughout. Off to the side, toward the floor-to-ceiling windows, was a small conference table and a half dozen armchairs. The most eye-catching feature of the office was the view, a panoramic vision of the Charles River, winding away from its basin, Cambridge and the buildings of MIT on the right, the calming brick townhouses of the Back Bay and Beacon Hill to the left. Ray had been here for meetings on numerous occasions—this was, after all, the teaching hospital where his students worked. Still, he was struck by the nakedly corporate nature of the place. It could easily have passed as the redoubt of a corporate chieftain in finance or banking, whereas the dean's office that Ray had inherited at the medical school, while spacious and comfortable in its old-shoe way, spoke of books, learning, knowledge, medicine. He preferred the look and feel of the ancient Oriental carpet in his office, worn through to the threads. As he arrived the sun was beginning to set, sparkling on the surface of the water. Sailboats moved lazily between the Massachusetts Avenue Bridge across to Cambridge and MIT.

"Hello, Walter," Ray said to the hospital CEO, Dr. Walter Grinnell, a man whom Ray had known since medical school. In a sense, they had come up through the sprawling system along similar pathways.

"Ray, good to see you, but I have to say, I'm not sure why Mike insists on your involvement," Walter said. "No offense, but I think we can handle this." Walter was of medium height, clean-shaven, receding silvery hair, perfect teeth a shade of white not found in nature. He was a precise man, demanding of himself and his underlings and, at this moment, clearly quite tense. Ray noticed a single vein in his neck protruding above his white shirt collar. Ray, rumpled in dark suit, no tie, didn't quite fit in here, and he was pleased by that. He did not want to fit into this culture, this place where he had trained as a physician but which he had come to view as a corporate entity rather than a mission-driven organization focused on the health of the community.

"Mike wanted another voice in the room, Walter," Ray said. "Different point of view."

"From?"

"Your palace guard of lawyers," Ray said. He smiled. "No offense."

Walter clenched his jaw. He was used to this sort of talk from Ray and would never have tolerated it were Ray not holding such an important role at the medical school. While Ray's iconoclastic ways were appreciated at the medical school, even celebrated, Walter found his manner off-putting. Walter gestured toward one of the chairs at the conference table, but Ray preferred to stand at the window and gaze out at the scene. Boston really was a pretty city, he thought. He had been lucky to wind up here after the navy, after Phu Bai, blessed to have met Julia and Rob here. He had come to learn over the years that institutions such as this one, sprawling systems of hospitals, ambulatory care sites, physician groups, specialists and subspecialists and the heft to dictate terms to the relentlessly greedy insurance companies, were similar to other big institutions in a never-ending hunt for revenue, even if it meant flirting with antitrust laws and driving up the overall cost of care for millions of people within the marketplace.

Dr. Deborah Zack, leader of the RAND health care practice, whom Ray had known for some years, arrived carrying a fat briefcase. She was a slight person dressed in an olive pantsuit, low heels, a perky energy at age sixty, small eyes, narrow face, conveying the notion that she was all business.

"Hey Deb, it's been a while," Ray said warmly.

"I didn't know you were joining us," she said, glancing at Walter. "What a pleasant surprise."

"Mike Dwyer insists," said Walter with resignation.

At that point the health system's chief counsel, Rich "Dickie" Potts, arrived, turned out in a silk suit, light blue shirt with a stiff white collar, and, most obvious, an attitude. Dickie Potts was highly valued by the hospital for his ability to limit financial penalties in cases of liability. Dickie himself once estimated that he had saved the system upward of $100 million during his twenty-three years as head lawyer. It was probably more.

Settled at the table, Walter started the meeting. "I was informed by Mike, in confidence, and informed very recently I might add, that about a year ago, the executive committee of the board, five members, keep in mind, had taken it upon itself to engage RAND for a study. Nothing against RAND, you understand, Deb," he said, turning in her direction. "Nothing but the highest level of respect for RAND. However, I will say, and I told Mike this, that in principle I object in the strongest possible terms to the board reaching beyond its policy role into operations. Totally inappropriate by any definition of governance best practices, but done deal, horse out of the barn type thing. Mike informs me that RAND got all the data they asked for. Every scrap. Scares the bejesus out of me to have that stuff out over the wires to another organization, but that's another story. At any rate, here we are. The report is written. Dickie and I have read it. You as well, Ray?"

Ray nodded.

"Now Mike wants us to make a recommendation to the executive committee as to what to do with it," Walter said.

"Shredder," Dickie Potts interjected. "Absolute shit show. No disrespect intended, Deb."

"I agree with Dickie," Walter said. "This is nothing but trouble. But since I suspect Mike will not be pleased if we recommend shredding it, then I suppose we should make a proposal on how to revise it, massage it, *manage* it, whatever terms you want to use. Strain the poison out of it."

"Christ, Walter, why the charade?" said Dickie. "We know this thing is poison and we've got to bury it in some nuclear wasteland. It's radioactive. It's spent fuel. It's got a nuclear half life. Could bring the whole damn enterprise crashing down on our heads."

"Your thoughts, Deb?" Ray asked.

She leaned forward, hands folded on the table. "The document speaks for itself, really," she said. "We do not know of any comparable research document in the health care space. As we note, we think it could be potentially transformative for your system as well as helpful for others."

"Our competitors included," said Walter.

"Let's get serious, Deb," Dickie interjected. "This thing strikes me as a cut-and-paste job, a rewrite of the overhyped Institute of Medicine report in '99 which scared the shit out of the American people. *Hospitals dangerous! Infection factories! Getting the wrong drug, vegetative state, wrong limb amputated!* This stuff is in the dustbin. We don't make those mistakes anymore, Deb. Those were the old days. Everybody's cleaned up their act. Our doctors have made a heroic effort—you heard me—a heroic effort to improve quality and safety, and they have done so. And now this piling on. This is their reward?"

"Dickie, I agree that there's been great improvement since the Institute study in '99," she said. "But the data is the data. It does not lie.

There was a burst of progress back then, but has it kept pace? Are the hospitals of America as safe as they could be? Not even close. Without good data, we know nothing. A simple question: What's the standard of excellence in medicine been for years? Maybe academic credentials, maybe institutional prestige, maybe a physician's reputation. The 'doctors that other doctors go to' type of magazine feature. And people tend to believe in this approach. After all, if your brother-in-law calls you, Dr. Grinnell, and says he needs back surgery, you will have a ready name or two whom you will recommend as 'the best back guy in town.' And you will perhaps even use those words."

"That's on the money," said Grinnell. "Happens every day."

"And you make that recommendation," she continued, "but when you make that recommendation you do not do it on the basis of data measuring outcomes. You do it on the basis of reputation. You don't tell your brother-in-law that Dr. So-and-So has the fewest infections, readmissions, complications, etc., of any other surgeon in our system. That he has the best outcomes down the road for flexibility, mobility, absence of pain. The fewest patient complaints. Fair?"

Grinnell frowned. "We know who the best people are," he said. "The most skilled."

"Anecdotally," she replied. "You know it anecdotally, Walter. We ran the data." She passed a single sheet of paper to each of the men.

"You will note that on the left column is a list of the twenty-seven surgeons in your system who perform back surgery. The columns to the right of each name cover several things including number of operations, number of surgical infections, number of cases requiring follow-up surgery within eight weeks to fix mistakes, numbers of patient deaths in the OR, percent of patients willing to recommend that surgeon, percentage of patients readmitted to the hospital for acute care within three weeks after surgery, etc. The overall performance is, to be kind, mediocre. Some of these surgeons' numbers are outstanding. But others are poor. And there is no consistency. No indication of standard work. Among the three surgeons whom you told me yesterday are the best, Walter—the ones you recommend to friends and family—look at the data. Dr. Morrissey is, indeed, near the top in every category. Across the board, his outcomes are just about as high as any I have ever seen. When he does the job, it is done well. No infections, no need for extended inpatient stays, no need to redo the procedure, excellent pain management, and a uniquely effective rehab program."

"A good man," Grinnell said.

"But the other two from your top three, Drs. Greene and Windler, are in the fourth quadrant by this collective measure. Windler has the highest death rate of all. So if you were going to have back surgery based on this data, surely you would be comfortable with Dr. Morrissey, but if Windler arrived in the OR you would run and hide. Greene and Windler both have high rates of infections, readmissions, and questionable outcomes overall."

"So Morrissey has his own rehab program?" Ray asked.

"More rigorous," said Deb. "Top outcomes."

Ray shook his head. "Walter, if the data says Morrissey's rehab is the best, why doesn't everyone use his approach?"

"Christ, Ray, you know these guys," Walter said. "They have their own approaches. They're not robots."

"But don't you think every patient who walks through the door should get what the data says is the best practice?" Ray asked.

"We tried it and it didn't take," Walter said.

"Because the surgeons bitched about it?"

Walter shrugged.

"Ray, you know how these prima donnas are, Jesus," said Dickie. "Try something new, they threaten to defect."

"I know these men, Deb," said Walter. "Have worked with them for thirty years. These are good men."

"They both have top *reputations*," she conceded, "but if you are a patient, you might not like your results."

Dr. Grinnell rose from his chair and went to a small kitchen adjacent to his office suite. "I need a drink," he said. "Anybody? Deb?"

"Sparkling water, please."

"Dickie?"

"Scotch."

Grinnell brought the drinks and began walking back to the kitchen. "Ray?"

"What are you having, Walter?"

Grinnell laughed. "Bourbon, of course."

"Same, thanks," said Ray.

Grinnell delivered their drinks, sat down, and sighed heavily. "This is a nightmare."

"Of our own making," said Dickie.

"Maybe an opportunity, Walter?" Ray ventured.

"I like that word," said Deb, who removed three binders from her briefcase and handed one to each of the men. "I know you received emailed copies," she said. "Here are hard copies. Turn to the tables on pages seven through nineteen. It's all in the data. These are your numbers, Walter. We didn't make this stuff up. We analyzed what you sent us and ran a comparison to the other big systems around the nation. We ran it against CMS data, we ran it six ways to Sunday. You do whatever you want with it, gentlemen, but I would say Ray is right. It's an opportunity to improve. Patients here are being harmed. Walter, your mortality rate is double what it should be compared to other big systems. You're not alone in this, by the way. There are a few outliers who have shown excellent progress on safety, notably Mayo, Hopkins, Cleveland Clinic, but the other big systems like yours cluster in the middle of the bell curve."

Dickie frowned, rhythmically tapping his fingers on the table, eager to get it all over with.

"Deb, do you have comparative numbers on nondisclosure agreements?" Ray asked.

She flipped through the report. "Page 23," she said. "During the past six years you guys had an average of 30 percent more NDAs than comparable institutions, and three times as many as the best."

"Jesus, Ray, we've been over this a dozen times," said Dickie. "I understand your philosophical opposition to the NDAs, but the reality in the cold cruel world is that when we make a mistake, especially a very bad one, what choice do we have but to batten down the hatches, make the patient and family whole, and move on? Publishing these things would be an existential threat to the organization. And nobody would follow suit as you have argued."

"Make the patient and family whole, Dickie?" Ray said. "After you've made mistakes that shattered their quality of life or killed them? You are saying that money can *make them whole*? Families coming in, trusting us, eager for a fix or cure, and leaving heartbroken. No, sorry. We have a moral responsibility to seize upon our errors, share them with the medical community and the public, and learn from them to the benefit of all."

There was an awkward silence until Deb Zack asked, "Any other questions?"

Walter looked at Dickie and Ray and replied wearily, "I think we're all set for the moment, Deb." He rose from his chair and shook her hand.

"Thank you, Deb," Ray said, shaking her hand as well.

"Sorry, Deb," Dickie said. "It's not personal."

When she was gone, Dickie went into the kitchen and refilled his scotch.

"This was ill conceived from the start, Walter, and you know it," Dickie said, returning to his chair. "I hate to say I told you so, but I told you so. Never ask a witness a question to which you do not know the answer. And never assign a year-long research study with your brand on it when you don't know what you will find."

"Next steps?" said Walter.

"Disarm the bomb," Dickie said. "Remove the plutonium, rip out its nuclear capability, rewrite it in broad generalizations, no crazy speculative numbers, not a word about NDAs."

Ray sipped his whiskey, then set it down. "Walter, this needs to be published," he said.

"Published!" said Walter.

"Have you lost your mind?" Dickie cried.

"I am sorry this upsets you, Dickie," said Ray calmly. "But as we know, sunlight is the best disinfectant. We need to be truthful with our patients, physicians, nurses, and our medical students."

"We don't lie, damnit!" Walter shouted, banging the table.

"But we cover up, Walter," Ray said. "We conceal. We pay patients who have been harmed to go away and shut up. And who loses? All the other patients lose. All the other health systems that look to us for leadership. That look to us to teach. We have life-saving lessons that we could share with the medical world with a benefit to all and yet they are locked up in these NDAs. Walter, for God's sake, you want your legacy to be that you concealed, covered up, paid people off?"

"Dr. Witter," said Dickie, "the NDAs of which you speak so disparagingly have saved this organization tens of millions of dollars, and I suspect some of that money has wound up in the coffers of research labs under your roof, so I'm not so sure you are wise to condemn those agreements. Agreements, by the way, that compensated injured people in a very fair manner. In a generous manner."

"Dickie, I'm a teacher," Ray said. "A researcher. I want every one of my medical students to study our mistakes so they will avoid them. Doesn't that make the most basic sense?"

"Christ, Ray, our reputation," said Walter. "I trained here, my fellowship, I love this place. You cannot ask me to allow something like this document"—Walter slammed the palm of his hand down onto the binder—"to escape out into the wider world."

Walter rose from his chair and went to the window, hands in the pockets of his trousers. He stared out at the river for several minutes in silence. Finally, he spoke. "We have the finest medical care in the world here in America, Ray," he said. "We save lives every day. Thousands. Tens of thousands. Every day. We do make mistakes. We are imperfect, we are only human." He shook his head and fell silent. After a while he turned away from the window, appearing disconsolate.

"We'll sleep on it," he said.

By prearrangement, Ray drove to Mike Dwyer's home in Brookline the following morning. Dwyer led him through the house to the back terrace with a view of expansive gardens that must have covered several acres.

"Still think we should publish it?" Dwyer asked.

"I don't think we have any choice, Mike," Ray said. "Our obligation to share it with our medical staff is absolute. In which case it would get out to the press in five minutes and how would that look? Secret report shows *blah blah blah*. We also have an obligation to our medical students and to other hospitals around the country, many of whom do, in fact, look up to us, learn from us. So I don't think it's whether we publish. It's how."

"I love this hospital," said Mike Dwyer, plunging his hands in his pockets and staring down at the earth. "It's done so much good for so many. People come from all over the world to see us with the most difficult and unusual medical problems. People who live a block away who are poor and sick depend on us for free care. And we provide it. Forty million's worth every year. But that good doesn't offset or excuse our responsibility to make our hospitals safer. Ray, for me, as you know, the veil lifted when I helped out my BC classmate I told you about. Infection—our fault—killed him. I felt like we were slipping. Complacent. The elderly mother of an accountant who worked for me had some issues, and I got her in to see the specialists and assumed everything was fine, and a few weeks later I get the news that she died in the hospital. This guy is shattered, of course, and I look into it, and the docs said there had been some unavoidable 'complications.' And I realized that I had been hearing that word a fair amount. So I called in the team that cared for her, and it turns out that the medication instructions—there was a change in her medication—were left by the team going off duty, but, for some reason, never reached the doc coming on duty."

Dwyer started walking slowly along the garden pathways, with Ray falling in step. "After that I went to the chiefs and said, 'Okay, do we have a safety issue in here?' They acted like I was nuts. Safety?! Jesus, you can't find a safer medical facility in the lower forty-eight. Etc., etc. In other words, 'We know medicine, you know fundraising, leave us alone.' That same day, I was at a meeting with the fellow who runs my firm, and we were going through the performance numbers for the year. Did we beat the market? Outperform the prior year, outperform our competitors? And it was like a lightning bolt. I realized in that moment that my business is all about measurement."

Dwyer stopped abruptly and turned toward Ray, extending his arms in a gesture that said, *It's so obvious.* "But I missed it. I've been missing what was right in front of my face for years. That if you're going to claim progress or success or achievement, you have to prove it with measurement. Why is it that as a student you were measured to exacting standards through high school, through medical school, and then, all of a sudden no objective measurement? 'Well, medicine is as much art form as science,' Walter told me. 'You can't measure how good a great cardiac surgeon is or a radiation oncologist.' And I was stumped. And then I thought, and this is heresy, I know, but I thought, These guys are stonewalling me. They want me to give money, preside over a compliant board of prominent rich people, and mind our business when it comes to what we actually do for people. I did my own research a couple years ago and discovered, for example, that there are lots of things you can measure that are components of quality and safety. Is the patient's pain managed below, say, level four after surgery? Does the patient receive the right medication in the right dosage at the right time? Does the X-ray get read promptly so appropriate treatment can begin for the best outcome? How many of our older patients take a fall while in our hospital, resulting in a broken hip or head injury or something else that means their condition and health gets worse while they're in our care? What systems are in place to prevent falls? A year and a half ago I urged Walter to undertake a study of quality and safety in our system. He told me it would be a waste of money because he knew the answer already—we make some mistakes, but overall, we are solid. And I got pretty pissed off. I said, 'Walter, what the fuck are you talking about, *solid*? We tell the world we are great, the best, and you are telling me we are *solid*?'"

They walked along in silence for a minute or so. "I found articles in *JAMA* and elsewhere by some docs who question the orthodoxy. And one of those articles was yours, 'The Hubris of Modern Medicine,' and it gave me a new perspective I wish I had had twenty-five years ago. And that is why I need you to help me nudge this place along, Ray. Shake it up, get people out of their comfort zones. Too much smugness ingrained in the culture here for my money. Or, as you put it, hubris. And I think the shoe fits."

They had made a full circuit around the garden and were headed back to the terrace.

"If this is to be published, where and how?" Mike asked.

"*New England Journal*," said Ray. "You and I coauthor a brief introductory essay explaining why this was commissioned and why we're sharing it with the medical community broadly. We give the chiefs a week heads-up, they brief their teams that it's coming, and the piece appears online before publication of the magazine."

Mike Dwyer nodded and said, "Let's go."

26

Griswold Shame

When Andy Burns learned from a tip that Rob Barrow had been selected to receive the Griswold, she was surprised. In light of Barrow's comments this seemed particularly awkward. After thinking it over, she sat at her desk and drafted an editorial headlined GRISWOLD SHAME. It read:

> The proposed recipient of the Griswold Award for this year is Professor Robert Barrow, the Louis C. P. Gardner Professor of Constitutional Law, sources have told the *Crimson*. We state our unequivocal opposition both to the selection of Professor Barrow and the process by which he was chosen. It is undisputed that Barrow holds a position of significant standing in the nation's legal world. That does not, however, immunize him from criticism. The *Crimson* has reported two disturbing events concerning Professor Barrow. We reported in early September that Barrow told our reporter that he considered the *New York Times* 1619 Project "irrelevant." One may disagree with the *Times* initiative, but how can a tenured faculty member believe the matter of race, in the form of this unquestionably significant *Times* project, is not at the heart of the national conversation at this time?

The second matter occurred during an orientation class that included a number of Black students, where Barrow derided the *Times* initiative again. Barrow insisted that America was all about its founding ideals. Yet the lived experience of millions of Black Americans is powerful contradictory evidence. A student in the class came away from the experience deeply uncomfortable with what she described, in a recent interview with the *Crimson,* as a "powerfully racist impulse" from the professor.

This level of hubris is perhaps unsurprising from a white male who for decades has believed that he and his cohorts are the ones who set intellectual standards. Barrow's view is that the Founders and their ideals are sacrosanct.

The Griswold is so stale it gives off a bad odor. This year the *Crimson* has chosen to break with the tradition of writing a hagiographic portrait of the Griswold recipient. Instead, we propose the following:

One, dismiss all current Griswold Committee members.

Two, dean of FAS appoints a new board with broad representation, including undergraduates.

Three, establish preference in the selection for underrepresented faculty members, particularly women and people of color.

Four, the newly appointed committee in consultation with the Dean selects a new recipient for this year's award.

Faculty members from throughout the university are in the process of signing a letter protesting the idea of awarding the Griswold to Professor Barrow. In the coming days, the *Crimson* will publish both the letter and the names of the signatories.

This selection of Robert Barrow for the Griswold cannot stand.

Andy brought the copy to Rafik and said, "We have to move this for tomorrow."

He read it quickly. "Okay, so the original sin is his comment that 1619 was irrelevant, correct? The problem is that since I started here freshman year we've had the policy of audio tapes for important quotes. I know we waive it sometimes, or actually a lot, especially on sports stories, but we are not adhering to our own guideline. And you raised this issue earlier."

"We've been over this, Rafik," said Andy. "I trust my reporter."

"You are flat-out calling this man a racist on a campus where that is the most unforgivable of sins without adhering to our own journalistic guidelines. We cannot do it."

"We are quoting a student," Andy said, "who attended the orientation session. We interviewed two days ago. She kept using the term 'racist impulse.'"

"Which is calling him a racist."

"The students have a right to speak," Andy said, "particularly after he denigrated something they consider foundational to understanding the nation's racist past." Andy paused. "Anything else?"

He shook his head.

"The piece goes tomorrow," said Andy.

When Rob read the editorial online the following morning, he was annoyed. It was nonsense.

"I think when Jerry first told me I was going to receive the award, I didn't really absorb what it meant," he told Julia at breakfast. "I was distracted with the cancer stuff, and you know me: awards have never been my thing. But lately, I have to say, the idea of receiving it has really come to mean something to me. Some of the most distinguished faculty members in university history are on that list. Two went on to serve on the Supreme Court. One was secretary of state. Three Nobel laureates. Being in that company felt damn good. At the same time, of course, I understand the need for greater representation on prestigious awards. I get that. But that encounter I had with the dean was surreal. And what's my heresy? I have failed to embrace the orthodoxy that says the entire traditional understanding of our founding is pure bullshit."

Rob held out his arms, palms up. "How did we get to this place?"

27

We Tell the Truth and Ensure the Truth Is Known

The addendum to the RAND report included the names of patients and employees who had agreed to nondisclosure agreements, and Ray began to search. Were there particular procedures that resulted in the kinds of mistakes that produced an NDA? Were there particular physicians or nurses who were error- and thus NDA-prone? But getting into the hospital's legal files was not an easy matter, even for someone in Ray's position. The RAND report had piqued his curiosity and mistrust. Was he paranoid? Perhaps. But he also felt a sense of apprehension. Ray was sometimes accused of being jaded, but it wasn't that. Rather, his skeptic's view of the tendencies of large institutions to deflect, feint, and cover up was based on reality: Vietnam, the Pentagon, Nixon, big business, big tobacco, and on and on. He recalled the first sentence in the honor code at the Naval Academy: *We tell the truth and ensure the truth is known.* He recalled his first night as a nervous plebe in Annapolis and, *my God*, had he been inspired by that! What could be simpler? What could be a better way to live, to lead? He and his fellow middies lived by this code. Those very few who had violated the code were immediately "separated," as the navy called it. Through the years, tens of thousands of midshipmen had honored this code with their behavior. Why couldn't the government have done the same? Honor was required of soldiers, sailors, and marines, but there was no requirement for honor among those at the Pentagon and elsewhere who were in charge of those soldiers, sailors, and marines. Ray was a Christian, considered himself a forgiving man. But he would never forgive the government of the United States for what it had done. He would carry his bitterness, rage, resentment—whatever it was—to the grave.

He called his former student, Myron Song. Myron had come to the medical school from MIT with an undergraduate degree in computer science. He had performed at a high level in medical school but hit a bit of a pothole a few months before graduation, when he showed up drunk for an examination. The disciplinary committee recommended expulsion, but after having a chat with Myron, Ray suspended him instead, and after graduating Myron founded a start-up identifying new ways to apply AI in health care. He had become a significant donor to the school.

"Myron, it's Ray."

"Ah, *the dean!*" replied Myron. "How can I help?"

"I need to get into the legal department's files at the hospital," Ray said. "My understanding is that it's locked down tight."

"You're Mr. Bigshot. Just ask."

"No, they have a policy—nobody but the lawyers see the nondis-closure agreements," said Ray. "Is it possible to get into their system, take a document or a copy of a document without any trace that it was taken or who took it? You had those MIT friends who could do this sort of thing."

"Theoretically yes, but we'll have to see how advanced the defensive system is," Myron said. "But, Ray, there is the small matter of this sort of act constituting a felony."

"Yeah," said Ray.

"If we get caught, I think we maybe lose our licenses to practice, but I don't practice anyway!" said Myron with a laugh. "But they do lock people up for shit like this, and I would prefer to avoid that, as I suspect you would as well."

"So can you probe, see what's there, without leaving tracks?"

"I have an MIT classmate, an Israeli, who was caught fishing around the Pentagon's chamber of secrets on behalf of Israel. He was in the US at the time and served two years of a seven-year sentence. The Israelis used diplomacy, and a spy swap, to get him back. He runs a cybersecurity firm in Tel Aviv with very close ties to the Israeli government. This guy, he can get in anywhere. Used to read the Ayatollah's text messages for fun. No problem."

No sooner had Ray gotten off the phone with Myron than Mike Dwyer called.

"Bad news," said Mike. "Six of the department chiefs at the hospital have blocked publication." After Ray and Mike had written a brief introduction to the RAND report and submitted it to the *New England Journal*, they had received the green light for publication. But now these department chiefs had decided that they wanted nothing to do with the RAND document. "They filed suit in federal court today to enjoin us from publishing, fearing 'irreparable harm' to their reputations and livelihood," Mike said to Ray. "The lawyers tell me this could be tied up in court for months, maybe longer."

28

Thomas, It's Mum

The next morning, Rob was having coffee at the breakfast table when Julia entered the kitchen, her hair disheveled, her face drawn, her expression confused.

"You okay?" Rob asked, rising to greet her, taking her in his arms and holding her.

"It was . . . I don't know," she said. "I had a nightmare I was convinced was real." She sat down heavily at the table while Rob poured her a cup of black coffee. She sipped it and shook her head.

"I was underground," she said, speaking slowly, trying to piece together what she remembered of the dream. "I was in some kind of tunnel that was under a house I was in, and the only way I could get out of the house was through the tunnel. I walked in the tunnel. It was very dark, and then there were lights and there was this shiny steel kind of a mini-rail car, and I got in and it glided along this underground tube, and it came up out of the ground over by Fresh Pond, you know, across from Route 2, that neighborhood, and it was dawn or very early in the morning, and I was in this front yard and then . . . ."

She leaned forward, hands on her face.

Rob pulled his chair next to hers and put his arm around her shoulders. "It was horrible," she said. "Thomas came out of the house dressed for school, and I called out to him, but he didn't hear me, he didn't respond at all, and I called as loudly as I could, but he kept moving, Rob, and he was walking along and I ran over to him. I ran across that side street I don't know the name of it, but I ran across without looking and a car hit me. It wasn't going very fast, but it hit me in the hip bone, and I was knocked to the ground, and the driver got out to see if I was okay. And Thomas saw this happen and he didn't say anything or do anything. Jesus, Rob!"

She cried and he held her. She wiped her nose on her pajama sleeve.

"And I went over to him, and I was standing right in front of him and *it was him*! It was Thomas right in front of me, and we were looking at each other, and I pleaded with him to talk with me to say something. I said, 'Thomas, it's Mum, Thomas, don't you recognize me?' And I went to a neighbor, and I asked if she knew that boy, and she said, yes, he lives next door, why? And I said that is my son. And she looked at me like I was crazy. And I said, who else lives there? And she said he lives with his girlfriend, and they are a very nice couple."

She stopped suddenly and shook her head once again, her eyes wide. She was struggling to grasp the experience of the dream, the reality of the images of her boy.

"I woke up and went to get water and sat up for a while, but when I went back to sleep, it continued. I was walking in that neighborhood by Fresh Pond with a real estate agent and telling her about him. I told her I wanted to buy a new house for him, single family in a better neighborhood. At an intersection, I told her that there had been an accident at that very spot, and the problem was these teenagers not obeying the rules and speeding and whatnot and that a nanny on her way to work was killed by a drunk driver."

She paused and took a deep breath, exhaling slowly. "I remember getting into a car with the real estate agent, and we drove and then pulled up in front of a house for sale, and she said that the family selling it had already moved to the West Coast, so the place was empty.

She said several times, 'It's in move-in condition,' and she seemed very excited about this, and she had weirdly big white teeth, very white, and we went into the house—I think it was over on Burroughs, just over a few blocks from us, a grayish place with the big porch in front.

"We walked through the rooms, and she was explaining various things about the place that I don't recall, but I remember the kitchen had recently been renovated. It was identical to our kitchen here. *Exactly* the same. And I said to her, 'I feel growing enthusiasm.' Those were my words. How weird is that, Rob?"

"Crazy," he said.

"Anyway, we went out from the kitchen to the garden at the back of the house. There was a trellis with grapes growing up and over and a slate terrace with a brick grill and outdoor furniture. It wasn't exactly like our yard but pretty close, and she told me the asking price, which I forget, and I wrote her a check for the entire amount. And then I was back underground again, and when I rode the little silver subway car I came up and it was first light, and I was back in the first neighborhood where the lady had said that he was living with his girlfriend and they were very nice. The one I said 'That is my son' to, who looked at me as though I was completely out of my mind.

"I wanted to see him again, so I hid behind some bushes, watching, and then he came out of his house in workout gear and started jogging toward the river, and all I could think was, 'Yeah, wow, he's got his dad's height and easy gait and my facial features.' And I started jogging after him, leaving plenty of distance so as not to be discovered, and when he jogged back home I waited outside until he emerged a while later, and headed to work. And I followed him into Harvard Square where he caught a Red Line train to the Kendall/MIT stop, where he walked the two blocks to his office. And I decided that I would do this every morning to make sure he made it safely to work.

"In the dream I focused on Thomas being my soulmate, and I was thinking that as much as I love Rob, Thomas was more precious to me than anyone or anything."

Rob wrapped her in his arms and held her gently for some time. "I love you, Jules. And our son was so very lucky to have had you as his mom."

Julia wrote in her journal:

My dearest Thomas, today I walked along the river just as you and I used to do, following the winding banks toward the west, and as I always do, I thought about you. It is now thirty-one years since you passed away, which means that you have been gone nearly three times as long as you lived. It is true that I carry the grief with me at all times, although that's not quite right to say that I carry it as though it is something I do actively. No, it is part of me, the grief, that is, in the way my cells are part of me. The grief occupies space on the double helix embedded within my DNA. It is an essential part of who I am as a human being. It's a balancing act. There is weight to the grief. Grief also has independent power to tap into my energy sources and drain the power for its own purposes. It also translates itself into electrical impulses and makes its way up the vagus nerve all the way to the brain, where it is headquartered. But make no mistake, it lives throughout the body.

Thomas, I must tell you that there is another side to the grief, as well, and this is very, very important, because in my grief are my memories of you and our lives together. I am in the kitchen as I write this, and I have to tell you that when I went into the mud room this morning I was certain that the remnants of that unmistakable odor from your hockey bag hung in the air! It's like nuclear waste—it takes centuries for it go away!

And so, well, now I am crying. I admit that there are certain very specific rec-ollections that make me so happy that I grow sad at what we have lost. But I want to make an important point to you, which is that grief has another side in that it opens opportunities to think about all of the things in your life that were so beautiful and filled with love. It goes without saying that those were the best eleven years of my life. Dad's, too, of course. You made our lives perfect in so many ways. You were the person who completed life for us.

Thomas, I am worried about your father. His cancer has gotten loose in his body and the prognosis is uncertain. He is feeling quite sick lately, not from the cancer itself but from the treatment. So many side effects. He is just not himself and honestly I have never seen him like this. It scares me. If you were here, you would make all the difference. In fact, you do make a difference, because he has told me that when his time comes, even if it is soon, he will welcome the opportunity to cross into the realm over to where you now exist. We don't know exactly what that realm is, of course, but we know without doubt that you are there in some form somewhere because you still have such a presence. And because your life was so beautifully lived. You were our Big Bang. At one moment you did not exist, and seconds later you burst into the world and created an entirely new universe for us. You were everything to us, Tom. Everything.

29

Unthinkable

On a balmy evening in early May, Rob received an email from a faculty colleague with a one-word subject line: UNTHINKABLE. Rob opened the link to an article on the *Politico* website. Never in the history of the Supreme Court had a draft decision been leaked, and it was hard to say which was more shocking to Rob, the fact of the leak or the draft opinion itself, which suggested the court was about to strike down the landmark *Roe v. Wade* decision. Rob took his laptop downstairs to the den, where Julia was watching a movie. He placed the computer on the coffee table facing her.

"What?" she asked.

He had no words. He nodded toward the screen. Julia read for no more than thirty seconds. "Oh, my God, Rob!" she cried, her face flushed. She stood and glared at her husband. "God *damnit*, Rob! You said this wasn't going to happen! Roberts to the rescue, and all that. How can they do this? How does this not shake even your faith, Rob? So, after half a century of constitutional protections, they can just ignore precedent to *remove a constitutional right women have had for fifty years?*"

Rob shook his head and sat down heavily in the chair next to her. "I don't know what to say, Jules," he said.

Julia stood there looking down at him, conflicted, not wanting to make him feel worse, but she couldn't help herself. "The majority just flouts tradition, laughs in the face of precedent. They just denied a state's authority to regulate guns. Never mind that our public squares are routinely killing fields, but then they contradict themselves and rule that states have the authority to regulate women's bodies."

Julia started to cry, then caught herself, eyes narrowed, as she looked accusingly at her husband. "The court has become the tool of the extreme right, out of step with Americans, and what's our recourse? Now what do you think about the great experiment in democracy? A democracy if you can keep it, Rob. *If.*"

She would realize later that she was angry not only for the loss of rights to women but angry as well that the court was possibly proving her skepticism right. In their decades-long quarrel over who was the dreamer and who was the realist, Julia wanted Rob to be right. But perhaps she was the one who saw the ominous signs in a more clear-eyed manner. Maybe the country really was crashing.

After Julia had gone to bed, Rob sat up in his study, a tumbler of scotch on the side table, and reread the full text of the Alito draft. There was something about Alito's tone that bothered him more than anything else. It seemed a mix of I-told-you-so and arrogance. Was it malicious? Maybe in a few spots. There was a burn-down-the-house undertone to it that offended his sense of restraint. He knew it would offend the chief, as well, and that was when Rob recovered his sense of hope. He came, in that moment, to believe that Roberts would figure out a way to navigate a more restrained middle ground.

Rob awoke to the light of dawn slanting through the eastern-facing windows. He had fallen asleep in the chair and woke with his back and neck stiff. He stood and stretched. Yes, Roberts would be able to fix this. He was cheered by this thought. The chief justice wouldn't permit the court to self-destruct. He had saved the day with the Affordable Care Act, and he would do so again with *Roe*.

"I'm sorry, Rob."

Julia was there all of a sudden in her robe, hair disheveled, eyes puffy. "I was venting too much last night. I was just so shocked by the whole thing."

"No, Jules," he said, smiling at her and taking her in his arms, "you have nothing to apologize for. I got your hopes up. But, Jules, it's not over yet. The chief can be counted on. The center will hold."

30

God Keeps His Eye on Us All

In the garden, Rob hung up the phone and turned to Ray, who was in the process of lighting a joint. "Am I wrong to care about this award, Ray? Because I do."

"These symbols matter," said Ray. "And you deserve it. Forty years, brilliant teaching, writing, advocacy. What the fuck else do they want you to do, serve breakfast?"

Darkness had fallen and there was a bright moon. "I look up at the sky, and I think, an award for a teacher, how can it matter in the scheme of things?"

Rob got up and went inside, grabbed two beers, and returned.

"Something else is on your mind, my friend," said Ray. "Lupron?"

"Not due for the next shot until July," Rob said. "But I'm not myself. I'm just kind of . . . I don't know how to describe it. I feel sick all the time on the Lupron and enzalutamide. The whole thing has turned me into a worrier, and you know me, was I ever like this? Anxious, unfocused?"

"Never," said Ray. "Literally never." He started laughing. "You're a freak of nature, Rob! You know, my friend, you've been through brutal times in your life, and you are reacting in a very human way. The cancer business is scary as hell, so much uncertainty."

"I'm afraid for Jules," Rob said. "I just . . . Ray, I have a hard time seeing her without me."

"I know," Ray said, "but there are other options. And regarding Julia, yeah, I have a hard time seeing her without you as well. Hell, yes." Ray leaned forward and placed his hand on Rob's shoulder. "But I don't think she's going to be without you, my friend, at least not for quite a long time. Let me tell you about one of the other potential arrows in the quiver. My former student, Nita Gretzle, is back in the US. I hired her for our faculty. She trained with us, went to NIH, then Novartis in Switzerland where they are doing some radical stuff with targeted therapy, and they have more latitude with human trials than we do. I sent her your file, and I want us all to sit down with her and get her thoughts. Let's consider a plan B."

Rob nodded. "Okay, thank you, I hope, Jesus, honestly, I hope it doesn't come to that. But you have to promise me that if anything happens to me—"

"You mean if you die."

"Yes, or more precisely if I predecease Jules, you have to promise me that you will—"

"Rob, please," said Ray, leaning forward, elbows on his knees, looking intently at his friend. "I already have committed to be there for her forever. And the same is true if she predeceases you. Christ, you *know* I am there for you both."

Rob was a bit tearful. "I do, Ray, I do. I just am not myself these days. All of a sudden I'm fragile. Never before. Never in my life, you know that."

"Cancer messes with the mind," Ray said. "Sometimes the psychological damage is as debilitating as the physical disease itself."

"In the middle of the night, waking up in the old days, I used to think about legal issues," Rob said. "There was comfort in that. Now, though . . ." Rob sighed heavily.

"It's the big questions," Ray said. "The scary ones."

"Exactly," said Rob.

"We're the only species that knows our fate," Ray said. "It's a blessing in a way and a curse. Our entire adult lives we know where this is going, never a doubt. Eventually, all the systems fail, and any sort of life within flickers, goes dark. But then, Rob, comes something else. What is it exactly? Nobody knows. No one ever in the history of mankind has known before the body dies what happens next. Or whether *anything* happens next. But, as you know, I am a believer. I have to be. It was confirmed in my mind while I was in Phu Bai. The suffering of those boys. And I realized while I was there that, like the song goes, *God keeps his eye on us all.* And because I believe that he is a benevolent being, I believe that God has a place for those who have suffered."

"Ray, I know you've told me this, but come on, was that to soothe us in some way after we lost Thomas or is that something . . . I mean, it seems so improbable."

"I get it," said Ray. "Galileo and Newton were men of faith, but it was easier then. You were expected to have faith, almost required. And they did. Newton was emphatic. He said the universe was a beautiful construct guided by an 'intelligent being.' I was with a colleague a few months ago, a Mormon who has unshakable faith. This is a really smart woman from MIT, and she says she has absolutely no difficulty in reconciling science and faith, and part of what she meant by this is that it is deeply unfashionable within science to have faith and, more to the point, to *express* faith. The scientific establishment laughs behind religion's back. I don't like that. The light that we can see from the most powerful telescopes goes back eleven or so billion years ago—not all that long after the Big Bang. What will we learn in the future when we have more powerful instruments? Will we see the explosion itself? We see remnants of it now. But the big question is will we ever see what came *before* the Big Bang. If there was anything. Think about it, Rob. There is a possibility that there was *nothing* before there was something. Or maybe there was something but the something was infinitesimal. And some nuclear force triggered an explosion that caused all of this. Or a benevolent being triggered the forces of nature, and *boom!*"

Ray took another hit on the joint, then carefully extinguished it, setting it on the side table.

"It's humbling," muttered Rob.

"Humbling because we don't know anything about what is beyond the known universe. Places where the laws of physics do not apply. Where there is a God who rules by whatever laws or construct he or she wishes. At MIT there's an oral history of faculty members who were part of the Apollo project, and it shows that virtually all of those mathematicians, engineers, physicists, etc., were *praying* on the day of the launch. The best scientific minds at one of the world's great universities asked God for guidance and inspiration. Maybe we should take note of that. So yes, I absolutely do believe. Peace itself. Grace itself. And I believe Thomas is in that state, Rob. His spirit, no question in my mind, his spirit is in a perfect state of peace and grace and will be for all of eternity. Perfect harmony. And I believe the same is true for all the boys I cared for in Phu Bai. I believe that every name on that granite wall in Washington is in this state."

Ray stopped, looked at the darkened sky and then at Rob. "That's what I believe."

Later that evening, Jerry called Rob. "You saw the editorial, I assume?" Jerry said.

"Read it online."

"Rob, the committee is unanimous, locked in full support of you, and we are going to fight like hell, I want you to know that. You deserve this award. There is no question, and if I have anything to say about it, you will receive this award. If they want to blow the whole thing up next year, fine, blow it up, Molotov cocktail, Weather Underground, Mark Rudd, whatever the hell they want. But not this year. Keep the faith, Rob."

"Will do, Jerry, and thank you."

Jerry and several colleagues had organized a letter-writing campaign on Rob's behalf to the president, supporting Rob as a worthy recipient of the Griswold.

"Everybody wants to sign, Rob!" said Jerry. "All the old guys, anyway. Our vintage, you get the picture. It's sad. And I get that these kids, they make some excellent points. The deck *has* been stacked! Women, Blacks, immigrants, the historical discrimination is a crime, literally. So let's unstack the deck! Let's correct past mistakes. Sign me up! But do not, do not on my watch deprive one of the finest faculty members in this fucking mental institution of what he has earned because he disagrees with your particular orthodoxy or, worse yet, disrespects your *lived experience*."

As he and Jerry were wrapping up the call, one of the medical office phone numbers showed up as a new call on his cell phone. These were perilous technological waters for Rob. How to shift from one call to the other. "Jerry, hang on one sec, please," he said as he managed to cut Jerry off and worried he might have cut off the doctor's office as well. Annoyed, he feverishly pressed buttons on the phone, hoping the doctor's office was still connected, but then suddenly, weirdly, he heard a voice that he did not initially recognize. It was the voice of that *Crimson* reporter, Judith Jansen. Somehow, Rob had inadvertently hit random buttons on his phone that had recorded their conversation.

"Professor Barrow?"

"Speaking."

"Hi, professor, it's Judith Jansen at the Crimson, *and I wonder if you have just a minute?"*

"Ahh, well, Judith, I am a bit distracted at the moment."

"I promise it will be quick, professor. I'm writing a piece about progress on the New York Times *1619 Project. It's the two-year anniversary of the project, and I'm asking faculty members their thoughts about its impact thus far. Any thoughts, professor?"*

"I read the article, of course, some time ago, but, to be honest I haven't given it much thought since then."

"Is it something that you have considered integrating into your courses?"

"In Constitutional Law? Well, never say never, I suppose, but I don't think, at least from what I know about it, I don't think it's quite relevant for what I am teaching these days . . . Judith, I apologize, but I have to run, My wife just got home. Sorry I can't be more helpful. Call any time."

31

Subatomic Particles

Rob marveled at the science. He had come to understand from his reading as well as from discussions with Drs. Chen and Lee along with Ray that men stricken with his disease back before the 1970s had little hope. Medical science at the time had no answers for the proliferation of cancer cells, but since then the subspecialty of radiation oncology had advanced. Big Pharma had become an enemy of the left, but a heroic force for people with various diseases. But while Rob was grateful for the power of Lupron every ninety days, the high daily doses of enzalutamide were driving him nearly mad. The drug grew more punishing over time, crushing his energy and gradually reducing his ability to concentrate. Not even halfway through a walk one day, strolling at a snail's pace, he was forced to rest on a bench while Julia hurried home, got the car, and came to pick him up.

"I'm becoming a zombie," he told Julia.

Rob had a catlike ability to move silently during the night when the side effects of treatment often wrested him from sleep. Rarely did his movements awaken Julia, but they did on this night. He made his way unsteadily downstairs to the library, where he sat glumly trying to read. But he could not.

"Not feeling great, huh?" she said, as she came down and sat in the cushioned chair across from Rob's. She seemed to have aged. She looked so vulnerable.

"I'm not doing this anymore, Jules," he said.

"But Rob . . ." she started.

"I know," he said. "I know."

Julia was about to interrupt to protest, but she caught herself. She knew her man. She knew that this was no way to live.

"I drag myself into class and give distracted lectures. I can't even focus when I read. I'm not taking those pills anymore."

"Rob, really, you—"

"I talked to Ray," Rob said. "He told me to take half the dose starting in the morning."

"Oh, I wish you had told me," she said.

"You were asleep when I talked with him," Rob said. "He sent my whole file to a former student of his, researcher from Novartis. Ray just hired her for his faculty. Dr. Gretzle. He's going to let us know when she can meet."

"We will find another approach," she said. "I am sure of it."

They went back to bed, to restless sleep that was better than nothing. After breakfast, Rob said he was going to go for a short walk.

"I'll go with you," she said.

"Thanks, but I have to think."

He hugged her and headed out the back door, down the flagstone steps and along the walkway to the street. She went out the front door and stood by their gate watching him trudge along. Rob made his way through a series of back streets to the banks of the Charles. Until he reached the river, he'd been too glum to notice what a glorious morning it was on the seventh day of May. He found a bench with a view across to the Boston side of the river and settled down to watch the scullers— they were disciplined and determined people, he thought—move at a slow, steady pace. He was letting his mind wander when, suddenly from his left, the eight-man crew emerged from under a bridge rocketing west at what seemed, compared to the single scullers, an astonishing speed. Eight fit young men committed to a collaborative enterprise. Rob marveled at it. In less than a minute, the boat had disappeared in the distance, headed upriver. Rob gazed across toward Boston. What a lovely city it was—centuries-old bricks and mortar and nature and institutions that collectively cradled the city's accumulated traditions and wisdom. It really was a place where people with particular types of brains were drawn. He liked it, was comfortable here.

It was a very unusual time in Rob Barrow's life, and not only because he had cancer. He never recalled being disappointed in himself the way he was now. He had committed the cardinal sin of reacting to it with emotion rather than reason. Not that an emotional reaction was unwarranted. His life was at stake, after all. But for Rob, reason had been the North Star that had guided him throughout his life. As he sat on the bench watching high clouds drift by, feeling the soothing spring air, he resolved to get a grip. The best antidote for all these swirling emotions, he thought, was to try to focus on gratitude. Rob knew the power of gratitude. It had been the force he had harnessed in the years since Thomas. *I am blessed*, he thought. He had so much in his life to be thankful for! Julia, Ray, work he loved, friends and colleagues. And, of course, Thomas. He had a son. And perhaps, if Rob's time was coming to an end, he would be guided by the spirit of his son, perhaps even reunited with him! He thought of their home, their refuge, where the most joyous times happened; where Thomas had lived and grown and embraced life. *If only they could have switched places.* Rob had often thought about that, and he realized that if God was a negotiator, he/she might have allowed for switches at the time of death. If Rob had died back then on August 15, 1991, Thomas would now be forty-two years old. Oh, how Rob wished this were true. If Rob had been able to trade places with his son, what would Thomas's life have been like? This was a question Rob carried with him at all times, no matter where he went or what he was doing. He knew that Julia and Thomas would have mourned his death, missed him, but moved on. Natural progression. Rob took a certain satisfaction in thinking about Julia and Thomas together, closer than ever after Rob's passing, Julia guiding Thomas, watching over him, protecting him, measuring how much freedom to grant him through his teenage years. Rob smiled as he thought about what he felt sure would have been one of the biggest days of Thomas's life—when the listing of those making the school's varsity hockey squad was posted just prior to Thanksgiving weekend. Making the team had been so important to Thomas that he now felt nervous worrying about whether his son would have made the roster had he lived. *How crazy am I*, Rob thought.

When he arrived home, he went upstairs and gathered several vials of painkillers and sedatives and tossed them into the kitchen trash.

"What are you doing?" Julia asked, surprised. "Don't you need those?"

Rob shook his head. "That's not me," he said.

32

Thirty-One-Year Secret

Thunder had been rolling in the distance as Ray, Julia, and Rob gathered in the garden when a lightning strike chased them into the kitchen. Ray had come over that morning with documents he wanted Rob and Julia to see.

"Let's be very careful with this," he said. "We really don't know what it has to do with anything, but I wanted to follow up. I told you about my old pal Myron, right? His friend was able to access this document." Ray did not tell them that the document had been hand-delivered to his office out of fear it was too sensitive to email. Nor did he tell Rob and Julia that Myron's Israeli friend told him that after multiple probes they had been able to penetrate the hospital's security systems.

Ray placed a document on the table. Julia and Rob read it together.

"What's this about?" Julia asked, clearly puzzled.

"Mary Meagher Moore was one of the nurses involved in caring for Thomas. This is a nondisclosure agreement between Mary Meagher Moore and the hospital. Personnel file shows seventeen years as a nurse, retired a few years after signing the agreement."

"Sorry," Julia said. "I'm not getting it. Why secrecy?"

"These sorts of contracts are not done casually," said Rob. "Two possibilities. There's something the hospital does not want us to know, or there is something we *do* know that is not of particular note to us but is to another party, something the institution feels would be somehow sensitive in public."

"Right," said Ray, "and it may be absolutely nothing of interest to us, and that is probably the case. But I want to follow up on it to make sure."

"But, I mean, these contracts are hardly routine, correct?" Julia asked.

"Not routine," Ray replied, "but more common than they should be. The hospital projects an image, but it's like any other large organization. It's about self-preservation, and if that requires deception, deceit, no problem. All these companies and organizations are essentially the same—the Pentagon, the mega hospitals, corporations, media, etc. It's all about them. Collateral damage, hey, sorry guys, cost of doing business."

"Does the nurse still live in the area?" Julia asked.

"West Roxbury," Ray said. "I have the address."

"I'll go talk with her," said Julia.

"But what could make her violate the terms of the NDA if she has a financial stake?" Rob asked.

"Mother to mother," said Julia.

A new storm approached the area and intensified overnight. The next morning Rob drove carefully, avoiding pooled water in pockets along the West Roxbury Parkway. The section where Mary Moore lived stretched to the farthest reaches of the city boundaries. It was an area of three-bedroom homes clustered closely together, populated largely by city workers, cops, firemen, and others who, through their own work or pluck or connection to a local politician, were able to gain a city job and the security and pension that came with such positions. Rob eased the car along the side of the street just shy of Mary's home. As Julia turned to him, about to open the door, Rob said, "Good luck."

She smiled. "I'm glad you're with me, Rob, but I have a feeling that it's some oddball thing, technical in nature, and I'll be out the door in ten minutes."

Rob nodded. "Run between the drops."

She got out of the car and opened her umbrella, holding on against the gusts. The white clapboard house had paint peeling, half a gutter hanging from a corner of the roof, a wrought-iron railing on the right that had long since broken off. Julia pressed the doorbell, and a doughy woman with thinning hair and a kind face answered the door. Mary Meagher Moore had been one of the five daughters of a Boston police officer and his wife, who worked as a school nurse. She married Gerard Moore, a Boston fireman, and they had three children, two boys and a girl. Mary and Gerard were a popular couple. They were regular attendees at Mass, volunteered at church functions, and worked diligently to raise their children well.

"Mrs. Moore?" Julia asked.

"Yes," Mary Moore said.

"Mrs. Moore, my name is Julia Barrow."

Mary Moore stepped back, hand to her mouth, eyes wide. "Dear God," she said. "Why . . . what . . . ?"

"Mrs. Moore, I would like to talk with you privately, if I may," said Julia.

Mary hesitated, then said, "Oh, I don't know, I mean . . ." She seemed stunned.

"May I come in out of the rain?"

Mary admitted her to the house, where Julia set aside her umbrella.

Mary stood in the entry, apparently not wanting Julia to get any deeper into her home.

"If we could talk for a minute, Mrs. Moore," Julia said. "As a mother like yourself, it would mean a lot to me."

Mary considered this and then nodded. She led Julia down a hallway to a kitchen at the back of the house. There was a worn linoleum floor, an ersatz walnut table in the corner, a Formica countertop on either side of the sink, and knotty pine cabinets lining the walls. It had the air of something not old exactly, but tired. Mary was a heavy woman, brunette, pasty skin with a double chin. She wore a loose-fitting top and sweatpants.

Julia followed Mary's lead and took a seat at the kitchen table.

"I apologize," said Mary as she sat down. "I am very nervous, and I don't hide it well. I'm retired now. Putting this old place up for sale. My kids are grown, my husband passed a number of years ago."

"I'm sorry to hear that," said Julia. "Where will you go?"

"My sister's on the Cape," said Mary. "I'll be with her. We're close."

Mary looked around the room as though reminding herself what it looked like. "There were a lot of good years here," she continued. Mary sat back in the chair and struggled to take in a deep breath. Anxiety was fighting to get the best of her.

"How many children do you have?" Julia asked.

"Three," she said, "my oldest is married, three children of her own. She's a nurse also. Then my middle one, a son, he's out in Norwood, a cop. My youngest boy is down the Cape, a school aide."

"Grandchildren?" Julia asked with a smile.

"Oh, good lord, yes," she said, the hint of a smile. "My greatest blessings, I will tell you."

"Wonderful," said Julia.

Both women fell silent, uncertain where to go beyond small talk.

"I have had a very difficult time with this going back to that night when your son passed, may he rest in peace," Mary said, making the sign of the cross. "I had hoped to talk with you years ago, but the lawyers make things complicated."

"The lawyers?" Julia asked. "You mean, related to this?" At which point Julia placed the document from the hospital system indicating the existence of a private pact between the hospital system and Mary.

Mary appeared confused. "How . . . where did this come from?"

"Someone gave it to me," said Julia. "I wonder whether you could share with me why you were asked to sign a privacy agreement?"

Mary drew a deep breath and bowed her head. She mumbled something to herself. "They were vicious."

"Can you tell me how it happened that they made you sign this?" Julia asked.

Mary hesitated.

"Mrs. Moore, put yourself in my position," Julia said. "Please, put yourself in my shoes and talk with me, one mother to another. Over thirty years ago I lost my only child, the most precious thing in my life. All I am asking is that you explain to me what is behind this piece of paper."

Mary remembered it clearly: *A crowded room, doctors, nurses, techs, packed around the child's bed. Mary tucked in the corner. She could see the child's parents stood, paralyzed by fear and shock. Boy's mother turned and vomited into the metal sink. And then came the moment when the doctors and nurses parted, allowing the parents to go to their child. It was at this point that Mary left the room.*

And then Mary's demeanor shifted as she sat up straighter, eyes no longer downcast. *Yes, of course. This is what I must do.*

"A report was filled out for the coroner by Dr. McNamara, the attending," Mary said. "I wrote the nursing report. I told the truth, Mrs. Barrow." She leveled her gaze at Julia. "I told the truth," she repeated. "Dr. McNamara lied. But I was the one called on the carpet the next day by a man I didn't know, who said he was a lawyer for the hospital. McNamara was there, too. He was a bully. None of the nurses liked him. I was shaking, I was so frightened. I was sick about what had happened. They had been telling us for years, 'We're all human, mistakes are made, and when an error occurs we report it and we get back on the learning and improvement track.' That's what they called it, the cheery little ladies from the central improvement office who came by once every few months to say *do it this way, do it that way*. I thought I was being fired on the spot. My heart was beating so hard. I was worried because my family, my husband and me, we *needed* this job, the income. I started crying. I couldn't help it. McNamara said to me, 'Mary, do not allow one mistake to ruin your career. Lose your job, have to testify in a courtroom, get sued, maybe lose your home?' I was hysterical, like, *Oh, my God, no, no, no.* I was in shock," she said, looking at Julia imploringly. "All I could think about was my husband and children."

Mary sighed. She looked at Julia, her eyes wet, sad.

"They had papers on the table; one was the nursing report I had written. The other was a new nursing report that I did not write. The new version had a space for my signature at the bottom. It listed the cause of death as a seizure. I read that and I looked at Dr. McNamara and I said, 'But Dr. McNamara, you know that is not true.'"

Julia was stunned. "Not true? What do you mean?"

"He had written that the cause of your son's death was a seizure and—" Suddenly, Mary Moore froze. She looked as though she had just witnessed a terrible accident, a wreck, bodies everywhere. Her eyes got very wide and she stared at Julia, absorbing the reality that she found so incomprehensible. *Dr. McNamara had never told them,* she thought. *He never told the parents what happened.* Mary Moore sat quite still, fighting to calm her heart rate, working to clear her mind so that she would find the right words for this mother who for so many years had been deceived. Mary had always believed the nondisclosure agreement was so that the truth of the matter would not be known publicly, but she had also believed that Dr. McNamara would have met privately with the parents and told them the truth.

"Excuse me for one moment, Mrs. Barrow," Mary said. "There is something I would like you to see." Mary went upstairs in the house and returned a few minutes later and handed a sheet of paper to Julia.

"At the end of my shift that morning, right after I wrote up the nursing report, I printed out a copy for myself. It was a terrible night. I really believe I was in shock when it happened, and I was just moving by instinct. This is what I wrote. This is what happened to your child.

This is why I was forced to sign the secrecy papers. You can keep that, Mrs. Barrow, but I want you to hear from me in my words exactly what happened that night. And I want to tell you I live with regret every day of my life.

"In the pharmacy area at the end of the hallway it was chaos," she continued. "It's always chaos. Some of the nurses from upstairs on the adult floor were coming down to our pharmacy to pick up their meds. Dr. McNamara wrote an order, which I went to fill. Eight hundred milligrams liquid Motrin, which in adults does not require a script, but in pediatrics it does. I got the one with your son's name on it, went back to his room, and placed it in the IV. The medication had been mislabeled in central pharmacy. The packet with your son's name on it actually contained a prescription for an adult patient on the floor above. I was supposed to cross-check two things, name and medication. I did not check the second and what I administered to your son, Mrs. Barrow, it was an adult dose of morphine. That is why he passed away."

The world was suddenly out of focus, spinning like one of those pinwheels on the boardwalk, blue and red and orange and yellow and pink, round and round in the breeze and then, with a slight shift in wind direction, spinning in the other direction, the colors bright and then blurry, and Julia got up from the chair and staggered to the side, bracing herself on the counter, Mary moving to support her. A cuckoo clock Julia had not noticed announced the time, and it seemed deafeningly loud, so piercing and cruel that it hurt Julia's ears, hurt her head, and she felt pressure behind her eyes as though something had gone very wrong in her brain. She went outside into the downpour and walked slowly down the cinderblock steps and shuffled to the car, but then she stopped and stood still, her shoulders slumped, head bent forward, arms dangling by her side. Rob got out of the car, and Julia did not acknowledge him. She stood motionless, her face expressionless, her clothing soaked by the rain, hair matted against her head.

Rob took hold of her and looked at her eyes, lifeless. "Jules, what . . . ?"

She took his hand and led him back into the house and through the hallway into the kitchen where Mary Moore was still standing, and she picked up the nursing report Mary Moore had written on the morning of Thomas's death and she handed it to Rob and she went back outside and stood for a while in the rain, her body slumped against the car.

33

Shattered

It was end of days. Energy, vitality, beauty, light, hope, joy—all drained from their world. How could the truth of their son's death lie buried in legal files for so long? How could anyone, any institution, resort to the cruelty of withholding the truth from grieving parents? For Julia and Rob there was no solace. Their home was a lifeless place, with two people who seemed unable to speak or do anything other than sit staring—in the kitchen, the library, Rob in his office, Julia in hers. Sitting for hours on end, staring, nothingness. Ray stationed himself in the kitchen when they were in other rooms, and when one or both of them came into the kitchen Ray quietly moved to the library. This was a new kind of shock, he thought. A fresh detonation with Julia and Rob in the midst of the blast radius.

"She hasn't said much for three days," Rob said to Ray. "We're both lost, Ray. Too brutal. Normal processing impossible. Sit down and try to read a book. *Not possible*. Have a coherent discussion that lasts more than five minutes. *Cannot be done*. All the essential mechanisms—physical, emotional, spiritual . . . do not work. There is no order. Things fall apart, the center cannot hold, mere anarchy is loosed upon us."

Rob's skin was pale, eyes puffy, bruised. He had not shaved in a few days. His shirt had sweat stains under the arms, and Ray noticed that it was the same shirt he had been wearing for about a week. And it was clear that he had not bathed.

"You know what it feels like, Ray? It feels like death. Or something just before death. Forget the white light and a silvery pathway. *Fuck that.* This is all darkness and suffering, and I tell you, my friend, and I would never say this to Jules obviously, but I wish the cancer had killed me so that I would never know the truth." Rob looked away and began to cry, heaving for breath. He leaned forward in the chair and covered his face with both hands, shaking his head. Ray knew enough to say nothing. What could be said in a moment such as this, at a time when a good man was suffering in such a way? Ray knew that his presence conveyed the simple message: *I am here for you. I am with you and Jules, and I will always be with you and Jules, and, somehow, we will find a way forward.* They had survived Thomas's death. They would survive this, Ray knew. He sat silently and he would remain there, silent, for minutes, hours, days, weeks, whatever it took.

Ray stood guard over his friends for ten days before he felt comfortable leaving for a couple of hours. He called Mike Dwyer and said he had some bad news he needed to deliver in person, and Mike told him to come to his home. When Ray arrived, Mike was at the front door to greet him.

"I don't like bad news," Mike said. "So no preliminaries. Just tell me."

Seated in Mike's home office, Ray told the story of learning about the NDA signed by Mary Moore, and of Julia going to her home and learning the truth.

"Jesus God," Mike said when he heard about the morphine mistakenly administered to Thomas. Mike bowed his head and made the sign of the cross. He sat trying to absorb the enormity of this tragedy.

"And they hid it all this time," Mike said. Mike had the kindest face, open, ruddy, the face of an Irish farmer in an old village. He exuded warmth. But now his face was twisted into a mask of pain.

"This happened on my watch," he said to Ray. "Under my chairmanship."

Ray was quiet. Before leaving his medical school office, he had clicked on the hospital's mission statement and printed out a copy, which he handed to Mike.

Our mission is to deliver leading-edge patient care in a safe, compassionate environment and to alleviate physical and emotional suffering of our patients and their family members. We pledge to teach and learn in a transparent environment where we identify and adopt the very best medical practices.

Mike read it to himself, then looked up at Ray like he had seen a ghost. He looked back down at the page and shook his head slowly in disgust.

"A safe, compassionate environment," said Ray, speaking in the monotone of a prosecutor outlining the charges in a murder trial.

"Alleviate the suffering, physical and emotional, of our patients and their family members," Ray continued.

His gaze was level, focused on Mike.

"Teach and learn in a transparent environment," Ray said. He shook his head. "It's all a lie. It's all deception, Mike. When push comes to shove, they protect themselves."

"We've done an awful lot of good for people over the years, Ray," Mike quickly countered.

"Absolutely true, but no excuse for this," Ray said. "You knew the train was off the tracks, Mike. That's why you commissioned RAND, and if those pompous asses would drop their lawsuit or we get a thumbs-up from the court, we can shine a light, get it out there where it belongs."

Mike got up, and Ray followed him out to the garden where they walked slowly, surrounded by the wonderful earthy scent and the buzzing bees, the tranquility of nature. How perfect some things were, Ray thought, and how utterly imperfect were others. They were halfway around the loop of the garden when Mike stopped suddenly.

"Ray, is there any chance the Barrows would allow the story to be made public? I understand nothing could be more intensely personal, but something like this, maybe it could break the dam."

"How so?"

"If, and I know it's a big if, but if the Barrows were willing to have the story made public in some way, perhaps a newspaper article, then we could say, *And oh, by the way, in addition to this, our own doctors are trying to prevent publication of a RAND report that highlights precisely this problem. A document we believe could lead to improvements in safety and possibly prevent tragedies like this from happening in the future.*"

Ray thought about this. What would Jules think? How about Rob? Finally he said, "Mike, if Julia and Rob could do anything to prevent this from happening to another child, to another mother and father, they would do it. No doubt in my mind."

Mike Dwyer called Steve Berubien that night. He had known Steve for decades and they had developed a mutual trust. Both were Boston fixtures, Mike as chair of the important community boards—cultural and medical—and as a leader in the city's financial community, while Steve had long been a top reporter in the city. Steve was in his mid-seventies, still grinding away, writing fascinating articles about various obscure theories of who might have stolen the paintings from the Isabella Stewart Gardner Museum, the biggest art heist in history.

"This must be important," Steve said as he answered.

"Very," Mike replied. He then summarized the situation.

"Which hospital was the child at?" Steve asked.

Mike told him.

"You are telling me that the child's death was caused by hospital error, that it was covered up for years, and it was at *your hospital*? Are you serious?"

"I am."

"Why would you reveal such a thing?"

"Because we need to put better safety protocols in place. I want to grab our doctors and nurses and everyone else by the neck and have them figure out a way to prevent this from ever happening to another child, to another family, ever."

Was Steve interested in writing the story? Mike asked. But he knew the answer already. Mike set ground rules. "The individual at the hospital who was principally involved in the mistake cannot be in any way, shape, or form identified in the article."

"Can I interview the individual on background?"

"Absolutely not," said Mike. "That's a deal-breaker."

"I need you on the record," Steve said, fully expecting pushback.

"Done," said Mike.

"And the parents?"

"The mother will sit down with you. Tomorrow."

"Wow," said Steve. "This really is important to you isn't it? But, Mike, let's roll the tape back here a minute," said Steve. "You are synonymous with the hospital and have been forever. Your mother's name is on one of the biggest buildings. You've given I don't know how many tens of millions of dollars to this place that you obviously love. Why would you want a piece in the paper that reveals a tragic mistake and subsequent cover-up? It makes absolutely no sense."

"Why?" said Mike. "*Because* I love the place."

34

Julia Tells Their Story

Late the following afternoon Steve Berubien arrived and was greeted at the front door by Julia. She wore dark gray wool pants, a cream silk top, and a black cashmere sweater for the interview while Steve was dressed in a sport jacket and tie. It was a cool, breezy day and she had a jacket handy if needed. Steve Berubien arrived exactly on time at 10:00 a.m. in a sport jacket and tie. Julia led him through the kitchen and out to the garden.

"I made us some coffee, if you like, Steve," she said.

"Black please, thank you, I'll help." He got up from his chair and followed Julia into the kitchen and carried his own cup back outside. He stood at his chair looking out over the property, a broad smile on his face. "What a beautiful place you have here, Mrs. Barrow," he marveled. "This is where you raised your son?"

"Yes."

Steve was beaming. "God bless him, what a perfect home for a child! Such a place to play with your friends, cowboys and Indians, hiding places. It's so special," he said. Julia was drawn in by his warmth and authenticity; it helped her relax in his presence.

He sat back, drinking coffee, asking her about the neighborhood and did this famous Harvard professor live nearby, how about so-and-so?

Finally, he said, "Mrs. Barrow, I want to say two things before I turn on my recorder and we start. The first and most important is that I am very sorry that you suffered the tragedy of losing your son. And the second is that I admire your courage and appreciate your willingness to share this very difficult story with me."

With that, Steve switched on his recorder and fell silent, and she told the story of learning so many years later the truth of what had happened. She was so calm, so precise in the telling that only infrequently did he interrupt to ask for an additional clarification or explanation.

The *Globe* ran the story on the following Sunday. In addition, Steve wrote a sidebar to the main article focused on Mike Dwyer and the extraordinary circumstance in which the chairman of the board of the hospital was criticizing his own department heads for blocking the RAND report.

"I think what they are doing is self-interest bordering on the unethical," Mike was quoted as saying. "If these six doctors find themselves pledging their allegiance to themselves rather than the patients, they should go work somewhere else. We had a top-shelf study done by RAND and the whole point was to improve safety, and RAND did a fantastic job. We were ready to publish, the *New England Journal* wants to publish, but six of our own doctors, I am ashamed to say, prevented it. This RAND report, which I have read very carefully, highlights our faults and helps define a pathway for improvement. If the tragedy suffered by the Barrows doesn't move these doctors to accept change, then nothing will."

The day the articles were published, Mike Dwyer phoned Ray and asked for the Barrows' home address. "I'd like to apologize to them in person," Mike said. "Would they be okay with that? Maybe you could meet me there and introduce me to them?"

"Good for you Mike," said Ray, who phoned Julia to give her a heads-up that Mike was on his way.

Ray was waiting when Mike pulled into the driveway. "How are they doing?" Mike asked.

"Obviously, they have been through the mill, but these are two exceptionally strong people and they have a great bond in their marriage," said Ray. "And the calls have begun to pour in from friends and long-lost acquaintances offering support does make a difference."

Ray led Mike around back to the garden and introduced him to Julia and Rob. "I want to thank you for what you have done and for what you said in the article," Julia said to him.

"You beat me to it," Mike said. "It is I who should be thanking you. What you have been through is unthinkable. I want to thank you for your willingness to tell your story, because I believe this will make a difference. But if you don't mind, maybe you could tell me a little bit about Thomas. I've heard from Ray about what a great kid he was."

Julia smiled. "I love talking about our son," she said, "but it is very rare for anyone to ask about him. They hear that you lost your child some years ago and most people say sorry and then shut down for a moment and move on to another topic. Golf, politics, anything but having to listen to the recollections of such a parent. So he was a little wild man, really. Most of all he loved the people in his life, his mom and dad, his uncle Ray, his friends, most of his teachers, his teammates. He said once, and I think this says a lot about who Thomas was, he said on the way home after hockey practice one evening, 'I'm not going to be the best player on any team, but I want to be the best teammate on every team I play on.' That was Thomas to a T."

"Wow," Mike said. "What a remarkable sense of himself at such a young age. He would have been a leader for sure."

"He really loved—" Julia broke down under the weight of it all. The loss of her boy, the years of grieving, of missing him it seemed every second of every day and every night. The new revelations. The idea that he might have suffered terribly in his final minutes of life—it all came crashing down on her in the moment, and she simply could not go on.

When Julia stood, the men did the same, and she wrapped her arms around Mike Dwyer in a tight embrace.

"Thank you," she managed through her tears as she headed into the house and up to her room with Rob following after her.

Ray and Mike walked slowly out the flagstone pathway leading to the driveway. They stood together in the sunshine in silence for a couple of minutes.

"I think we can do something," Mike said. "Mrs. Barrow, Julia, and I. People might listen to us. I got a call this morning from an old friend—he's president of CBS now. He said he was blown away by the *Globe* articles and asked whether it might be possible for Julia and me to be interviewed together by CBS News, or one of their shows. He said, 'Mike, do you realize the power of the message you convey together? Independently, you both tell compelling stories, but put the two *Globe* articles together with a skilled interviewer, it would be riveting.'"

Mike paused. "I think he's right, but I also can see how brutal this is for her, for Julia and Rob. Think about it, Ray, and, only if you think it is appropriate, maybe raise the issue with her. See whether she might be willing to do something like that."

"Mike," Ray said, "if it could save one child, prevent one parent from suffering . . ." Ray paused, then added: "Count them in."

35

A Generous Spirit

R ob had made an appointment to sit down with Andy and Judith. While many of the students had left for the summer, seniors remained for commencement, which Judith would be covering two days hence. When Rob arrived at the newspaper office, Andy led him to the conference room, where Judith sat stone-faced, clearly annoyed by Rob's presence.

"I would like you to listen to something," he said. With that, he took out his cell phone and pressed a button.

"Professor Barrow?"

"Speaking."

"Hi, professor, it's Judith Jansen at the Crimson, *and I wonder if you have just a minute?"*

"Ahh, well, Judith, I am a bit distracted at the moment."

"I promise it will be quick, professor. I'm writing a piece about progress on the New York Times *1619 Project. It's the two-year anniversary of the project, and I'm asking faculty members their thoughts about its impact thus far. Any thoughts, professor?"*

"I read the article, of course, some time ago, but, to be honest I haven't given it much thought since then."

"Is it something that you have considered integrating into your courses?"

"In Constitutional Law? Well, never say never, I suppose, but I don't think, I don't think, at least from what I know about it, I don't think it's quite relevant for what I am teaching these days. . . . Judith, I apologize, but I have to run. My wife just got home. Sorry I can't be more helpful. Call any time."

Andy and Judith sat stunned.

"Professor Barrow," Andy began, "I . . . I am at a loss. I don't know what to say. Obviously I had had no idea there was such a recording."

"It was quite inadvertent," Rob said. "I am not all that familiar with my phone beyond the basics. I didn't know it had a recording capability or how to use it. But apparently, in my fumbling, I hit the record button when Judith called me."

"I'm just speechless," Andy said. "I don't even know where to begin."

Judith Jansen had gone pale.

"Here is the article where I am quoted as saying the *Times* project is 'irrelevant,'" Rob said. "It reads: 'Professor Robert Barrow was clearly uncomfortable discussing the topic. He dismissed the 1619 initiative as "irrelevant" and abruptly ended the brief phone interview with the *Crimson*.'"

"Here is a transcript of the recording," Rob said, passing sheets of paper to Andy and Judith. "And if you look at what is written in the *Crimson* and compare it with the recording, clearly your reporting is false. Central to all of this, of course, is the word 'irrelevant.' Do you see in the transcript that I use that word at all?"

"No," said Andy.

Judith shook her head.

"Okay," Rob said, "I'm now going to play the brief audio clip one more time." He pressed the button, and they listened. When the recording ended, he continued.

"The article said, and I am quoting from the *Crimson* now: 'Professor

Robert Barrow was clearly uncomfortable discussing the topic.' Listening to the tape, does it sound as though I'm 'clearly uncomfortable'?"

"No," said Andy.

"And listening to the interview, does it sound as though I 'abruptly ended' the interview?

"No, professor," said Andy. This was torture for her. She couldn't help but think of Rafik all but insisting that she not use the word 'irrelevant' in the pieces they wrote unless they had it on tape.

"So is it fair to say that the article—in the portion related to me—was substantially if not entirely false?"

"Definitely," said Andy.

Judith at this point seemed catatonic. She not only was not speaking, she seemed unable to do so.

"Let's move to the 'Griswold Shame' editorial," Rob said. "Again the 'irrelevant' quote, which we have established beyond doubt is false. Let's focus on the key sentence in the editorial, at least from my perspective. It states that the comment that we all agree I did not make 'is, at the very least tone deaf, but, worse than that, it is racist.'"

Rob sat back in his chair, hands folded on his midsection.

He let the silence settle. "In this political environment, as you both know very well, particularly on campuses, there is bloodlust for anyone who dares to challenge the orthodoxy. But the wholly unsupported accusation here is far worse. To be accused of being racist is to disqualify that individual from serious conversation or debate about American law. I never really gave much thought to my reputation. I just went along through the years very happy, and grateful by the way, to be able to teach, and write, and litigate constitutional issues. If you had said to me before these articles, *Hey Rob, how would you describe your reputation?* I would have said, *Yeah, solid, pretty damn solid.* But then to have people come along and try to tear it down, I thought, Wow, very easy to see how a reputation earned over forty years can be tarnished over forty days. I'm older now. It matters to me. I don't know why you did this. I don't know your motivation. I am going to assume good faith on your part, Andy. On your part, Judith, I am going to assume you got confused. Easy enough to do making dozens of calls to faculty members. Perhaps you jumped to an erroneous conclusion. You got stuck with your story. You lied and couldn't figure out how to extricate. And I suppose, you assumed that it was okay to continue with the lie because, after all, I am an old, privileged white male and I probably hold the sorts of views that you ascribe to me."

"Professor Barrow, I'm ashamed and embarrassed, and I want to apologize to you," said Judith. "I was rushing somewhat to get the interviews done. After you and I talked, I realized I hadn't turned on my recorder. I was looking at my notes after we talked, and I *thought* you had said the word 'irrelevant,' but it wasn't in my notes. And I know that's not what I told you, Andy, and I am so sorry for letting you down when you really, really trusted me, believed in me. I think because you are who you are, professor, as you say, a privileged white male, that I just completely convinced myself that *yeah, of course he said it*. And at the tail end of the piece, I don't know, I just wasn't focused. I apologize to you, professor, and to you Andy. I just . . . I don't even know what to say."

Andy leaned forward, elbows on the table, head in her hands. Silence settled upon the room until Judith could be heard softly crying. Finally, Andy spoke. "Professor, I will write a correction, apology, explanation," she said. "Tell the story of what happened, put it on page one. We will own up to everything. I will write it today and publish tomorrow. I will include any and all quotations you want included, however critical you wish to be. I'm ashamed."

Rob was silent for a long moment, considering this. "I appreciate that, Andy, and if you feel you must do that, then you must. I hope you will not. I hope there is another way. I say this out of concern for the two of you. There is a level of vitriol these days, savagery, when people make mistakes. How old are you, Judith, if I may ask?"

"Nineteen."

"Andy?"

"I am twenty-two, professor," she replied.

Rob smiled. He extended his arms wide as though about to receive an embrace.

"How wonderful!" he said. "You have your whole lives ahead of you! Who knows where you will go or what you will do. I had decided last night to demand a full correction, clarification, explanation, etc. Every detail. Hang the bastards by their thumbs! But when I woke up this morning I realized that would be humiliating to you both. And maybe even, who knows, have an effect on your career paths."

He took a deep breath and frowned. "I assume, Andy, that as editor you will figure out appropriate discipline for Judith, whatever that may be. But I ask that we keep the existence of this bit of audio confidential. And further, I ask only for a very brief 'amplification,' I would call it, stating that recent articles erroneously implied sentiments of racism to Professor Barrow that were in error. Something along those lines. Something unobtrusive, yet that rebuts the accusations of racism and remains in the archive attached to those articles. And pretty soon everyone will be on to something else, the record will have been corrected, and you can still bash me as the wrong choice for Griswold."

Rob laughed as though he found such a prospect immensely amusing.

"So is what I am asking something that can be done, Andy?"

"Professor, I'm speechless," she said. "If that is how you want the situation resolved, that is how we will resolve it, but I have to say I'm flabbergasted at your generosity. May I ask why?"

Rob shook his head and stood to go. He plunged his hands in his pants pockets and looked down at the table for a moment. "Because I'm afraid mistakes in this new extremist culture are too costly," he said. "Because you will be better journalists because of it, and, this I really hope, maybe a bit kinder. Small acts of kindness and generosity bring much joy to life."

36

Smash the Patriarchy

That evening, Ray met for drinks with his old friend William Mercer Calhoun, the Harvard president. Bill had long been a prominent economist, often called to Washington to consult on monetary policy. He was a thoughtful, affable man, gangly, and a bit awkward. He had been raised in rural Tennessee—his father a tractor repair man, his mother a seamstress—gone to the University of Tennessee, completed his BS in physics in two years, and gone on to complete graduate work in economics at MIT before joining the Harvard faculty. His appointment as president had been celebrated for his ability to get along with almost anyone and for his thoughtful, reflective manner. Over time, of course, his popularity dipped a bit because he had to use a word that faculty, staff, and students did not like to hear: *No. No, we don't have the budget. No, we don't think that's a good idea.* And most recently, *No, we do not think it wise to replace the university's American history curriculum with the 1619 curriculum designed by the* New York Times.

Rob and Bill Calhoun had become friends some years before Bill's ascension to the presidency, when Bill's mother fell ill in Tennessee. Doctors at the community hospital nearby were uncertain what the cause of her condition might be, and Bill asked Ray whether he might help. Ray got on the next plane south, examined Mrs. Calhoun, reviewed her records, and had her flown by medical ambulance to Boston, where she was admitted to Beacon Hospital. Ray put a team together, and one of the oncologists discovered that Mrs. Calhoun was suffering from a rare form of blood cancer. A new treatment, by no means guaranteed, worked beautifully, and Mrs. Calhoun was restored to health and lived for many years. Bill's gratitude to Ray was boundless. They became close friends.

"Rob's been through hell, Bill," Ray said as they gathered in a private alcove within the Faculty Club, a private preserve within a private preserve, hushed tones, the smell of wood polish and old money. Early evening, a time to relax. Each man enjoying a Manhattan straight up, served by white-jacketed waitstaff.

"Tough time for Rob," Ray said. "Metastatic prostate cancer."

"Jesus," said Calhoun, wincing.

"And now this *Crimson* smear," said Ray.

"Yeah, I saw that," said Bill. "Bad juju. Accuse someone in print of being a racist and, *whoops, sorry!*" Bill shook his head. "They should be tarred and feathered."

"Bill, you know Rob," Ray said. "He is as fine a man as I have ever known. And you know what he and Julia have been through."

"The ultimate nightmare," said Bill. " I cannot even contemplate it, Ray." He shook his head.

"Look," said Ray, "I like Pauline, but she's got a thing against Rob. It annoys her that she cannot bring him to heel. He won't genuflect at the 1619 altar."

"Issue du jour," said Calhoun. "The editors will graduate and new kids will have new issues to be enraged about next year. Their capacity for moral outrage is limitless. But you know, Ray, these kids we have, Jesus, they're good kids. By and large, they are something special. Their ambitions are lofty, as they damn well ought to be. Noble intentions. Are they full of themselves? Arrogant? In spades!" said Bill, laughing. "But they're *kids*! Ten years from now, twenty years from now, look around the world—these same kids saying stupid things today will be doing work that *matters*—in science, government, international affairs, literature, journalism, you name it. They will do good stuff, and some of them will do truly *great stuff.*"

The president of the university signaled to a nearby waiter, and two fresh drinks were promptly produced.

"I got the seniors finishing up, and they have been a hell of a good class. A pain in the ass here and there, but smart, constructive. And likeable, I have to say." Bill raised his glass. "To the kids," he said.

Ray did the same.

"I'm worried about Pauline fucking up the Griswold for Rob," said Ray.

Bill gave Ray an are-you-kidding-me look. "Ray, *please*," said Bill. "Rob will be awarded the Griswold. Period, end of story."

"How can you be so sure?" Ray asked.

Bill laughed. "Because I have final say on the matter. We'll have a small dinner where I will present the award to Rob. Nothing ostentatious. Discreet."

"And the disciplinary process Pauline said she would subject Rob to?" Ray asked.

"Jesus," said Bill. "It was, what's a good word? *Tabled*, maybe." Bill smiled. "Yeah, it was *tabled.*" He raised his glass.

"What about Pauline?" Ray said. "How will she handle this?"

"She will voice her disapproval, and I suspect she will be pretty compelling about the need to change how we go about selecting the Griswold in the future. And we need to look at that. She's right—of course it needs to change. The committee and selection process need an overhaul. Bring it into the twenty-first century. I'm all for it. But, like everybody else, Pauline has her own agenda."

Bill glanced around to see if anyone was within earshot. He lowered his voice and said to Ray, "She's shortlisted for president of Wellesley. *Really* wants it. Doesn't think I know about it." Bill allowed himself a slight chuckle. "One more step in the vetting process: Wellesley search committee visiting me right after commencement."

Bill sipped his drink, then nodded at Ray. "I'll have a word with her," he said. "All will be well."

Not an hour later, Ray was in Rob's backyard filling him in on his conversation with Calhoun. When Ray told him the Griswold was a done deal, Rob felt a physical sense of relief. He realized in the moment just how much this award meant to him.

"It's ironic," said Ray. "We've actually proved the kids' point about white male privilege. Who else can meet in a private corner of one of the world's elite faculty clubs, waiters at the ready, ice cold Manhattans served straight up, while at the same time gaining an inside assurance that *no, the dissidents will not win this battle.* An aging, bearded, disheveled, disgruntled, half-stoned white male! Will it be one of the last acts of a dying breed? They're coming for us, Rob. The barbarians are at the gates! It's their time now. Ours has passed. Or nearly so."

Ray seemed amused by this. "Everybody's tired of having us around. We talk too much and too loud, we interrupt, we bully, we dominate positions of influence in politics, business, etc., throughout the country and the world for that matter. We've been in the driver's seat for centuries. These kids coming up—female, Asian, Black, Hispanic, etc., etc. They've got brains, they've got balls, and they've got big plans—it's time to get out of their way."

37

Touching JJ

During the first week of June 2022, Julia, Rob, and Ray caught a morning flight out of Logan and landed at Reagan National a few minutes after ten. It was a pleasant day in Boston but a steamy one in DC, and they crammed uncomfortably into the back of a cab. Julia and Rob had dressed quite casually, anticipating the Washington heat, but Ray wore a newly pressed suit, a crisply laundered shirt, and a necktie, which was unusual for him.

"Sorry to be taking up half the room," Ray said. He was trying for lightness, but it was clear he was tense. He hadn't uttered a word on the flight down. Julia and Rob had suggested the trip. Ray had visited the Vietnam Memorial nearly forty years earlier, in 1982, soon after the dedication. But he hadn't been back since, though he had been to Washington dozens of times in the ensuing years. By late morning, having arrived on the National Mall, they approached the memorial from some distance. It seemed to rise from the ground gradually, presenting itself with a sense of modesty and grace.

"It's so beautiful," Julia said as they drew closer. The understated elegance of the black granite with the names carved, so many names, it was overwhelming. Ray had his list with him, originally made while he

was in Phu Bai but updated in 1982 to indicate the location of each of
these names on the wall.

"This way," Ray said, and he led them to the start of the memorial
where the names were listed in chronological order based on the years
in which the deceased had served in Vietnam. The crowd that morning
was sparse but beginning to build. Julia was struck by the quiet. There
were hundreds of people, and while you could hear a dog bark now and
then over on the Mall, no noise to speak of came from the vicinity of
the wall itself other than whispers, hushed conversation. People spoke
as though in church, a holy place, a sacred place, and of course it was
just that. They were on sanctified ground. Moving slowly along past
the names of those soldiers, sailors, and marines who had been killed
in the early and mid-1960s, they progressed to the late 1960s and early
1970s, when Ray had served, when the number of names increased
exponentially.

Julia grew cold with sadness and fury, wrapping her arms around
her shoulders and making sure to walk slowly enough to stay behind
Ray, who led the way. She did not want to show any emotion. She
wanted to be sure and steady. This trip was for Ray, and she and Rob
were here to support him. But she needed a moment. She was rocked
by the brutality of this monument to all of these young soldiers sent off
to die. It galled her that mostly it was parents sending the children of
other parents—but very rarely their own sons—to fight and die. As she
read the names, she envisioned the proud parents at home when, without warning, came a knock on the door, two uniformed officers, deliver-
ing the unthinkable news that changed everything in a heartbeat.

She looked ahead and saw Ray moving at a glacial pace, reading
name after name. It took over an hour for them to reach the section
listing the casualties from the time period in which Ray had served. He
stopped and removed the list from his pocket. Julia and Rob hung back.
The sun was high in the sky, and Ray's jacket remained on, tie firmly in
place, perspiration stains forming on his back and under his arms. He

was in his role as a high priest conducting a service guiding the spirits of the boys to God. He would glance down at the list and reach up on the wall and place his right hand on a chosen name, and he would bow his head and pray silently for several minutes, and then he would move to the next name on his list. When he came to a name of one of his boys on the lower portion of the wall, he knelt, carefully lowering himself, a hand extended to the granite enabling him to settle himself as though kneeling in a church pew. At certain points, Ray would place his hand on the name and remain in place, head bowed, unmoving for a full fifteen minutes.

Hours passed until he came upon the name of John Joseph Smith of Lebanon, Kansas. At this point, Ray turned to them and whispered, "JJ." Julia and Rob knew the story. They gathered at Ray's side and all three, together, reached forward and touched the name. That visit to the family farm, JJ's father. There were no words to describe such a loss. You could say that JJ's dad had been crushed or shattered or any number of other vivid, active verbs. But it still would not describe the reality. No language had ever been invented that was capable of doing that.

Julia cried quietly for JJ and his dad and for all these boys and all the dads and moms. And, human nature being what it was, she cried for her son and for herself. This place was, first and foremost, a monument to all of these service members who had made the ultimate sacrifice for their country. But it was also in a way a monument to all of the mothers and the fathers and to the burdens they bore.

As Julia cried, Rob embraced her. Ray embraced them both, and they stood there, enveloped in silent grief, as people passed them by, many of those people touching them lightly on the shoulder or back, a gesture of support and shared grief.

It was a somber trip home. They gathered that night in the garden, where Ray seemed eager to talk about the day.

"What did you think, Jules?" Ray asked. He and Rob had their scotches, Julia a glass of red wine.

"Overwhelming," she said. "All those names and all that suffering, but I found that the longer we were there the more jumbled my emotions became. I felt quite angry at one point and I thought about Rob telling me through the years about the majesty of America, and, sorry Rob, I grew angry at everyone and everything."

She paused and reached over and grasped Rob's hand.

"It made me angry, too," Rob said. "They trusted us. They placed their trust in the so-called elites and we betrayed that trust."

"Love is a strange emotion," Ray said. "It has a nearly mathematical balance to it, I think. It brings the most extreme joy and the most extreme sorrow, suffering. I felt both today, not in equal measure, of course. But I felt joy that those boys were born into this world and experienced the love that comes with being a child in a family. Such a precious thing. They experienced the beauty of life, even if only for a short time. They gave their young lives, and how were they to know that they were being lied to? Deceived?"

He paused and sipped his scotch. "Those kids . . . dear God."

38

Return to McCann's

The Griswold Award was presented to Rob during a small dinner at the Faculty Club. Twenty faculty members attended while eight students picketed in a light rain outside. People said nice things about Rob. Jerry Katz was over the moon. He had a few drinks, thanked Bill for standing up to "the mob," and cried during his toast. The real celebration, though, came the following night, when Julia surprised Rob and Ray with a return trip to McCann's. On a balmy June evening the three of them drove there, with Julia explaining en route that she had read an article online about how Eddie's grandson had bought the place, renovated it, and turned it into an upscale restaurant.

"I remember walking down the hill from the VA and meeting you guys there," Ray said. "How long ago was that?"

Julia laughed. "Too long!"

The place was unrecognizable. No more buzzing, faltering neon sign outside, no more beer smell inside, no broken barstools or tables or ceiling leaks or scarred pool table. There was an understated elegance to it, soft lighting, but a very fun vibe.

"That's where we used to sit, right over there," Julia pointed out. "And this," she said, "was the place where there was some kind of leak, remember?"

"Yes!" said Rob. "I cannot believe we both remember the leak."

Halfway through dinner, Julia got up to go to the restroom. When she returned to the table, she said, "Come with me. Come on."

"What?" said Rob.

"Just come," she ordered.

They followed her a short distance back to a bar area, where on the wall was a display of old photographs from the original McCann's. These were black and white five-by-sevens of various patrons, including bus drivers, cops, and firemen in uniform. And there, amid the pictures, was the photograph of Julia, Rob, and Ray, taken by Eddie McCann on July 24, 1974, the day the Supreme Court ruled on the matter of *Nixon v. the United States*.

"Some good ones there," said the bartender, a friendly woman in her thirties. Julia pointed to the picture and said, "That's us."

The bartender looked closely at the picture, then turned and studied their three faces. "It *is* you guys," she said. "This is crazy. I have to go tell Ed."

It was jarring to see how youthful they looked in the photo—their. faces young, bright, their bodies slim, fit. They exuded confidence and ambition—they would make their mark on the world. The bartender hurried back to the kitchen, and a minute later a young man emerged in full chef's garb. "I'm Ed McCann," he said. "My grandfather owned this place years ago. You're in one of the pictures?"

"That's us," said Julia, pointing.

Ed McCann did not have to study the picture—he merely glanced at it. He knew it well. He turned to the three of them.

"You're the brainiacs!" he said.

"Oh, my God," said Julia. "That's what Eddie called us!"

"This is crazy," Ed said. "He used to talk about you guys. He said that some of his customers were very 'high class,' was the term he used, and you guys were the examples. One of you was a doctor at the VA, right?"

"Ray Witter," said Ray, shaking Ed's hand.

"And one of you was in law school."

"Both of us," said Rob, indicating himself and Julia.

"I'm speechless," said Ed. "And now I remember. You, the doctor, you drank on the house, right?"

They burst out laughing.

Ed called to the bartender. "Bea, would you mind taking a picture? You guys okay with that?"

"Love it," said Julia.

"I'm going to put it up next to the original," he said. "This is so cool. All these years later, you're still friends."

When they arrived home, Julia went up to bed while Rob and Ray sat outside with brandy.

"How are you doing?" Ray asked.

"Okay," Rob said. "Apprehensive, of course. Eager to hear what Dr. Gretzle has for us in the morning."

"I'm hopeful," said Ray, "but remember, there are other arrows in the quiver."

They laughed together, and it felt good.

39

Uncertainty

The following morning, Rob and Julia drove to the medical school and met Ray in his office. Nita was running a bit late, Ray said, waiting on results from Rob's most recent testing. A few moments later Nita Gretzle arrived, and Ray lit up in her presence.

"What a pleasure for me to be able to introduce my dearest, most beloved friends to my most prized medical student," he said proudly.

"My *most* prized mentor," she replied, beaming at Ray. Nita was of medium build, short dark hair, long white coat, dark skin, bright eyes, and quite pretty.

Ray gestured for everyone to take a seat, Julia and Rob on the sofa, Ray and Nita on the two chairs. "Okay, we have a problem that we need to solve, and there is nobody better on this specific type of problem than Nita," Ray said. "It's become clear that your case is a little different than others and resistant to the standard treatment. So, Nita, why don't you share your thoughts."

"First, may I say, Mr. and Mrs. Barrow, I have heard much about you from Dr. Witter, and I am honored to meet you both." She had a soft voice, steady and deliberate, and Rob had to strain to hear her. "And I am humbled that you have placed your trust in me to examine your case. I'm sorry, but I must begin with a disclaimer, which is that we are not permitted to use this treatment on patients in the United States. All of our trials are in Europe, where there is greater leeway. What leeway there is in the US lies with Dr. Witter. Our company shares these new therapies with the medical school for research purposes, not for treatment. If Dr. Witter then turns around and uses the therapies for treatment, that is a violation of our agreement and of FDA rules."

"Dr. Gretzle, would you be at any risk if Ray treated my husband?" Julia asked.

"Zero," said Ray. "She can share with our medical school and labs for study. What we then do with it is on us. Not her responsibility."

"But, Ray, you would have problems if anyone knew, is that right?" asked Rob.

Ray laughed heartily. "Of course!"

Dr. Gretzle started with a review of the chronology of Rob's illness, going back to the initial PSA spike. "I would say, reviewing the records, that you have received appropriate care thus far," she said. "Unfortunately, as Dr. Witter just noted, we would have hoped for a more robust response." She reached into her briefcase and removed her laptop, tapped a few keys, and showed a photograph. "This image is from your most recent scan, and it suggests that you may need a somewhat different approach. The heart of the matter is this opaque image here in the pelvic area, very close to the bone. You can see here that the hip area has been largely unaffected by hormones or radiation."

"Sorry for interrupting," said Ray, "but just so you understand the significance of the work Nita is talking about, the research paper on which she is lead author will appear in the next issue of the journal *Cell*. Major finding. Sorry, Nita, please go ahead."

"Thank you, Dr. Witter," she said. "So what is interesting is that your image"—she passed her laptop to Rob and Julia for a closer look—"shares similarities with structures we have observed in our research. We studied the medical records of several hundred patients who had similar images and, in most cases, the usual pattern prevailed. But in some, the cancerous cells accelerated their movement and got away from us. The paper Dr. Witter referred to finds that in some cases, images like yours were a precursor to a rapid metastatic event. And in those cases the increase in aggression by the tumor was fatal. These patients had a very particular and somewhat rare cellular marker. Unfortunately, the blood work shows that you, also, have this marker, Mr. Barrow."

Julia reached for Rob's hand.

"This seems like *really* not good news," said Julia.

"Hold on, Jules," said Ray.

"I have taken the liberty, Mr. Barrow, of scheduling you today for some additional blood work, which will get us a deeper look at the molecular structure of these cells. The good news is that at Novartis we have developed a targeted therapy for patients with these particular cellular characteristics. For such patients, the drug can be effective. Before I arrived here this morning, I received the most recent results from your blood work and from the new PET scan." She typed and called up a different screen.

"As you know, our immune system usually does a good job of protecting us from a variety of diseases," she said. "But cancer cells are smart, and to survive and grow they figure out how to effectively bypass immunosurveillance and switch off the immune system in some cases. They are criminals, burglars who disarm the bank's security system. Not easy to do, but it can be done. For some time now the focus of my research has been related to what is known as adoptive cell therapy. I suspect you've heard about CAR T cells, which are important immunity cells in the body. With adoptive cell therapy we are able in some cases to remove your own T cells, adjust them in the lab in a way that gives them more resistance to cancer, then reintroduce them into your system. We have developed—"

"*Nita* has developed," Ray interjected.

"—a new therapy that is taken in pill form after the injection of the newly modified T cells. And we find that it acts like a kind of steroid for the T cells. It is under study in Europe, and the results are promising. If it works, we know within six months. After that amount of time, we find minimal efficacy from the treatment.

"There are risks," she continued. "A few patients in the early trial, three people out of several hundred, were overwhelmed by an immune system rebellion so extreme that it led to organ failure and death. On the positive side of the ledger, in many patients the therapy blocked the cancer cells from progressing into the bones. Blocked it from progressing *at all*, in fact. And in the best cases we saw quite a few patients after six months entirely free of the disease."

Julia asked quietly, "How long does it take to complete the first stage of the process?"

"About a week," said Dr. Gretzle. "Painless, very simple. Everything would be done by Dr. Witter here at the medical school."

"Then the pill," said Julia.

"Correct."

"Side effects?" Julia asked.

"Fatigue, weight loss, sometimes alterations in the functioning of the lower GI tract."

Suddenly, the room was quiet. Rob's chest was tight, and he realized that if there was really good news to share she would already have shared it.

"What are the chances it will work?" Julia asked.

"There is an algorithm one of our people created," Dr. Gretzle said. "We feed in a patient's full profile, and it has proven remarkably accurate at predicting the odds that the combined therapies will have a significant degree of efficacy for a given patient." She looked down at her computer and tapped a few keys. "For you, Professor Barrow, the results are something we don't often see. Precisely 50-50."

No one moved, no one said a thing. Rob's heart was pounding. *The flip of a coin*, he thought. *Jesus.*

"So, doctor, what is the bottom line here?" Rob asked. "What does it look like over the horizon? What does my future life look like?"

Dr. Gretzle looked from Rob to Julia and back again.

"In a word, Mr. Barrow, it is uncertain."

They heard the news as they were leaving Ray's office. It was all anyone was talking about. The court did not merely uphold the Mississippi restriction on abortion, it went much further and overturned *Roe*. The chief had failed to persuade colleagues to his sensible compromise position. Rob had been wrong. He felt quite lost.

40

Next Spring?

It was the Friday of Thanksgiving weekend, November 25, the end of their season together in the garden. Rob, Julia, and Ray went about various pursuits during the day with a plan to gather that evening, bundled up against a chilly day that promised a cold evening. That morning, Rob Barrow had walked to his office at the law school where the hallways, offices, and lecture halls were empty. Everyone, it seemed, had taken time off over the long holiday weekend. But there were some case files Rob did not have at home that he wished to consult relative to a class action suit brought in federal court in Denver by inmates at the United States Penitentiary Administrative Maximum Facility near Florence, Colorado. The suit was led by Edgar Masoud, a bright, idealistic young lawyer who had been a student of Rob's a few years earlier and had set out to challenge the prison system on Eighth Amendment grounds. He had joined the regional ACLU office as part of an expanding team to sue the United States Bureau of Prisons, asking the court to shut down the famed Colorado Supermax facility. Edgar's brief asserted that "the very existence of the facility conducted in the manner in which it is conducted inflicts cruel, unusual, and inhumane punishment upon inmates and that the very nature of the prison structure and rules violates the Eighth Amendment."

At the office, Rob settled in his leather desk chair and put his head back and shut his eyes. He felt a degree of fatigue that had gotten steadily worse during the recent period of treatment Ray was administering. Blood draws to measure a variety of activities within his cells along with proton beam scans. Nita Gretzle had called Rob once to interview him about symptoms, a thin veil of pretense that this was a controlled research project. In fact, Ray had taken all of the information from the work that Nita had done at Novartis—work he had pledged in writing to use only for research and not for clinical purposes—and turned around and focused it exclusively on Rob's case.

Rob went down the hall to an ancient, sludgy coffee machine and got a cup of coffee, returning to his office where he sipped it and set to business. He was working on a memo offering thoughts to his former student, but the more he had been thinking about the matter of late, the more he focused on the idea of intent. If there was evidence anywhere that anyone involved with the design, construction, and management of the facility had expressed a cruel intent, that might be a wedge into a novel case that the court might entertain.

"If you could demonstrate intent, Edgar," Rob had said that summer while they were hashing out aspects of the case in a phone call.

"How would we do that?" Edgar asked.

Rob suggested going back to the beginning, when plans were being discussed about the construction of the prison. "I would gather any and all public documents related to hearings, meetings, discussions among leaders at the Bureau of Prisons," Rob suggested. "Subpoena any and all memos from the early days specifically related to intent."

"We filed those a while back, before I asked you to get involved," said Edgar.

"Good, that's good," Rob said. "But I would add one other suggestion. I would suggest going back and subpoenaing documents from the architectural firm or firms, the construction companies involved, and any correspondence between and among those entities and the Bureau of Prisons."

"Interesting," said Edgar.

"And one more thing," Rob said. "I would depose the architects, construction company personnel, including laborers who worked on the building. What was their intent? We know what they say in official documents, but were there common discussions about the cruelty of the place? Did they know that what they were doing, the architects and construction companies and the Bureau, did they know that by constructing this hellish place they would be inflicting an ungodly level of inhumanity on the prisoners? If this was common knowledge or a common belief among those who planned and executed the design and construction, who knows, maybe we would have something."

"So you're saying maybe the general understanding among those designers and builders was that the result of their work would be to inflict cruelty," Edgar replied.

"Precisely," Rob said. "There may not be anything in writing. But in sworn depositions the architects, designers, construction execs, and the workers, for sure, might reveal what was talked about at the time."

"This is great, professor, we'll get started on it," Edgar said. "Will keep you posted."

Rob sat scribbling some notes, thinking about various aspects of the case for a while and coming to a point where he thought it unlikely that the petitioners would prevail in light of the truly depraved and heinous nature of the crimes most of the prisoners there had committed. The whole thing bothered Rob. He read through Justice Brennan's guidelines from the 1972 case of *Furman v. Georgia*, where Brennan wrote that there were "four principles by which we may determine whether a particular punishment is 'cruel and unusual.'"

Rob examined the map of a standard cell at the prison, a seven-by-twelve-foot space with a poured concrete desk, bed, and stool, along with a stainless-steel structure that served as both sink and toilet, and reinforced steel doors. And one window forty-two inches long, but barely four inches wide, angled so that the inmate could see only sky.

Prisoners in solitary confinement were locked into a windowless version of the cell. What did it do to the human psyche to be prevented from ever again seeing the creations of God and nature? Trees, shrubs, shifting colors and hues of the landscape through the seasons, wildflowers bursting forth in the foothills after spring rains. Rob tried to imagine being confined to his home but never again being able to see his garden; knowing it was right there, a place that brought joy and peace to his soul.

Wasn't such deprivation "degrading to human dignity" under the Brennan rule? Wasn't it also "patently unnecessary"? But perhaps Rob was thinking on a visceral level. He was so deeply connected with his small share of nature that had calmed him and, in fact, been central to sustaining him through the years, that he found the prospect of being without it unimaginable. He wondered whether he would be around to see the district court's ruling. Could this be the last case in which he played any role at all? He was unsurprised by how calm he now felt in the face of the cancer. He had found his equilibrium. He had always been a steady, solid person. It was what had drawn Julia to him in the first place. Rob gathered documents, filed them into his briefcase, and headed out of school for a leisurely stroll back home. The air was sharp, the late afternoon sun thin and weak, as though fighting a losing battle against the earth's rotation. Rob looked around, saw the mothers and children playing in the park, the kids running and shouting with glee, the mothers huddled off to the side, shivering. Oh, how he envied them.

Rob made his way home the long way, which gave him time to reflect and to embrace a sense of appreciation for all that he had in his life. I have been so blessed, he thought. He had married the love of his life. He had a friend in Ray, who had always been there to guide and support. He had had a career for so many decades doing work that mattered and that he loved. And, of course, he had had his precious son, whom he had loved in a way that could not be described by words, certainly not in any language Rob knew. Thomas had been everything to Rob. Thomas had been given the gift of life for far too short a time, but he had loved the life he lived. So exuberant and joyful in every way! Rob Barrow headed home for an evening in the garden, feeling a bit of sadness but, much more, that life had been good.

As Rob was making his way home that afternoon, Julia was sitting in an ornate reading room in the main library on the campus of Boston College. She had been invited to speak to a handful of faculty members about her book. She was also often invited now to speak at medical conferences about transparency and the lessons of her family's experience. She attended as many as she felt like she could handle, but they took a toll in requiring her to recount and, in some respects, relive it all. It was not always a comfortable juggling act. One week on an academic panel focused on the decline of the country, the next talking about the loss of her son and the failure of the medical system. Sometimes she felt as though she was the inheritor of the fate of Sisyphus, rolling the rock that was her story of personal tragedy up the hill, only to watch it tumble back down to the bottom, then rolling another stone that was the American tragedy up to the top of the hill, only to have that roll back down too.

As Julia was finishing up at Boston College, Ray was in his research laboratory at the medical school puzzling over a series of numbers, letters, and abbreviations. This was Ray's calling now. He was also still teaching in the medical school, as well, but his devotion lay within the realm of research. Throughout that summer and into the fall, Ray dug deeply into the Novartis data from Nita Gretzle. In turn, Ray subjected Rob to a series of blood draws, experimental infusions based on the Novartis work, to try to determine whether the molecules in the therapy were binding with cancerous cells. That was the first of the two questions. Can you outfox the cancer cells? Can you get around the cancer cells' defenses and attach a healthy protein to the rogue cells? Then the second question: If you can do that, would the new drug carried by the healthy molecules kill off the lethal cells? Ray had explained to Rob and Julia that it would be at least a few months before they had a sense of whether step one would work. Beyond that was uncertainty, as Nita Gretzle had said. The underlying and unspoken concern was whether Rob would run out of time before answering both questions.

Mike Dwyer walked into the medical school lab on the south side of the ancient brick structure that hovered over Longwood Avenue. Ray was in his office going over data on his laptop when Mike appeared in his doorway.

"I can't believe you work in these conditions," Mike said.

Ray laughed, got up, and the two men shook hands.

"It's perfect," Ray said, "assuming you like the mixed aromas of rats, mice, and whatever other vermin we have around here. Not to mention blinding industrial lighting and an assortment of lethal chemicals."

Ray led Mike out of his office to the corner of the lab where there were side-by-side stools at a research bench.

"So, congratulations, I guess," Mike said. "But I wonder why now?"

Ray gestured, spreading his arms to encompass the laboratory. "I need to be in here more, Mike. Exciting stuff going on. Plus time to promote a bunch of talented people at the med school. You know Minh Li?"

"We've met," Mike said.

"She will be great as dean," Ray said. "Gets along with everybody except the people she should not get along with. Wonderful teacher and researcher."

"Changing of the guard," Mike said wistfully.

"Healthy," said Ray. "New blood, ideas."

Mike nodded. "Yeah, of course. But it's . . . well, I don't know."

"I'll walk out with you," Ray said. "Let me just check something first." He went into his office and quickly scanned some new data that had just arrived. He stopped for a moment and read it again—a half page of numbers, half words, abbreviations. He hastily folded the document and stuck it in his pants pocket before rejoining Mike and walking down the hallway, Ray greeting a security guard and exchanging brief pleasantries.

"How's this research with Novartis going?" Mike asked. Ray stopped walking and turned and faced Mike. "You're asking me about Novartis?" Ray said. "I wonder why you would do that out of the blue?"

"I had dinner with Ziegler, the CEO, the other night," Mike said. "He said that they had provided you with access to one of their new protocols and there was some question as to what exactly was happening with it."

Ray actually laughed out loud. "*Some question*, huh?" he said, smiling. "Maybe they should ask me the *some question*."

"Ziegler says they have," Mike said.

"Did he now?" said Ray.

They continued walking out into the chilly night air, a feel of winter headed their way sooner than anyone would like.

"He said something about being questioned by the FDA and your name came up," Mike said.

"Hmm," said Ray.

Mike reached over and gently grasped Ray's forearm. "This is serious stuff, Ray," Mike said. "Licenses can get revoked in matters like this. Is whatever you're doing kosher?"

Ray smiled and said, "Who's asking?"

Mike thought a moment. "Your friend."

Ray patted Mike on the back. "Kosher?" he mused. "Let me ask you this, Mike. Kosher according to government rules and regulations, or kosher in terms of trying to help a friend?"

"Both," Mike said.

"To the first, no. To the second, yes." Ray said.

The two men studied one another in silence, and Mike was about to speak, was about to caution Ray about breaking or circumventing the rules, but he realized that Ray knew what he was doing. They walked a block, Mike pulling the collar of his coat up against the chill, Ray seeming oblivious to it. They got to the small executive parking lot where both men's cars were parked.

"Before you go, Ray," Mike said. "I just . . . I wanted to say thank you for your courage and guidance, really, on the whole RAND thing. I get calls all the time about it, as I'm sure you do as well. Trustees at places around the country wanting to understand how you navigate the minefields of department chairs. How you use data to get safer and better. How to keep the patient top of mind. They've all read our piece in the *New England Journal*. I think we accomplished something there."

"You were the one who had the balls to hire them and let them run," Ray said.

Ray was trying to be light about it, but it was clear this was actually an emotional moment for Mike Dwyer. "It made a difference, Ray, and isn't that all we ever really want to do, something that matters, make a difference in people's lives? Old guys like us?"

Ray opened the door to his car. "Dinner soon?" he said to Mike. "On you?"

Mike managed a smile and a thumbs-up.

Rob was the first to arrive in the garden that evening, wearing a jacket, hat, and wool scarf against the chill of the crystal night air. He sat gazing around the garden and noticed that all of the trees had shed their leaves with the exception of the majestic sycamore. Like hibernating bears, these trees had settled in for the long New England winter ahead. They were essentially dormant now, in concert with the shrubs and brownish grass. Nonetheless, the sycamore retained a partial canopy, a mix of green and brown, the green ones muscular in appearance, healthy, powerful enough to fend off the declining temperatures and fading light. *How amazing,* Rob thought. *The tenacity and strength of this living thing through the centuries.*

Julia emerged from the house in thick wool pants, a down parka zipped all the way up, and a ski hat. She had a mug of hot chocolate and offered it to Rob.

"I'm going to get a scotch, thanks though, Jules," he said. He went inside and set about pouring drinks for Ray and himself. It was an end of season occasion that required good whiskey, and Rob found some in the back of a rarely used dining room cabinet.

While Rob was inside, Ray strode through the hedge at the far end of the yard in an old sweater, suede patches at the elbows, and stained chinos—his "lab pants," as he called them. He ascended the stone steps to the terrace and hugged Julia.

"How is he?" Ray asked.

"Fatigued," she said. "The treatments take a toll."

"Anything else?" Ray asked.

"No," she said. "He's been working a lot, and I think he's down but tries not to show it."

At that moment Rob emerged from the house with two tumblers of whiskey and handed one to Ray.

"Thanks, pal, how are you feeling?" Ray asked.

"Better now that you're here," Rob said. "All present and accounted for."

Ray raised his glass. "To your health, Rob."

They clinked glasses, and Ray reached into his back pocket and pulled out the sheet of paper, unfolded it, and handed it to Rob.

"Please read," Ray said. He couldn't help but smile, knowing the numbers and abbreviations on the page were hieroglyphics to Rob. The type covered barely half the page, a printout from Rob's latest lab work. Julia leaned over and scanned the page.

"What is this?" she asked.

"What is it?" Ray said. "It is something beautiful. Answer to a prayer. It is an analysis from a few hours ago of the latest data—" Ray hesitated, choked with emotion for a moment. "Nita's protocols," Ray continued. "The Novartis drug. The proteins have successfully attached to the cancer cells. The proteins have started to kill the cancer cells."

Julia said, "Ray, does this mean—"

"It means the process of killing the cancer has begun. Will it continue on course? Will the rogue cells hide, lie in wait to fight another day? Don't know." Ray hesitated, the slightest catch in his throat. "But we will do everything we can so that the three of us are together next spring. Right here where we belong."

Acknowledgments

I owe a debt of gratitude to the late Herbert Gutterson, a teacher of English at the Choate School for thirty years. Mr. Gutterson's encouragement mattered a great deal at a pivotal time in my life. I am grateful to Alice Martell at the Martell Literary Agency and Flip Brophy at Sterling Lord Literistic for their kindness and wise counsel. Tony Lyons, the CEO of Skyhorse, provided opportunity at the right time. I am grateful to my daughter, Elizabeth S. Kenney, for designing the cover of this novel. Three gifted editors helped me write *American Sycamore*, including my wife, Anne, who kept a sometimes ramshackle venture on track. Cal Barksdale at Arcade Publishing brought smart thinking and precision to the work. Finally, Laurie Bernstein at Side by Side Literary Productions made frequent use of the massive shredder in her office in the early part of our journey together. In the end, she worked painstakingly to help me write exactly the novel I hoped to create. I am forever grateful.